WALL OF
GUNS

WALL OF GUNS

Jim O'Mara

A SIGNET BOOK

SIGNET
Published by New American Library, a division of
Penguin Putnam Inc., 375 Hudson Street,
New York, New York 10014, U.S.A.
Penguin Books Ltd, 80 Strand,
London WC2R ORL, England
Penguin Books Australia Ltd, Ringwood,
Victoria, Australia
Penguin Books Canada Ltd, 10 Alcorn Avenue,
Toronto, Ontario, Canada M4V 3B2
Penguin Books (N.Z.) Ltd, 182–190 Wairau Road,
Auckland 10, New Zealand

Penguin Books Ltd, Registered Offices:
Harmondsworth, Middlesex, England

Published by Signet, an imprint of New American Library,
a division of Penguin Putnam Inc. Previously published in a Dutton edition.

First Signet Printing, February 2002
10 9 8 7 6 5 4 3 2 1

PUBLISHER'S NOTE
This is a work of fiction. Names, characters, places, and incidents either are the
product of the author's imagination or are used fictitiously, and any resemblance to
actual persons, living or dead, business establishments, events, or locales is entirely
coincidental.

Chapter 1

THE HEAT of this June day's halving was a stifling pressure, beating Landry into the saddle and touching with fire the metal rings into which his gear had been lashed. Since dawn, when he had dropped down across the southern slopes of the Buckhorns' east-west traverse, he had ridden away from green-growing things and the shade of trees. With mid morning, he had found himself pursued across the desert's shimmering expanse by dust devils and by the acrid tang of sage and mesquite. The taste of the desert, alkaline and hot, was in his mouth, and its brassy feel sat all through his tissues. Like a woolen blanket over his brain, it smothered his thoughts, leaving his responses dead and warped.

Upon leaving the hills where he had spent the night, he had swung wide into the desert, passing across the beaten trail which led directly southward to the town of Broken Wheel, and drawing a slow half circle through the waste lands toward the spot on the horizon's dim perimeter where he knew the town would lie. It was a small stratagem, yet he knew that he must make his approach indirectly, for here, in this country, danger waited. He must have time to study the game and to see how the first few cards might fall.

He had known this in Montana, and it had been kneaded into conviction by long, sobering thoughts while on the trail. It had ridden with him down through the Bitterroots and across the Yellowstone and Wind rivers; it had been a pushing voice at his back as he crossed the Park Ranges and

came into the headwaters of the Arkansas, and, finally, upon
the upper reaches of the Rio Grande.

Now, Mexico lay near, and all the days and miles had
come to focus upon this tract of desert and the little town toward which he was pushing his last weary miles. Somewhere ahead in the shimmering vastness lay Broken Wheel,
and there he would find the man whose life he had come to
take for another's.

As his shadow began to lengthen on his left, Landry became aware of a tall cottonwood with its surrounding clump
of willows, which slowly emerged from the distance. Knowing that here there might be water, he turned the black toward it, coming finally into its shade, and here he
dismounted. At the roots of the willows was a spring, green
and cracked, now, with the unrelenting heat. He stared at it
for a moment, his hand on the black's sweat-streaked withers, and then he called up his philosophical inward shrug
and threw off, letting the black seek the shade while he sat
down under the cottonwood to eat his cold rations. Afterward, knowing it was foolish, he drank the last of the water
from the canteen, then stretched out to rest, pulling the brim
of his hat down over his eyes.

For a time he dozed, tiredly and dumbly. Then the sun's
sharp heat came around, cut through the branches overhead
and slanted down upon his chest. With that he got up, threw
the saddle on again, and pushed out into the heat-swept flatness, knowing that he would not reach Broken Wheel before
night.

It was well into the afternoon, and travel had become an
unfeeling monotony, when the far, white shape of a ranch
house began to grow off to his right, and around this white
house the gray, dull shapes that gradually became barns,
buildings and sheds. For a little while he fought the impulse
within him, then he pulled the black's head around toward
the ranch.

From a distance he saw that there were people on the veranda of the house's shady side, and that three horsemen sat
their mounts in the yard, talking to the others. When these

facts had made their impress, he told himself that it did not matter. They had seen him now, and were watching his approach. Not caring, Landry rode past the corrals and buildings and into the yard, where he stopped and waited.

There were two men on the veranda, a young man and an older one. The latter regarded Landry coolly, out of dark eyes that held little patience and rather more of worry, somewhere beneath the surface. Other things, too, Landry read there: hard, sober, quick-forming judgments and inflexibility. He was fiftyish, lank and heavy-boned, with weather-darkened skin and thinning black hair, and his mouth was hidden by drooping black mustaches. The other one was slim and dark in a way the older man was not; he had the same frame and features, but his mouth was weak and there was no drive, save curiosity, in his gaze. Landry thought: "Father and son, but the blood has gone bad."

Now the older man put a long, questioning look on Landry, and when Landry said nothing, suspicion grew up in the man's gaze. He turned to the foremost of the riders sitting before the veranda and said in a thick, quiet way, "Another one, Steele? How high do you expect to stack this thing?"

Steele had been watching Landry, feeling out for everything that he was and what was behind his coming. He was a long man, lean and wide of shoulder, with sandy hair and a cold blue eye. His nose was high and thin, and his mouth was a slit which ran into loose areas at the corners. He turned to the man on the porch and said bluntly, "He's a trail runner, Wayne. Any damn fool can see that."

Landry swung his glance around the group, and let it rest on Steele. "I call my own brand," he said. "If someone reads it, let him read it right."

Something in Steele's wintry-blue eyes rose and fell. "Another hard man has ridden into this country," he said ironically, "full of small resentments and yearning for conflict." He was silent for a moment; then, "I really don't give a damn who you are, friend. Now. Are you happy?"

The man beside Steele shifted on the leather, bringing

Landry's glance his way. He was a squat, heavy man with an oversize head and smoke-colored eyes that seemed dead. Expressionlessly he watched Landry, and Landry felt waiting in the air all about him. He hesitated a little before he said to Steele, "You travel in style. I know the type: talk yourself out of every hole but the last one."

Steele colored. The man on his other side muttered something and threw his weight on one stirrup. He was a thin-lipped fellow with a tough, wild face and long, claw-like hands.

"All right, Kirby?" this one said in a flat tone.

Kirby Steele let go a meager smile. "Be quiet, Coulter," he murmured. For a moment he pondered over Landry. Then he said deliberately, "Too many around here think courage is identical with arrogance. That can trip a man up. There's your answer, my trail-worn friend." With that he dismissed Landry and turned to the man on the porch.

"Darby," a note of exasperation pushed along his voice, "you could have asked me up in the shade. But I will overlook that, since I understand your feelings. Before I go, I'll ask you again: do you want to deal for the Running W, or will we let this matter go into court tomorrow?"

The man on the porch waited a moment, as if adjusting his judgment. "Your trouble, Steele," he said finally, "is that you run with a pack. Makes you too damned sure of yourself."

Steele stared at Wayne, and for a moment it appeared as though he would argue the point. "That your answer?"

"That's it."

Steele nodded, drawing a still, tight mask over his face. "If you change your mind," he said, glancing at the younger man, "we can talk it over tonight at the hotel."

Darby Wayne's gaze slipped aside to his son, then came back to Steele. "I won't."

Now Young Wayne spoke up. "You think that, you're crazy," he told Steele. An overtone in his voice hit Landry's eardrum and stayed there.

Steele nodded shortly and reined about. Then he stopped,

looking hard at Landry. "There is something about you," he mused. "Could it be that we have met before—?"

Landry said sparely, "Don't run with your kind."

Surprisingly, Steele laughed. For a moment he studied Landry narrowly. "The arrogant tribe," he mused. "The savage courage of animals and brains to match—" Then he hit his horse with the spurs and the three of them rolled out of the yard, the dust rising heavily behind them.

Landry watched them go, then turned his gaze back to the others. Full of impatience with all this he said, "I don't give a damn about your shade either. But I'd like a drink of water."

Darby Wayne's eyes now lost their hard, speculative look. He nodded. "Pump's around back. Then come here and set."

Landry got down then, a tall man, wide of shoulder, whose strength sat easily through all his wiry limbs; a tired and dry and dusty man with a quiet arrogance that showed in his narrowed gray eyes and on the even planes of his weather-blackened face. Along with this arrogance was ease and the rider's grace, and it was in his walk as he led the black around the house to the pump.

He let the horse take the edge off of its thirst; then, mindful of the desert's heat, he pulled the animal away, still hollow, and had his own sparing drink. Afterward, he sloshed water over his face and neck and dried himself with his neck piece. Then he went around the house, and as he turned the corner, he saw that a girl had come out on the veranda to join the others. She stood watching him as he came up.

She was slim with the slimness of the girl not yet turned woman, but there was a full roundness to her upper body that brought a fleeting tightening to his throat. Coppery-red hair formed a corona about features that were pertly feminine in spite of the sprinkling of freckles over her nose and cheeks, and the loose strands of hair about her ears crinkled and sparkled with the light that came in under the veranda. These things Landry saw in an instant, and then his glance went to her eyes—deep, blue eyes that looked at him openly and with a frank appraisal that would have been boldness in an older or harder woman. He let his own gaze search hers, and for a moment it went beyond that, reaching out toward her boldly with all that was male in him, and telling her that she was a woman, and desirable. It brought a faint, excited flush to her cheeks, and she let it hold her for an instant. Then she looked away, and Landry turned his glance to Darby Wayne.

"Thanks for the drink."

Wayne said, "Come up and sit a spell. This"—he nodded to the younger man—"is my boy, Harry Wayne. And this one," he looked at the girl with a kind of good-natured irony, "is the boss of the outfit, my daughter, Mary."

Harry Wayne gave Landry a neutral nod, and Landry raised his hat to the girl. "Thanks. But I'll have to ride on. Want to get to Broken Wheel before night."

Now there was a small, tentative silence. Landry could see that Darby Wayne was wondering at him, and knew it when Wayne said bluntly, "Who are you?"

"Frank Landry. Montana."

"Long ways off."

"Yes." And now Landry's gaze was bleak and withdrawn.

Harry Wayne shifted his feet. "That name sounds familiar. Relations around here?"

Landry fiddled with the cinch a moment before he said, "Had a cousin somewhere hereabouts. Thought I might go to work for him."

There was another short silence. "I could use a man," Darby Wayne said, "any man who'd stand up to Kirby Steele and his guns."

"You need hands?"

"No," Wayne said softly, "but I could use a gun or two."

Landry threw the reins over the black's head. "Not in my line." He stepped aboard and sat in the saddle facing them.

Darby Wayne now drifted easily down off the veranda toward Landry. "You don't fool me a bit," he said. "And that's all right. I guess you're not one of the gunmen drifting in to back up Steele's play, and that's better. How about working for the right side if you're going to stay around here?"

Landry had kept his gaze off Mary Wayne. Now he pulled Wayne's query up before his mind's eye and looked at it from all sides, and then his gaze rose slowly to the coppery-haired girl. "Well," he said, "I've got my own business to look after. But I think I'll be around a while."

A touch of color came to the girl's cheeks. He thought a light smile touched her lips, but was not sure.

Darby Wayne said, "Watch your step in Broken Wheel. When you want to go to work for me, ride out."

Landry nodded, tipped his hat to the girl and reined away with her half-smile pictured in his mind. Riding down the trail toward the distant town, he remembered that. And, too, he remembered Darby Wayne's sidelong glance at his son, and the look Steele had given the younger man before he said, "We can talk it over tonight at the hotel." He wondered, then, if he had been wise to mention his own name in connection with Steve.

Darby Wayne watched Landry ride out, then turned toward the shade. He came up on the porch, thoughtfully pulling his mustaches, and stopped before his son. "Harry," he said, "that was damn poor business, asking about that other fellow—Steve Landry."

"Why not? Same name."

Darby Wayne frowned his disapproval. "You, born and raised in this country! You ought to know that curiosity is the worst damn thing a man can have. You've had too much of it lately."

Young Wayne shrugged. He was about to reply, but in that instant there arose the sound of running horses, and three riders burst around the corner of the barn and came up through the yard. Before the veranda they reined in and one of them got down. "Turn 'em loose," he said to the others, and came on to join the Waynes.

He was a long-faced man, running toward fifty, glum and sour. He had a weathered look about him, and the patiently weary air common to men who work with cattle for a living. He let a melancholy gaze run over the others, wiped his face and his hands free of dust with his neck piece, and afterward built a smoke, pursing square-cut lips as the cigarette took shape. When he had his first pull on it, he said to Darby Wayne, "They're settin' up that herd for the trail, all right. Over in the Putumayo Draws. Grass there." Then he waited.

Darby Wayne stared at him for a long five seconds. Then he sat down. "So." His gaze had hardened now, and visibly he was shaping some kind of judgment. Presently, "Just across the country line. Their sheriff has jurisdiction."

"Yes."

Wayne raised his dark glance. "How much of it is ours, Drav?"

"Well," Drav said laconically, "if we was to cut out our brand, they'd have to chouse up a couple of thousand head again."

Wayne shot to his feet, color running high in his face. "Two thousand head! We didn't have *that* much of a drift, bad as the winter was."

Drav McLain shook his head. He was older than his years, which were many, and wise with them. "No," he said, "I reckon not. We found lots of scattered fires over that way. They been working our brand with a runnin' iron."

Wayne swore. "You sure of that?"

Now Harry Wayne said, "I don't believe it! They might take the drift, but they wouldn't touch our calves or burn over brands."

"Who asked you?" Wayne demanded angrily. The boy drew his lips tight.

Quietly Drav said, "We haven't worked over that way. Fires have got to be theirs."

Darby Wayne stared silently at McLain, and the foreman eyed his burning cigarette with a frown. After a while the older man walked off toward the end of the veranda, where he stood squinting into the shimmering distance. Presently he wheeled and came briskly back, having the air of a man who knows his mind and has charted his course.

"Drav," he said curtly, "tell all the boys to saddle up after supper. We're going to that talk tonight in force."

McLain gave him a long, sober look. "All right, Darby." He turned away.

"Wait." Wayne's voice stopped him. "How many men with that herd?"

"Wagon, about six hands. Just a holding crew."

Darby Wayne's jaw set, hard. "All right," he murmured. "All right! If they listen to reason tonight, if the trial goes our way tomorrow, everything will be fine. If not"—he hesitated a moment—"we'll cut that herd. And by God—we'll cut Corralitos to pieces if they try to stop it. When Running W beef—Wayne beef—goes up the trail, we're going to take it!"

A slow grin came over Drav McLain's long face. Then, with a short nod, he stepped quickly down off the porch.

The three Waynes had their moment of indecision. Then Mary Wayne said, "Dad, was that wise?"

"Maybe not. But you can't always do the wise thing."

She understood, but said nothing, showing her approbation only in the look she gave him. Her father came up to her, placed his hand on her arm. "You'd better stay in town for a couple of days, honey."

Harry Wayne turned toward the door. "I'm going in now," he said. "I'll take you with me, Sis."

Darby Wayne stared at his son. "Not ridin' in with the crew? That's where a man belongs—at the head of his outfit."

Harry Wayne colored lightly, but shook his head. "It won't matter. You're coming in with them. I've got some things to do before night." Quickly he went into the house.

The older Wayne's troubled gaze came back to Mary. She smiled at him. "Weren't you that way when you started courting the girls, Dad?"

After a moment he grinned, then turned her toward the interior and gave her a gentle shove. "You're growin' up," he said gruffly. Then, as she went into the house, he murmured, "But I was careful about the females that I courted. I wonder—"

* * *

Landry rode into the town as night began to ease the day aside, throwing shadows over the dusty streets of Broken Wheel, between its gaunt-framed houses and stores. A little finger of coolness now felt its way through the day's last gasping heat, softening the acrid smell of dry, sun-baked pine lumber and of hot adobe, but still in his nostrils hung the bitter odor of dust, strong and cloying.

Past a scattering of 'dobe shacks on the fringe of the town he rode, until the trail turned easily left, and the black faced down the main street. A new liveliness then came into the animal's ploshing walk, but Landry curbed the eager quickening with a small pull at the reins, wanting time to see this place and what made it.

There were too many cow ponies racked along the street for this hour, too much coming and going for a small desert *pueblo* at nightfall. Most of these men should have been on their home ranges. A few nesters' wagons huddled at the far end of the street, and they said, *Plowland*; but the cut of the men who lounged before the stores and saloons was the cut of the rider, and they wore guns. They were, he concluded, waiting for something; because he knew that, his weariness fell away and he became wary and alive.

The town lay in the vast, flat expanse of the desert, hugging the banks of a small stream whose source lay in the hills he had left this morning, whence it meandered southward through the hard plains to cut into grass land again on the perimeter of the Santisima range. That much he had seen from afar out, when the distances were still bright against hazy-blue farness. He noted, now, that the main street was merely the widening of the trail he had joined as he rode in, running from the north onward through the row of buildings on either side of the street and the others scattered through the dusk in back of them, threading through this little town and snaking on into the southwest toward the foothills and plains rimming the desert's edge.

There was movement of riders in the street past him, movement of men across his path as they went toward the bars for their sundown drinks. Low conversation made a web in the cooling air, catching him up in the hidden mystery of the place.

Lights now began to wink on in the stores and houses. Down the street the hotel's faded sign, proclaiming it the Desert House, was dim in the shadow. Past the Wells Fargo and the Stage Post Landry rode, and a saloon on his right called the Casino. A knot of men stood on the boardwalk here, eying without humor the street and all who passed. Across the way from this saloon was another, labeled the Longhorn. From behind its swing doors came the low monotone of conversation and the clink of glasses. Beyond this saloon was the hotel, and below it a store whose sign said, "Lang's—Feed And Grain." Two doors farther down the street was a livery stable, and here Landry pulled up and dismounted.

A man drifted to the edge of the stable's shadows and stood watching. Landry loosened the cinch and when the other had not yet spoken he asked, "Where you want me to put him?"

"There's one back by the alley on the right." The man's voice was wholly neutral.

Landry let the black drink from the trough near the walk, then led him to a stall near the rear door. When he had pulled off the gear and pegged it, he slung the saddle bags over his shoulder and walked to the street. In the doorway he paused to build a smoke, conscious of the stableman's narrow regard through the half-light.

After a while the man said, "That black's had a piece of trail."

Landry pulled on his smoke, found it tasteless, and irritation bubbled up in him. He said nothing.

"You aimin' to be around a while?" The man's voice failed at unconcern.

Landry flipped his cigarette away and watched a little shower of sparks rise and fall into the dust. "Go in there and throw him some hay," he said sharply. "That's more in your line." He swung up the walk toward the hotel.

When Landry had gone a few yards, the stableman whis-

tled softly into the darkness. A barefoot Mexican, with a
dirty serape over one shoulder and his face half hidden by
the brim of his sombrero, came out of the shadows and stood
before him.

"Luis, go tell Kirby he's here. *Ligero.*"

"*Como no, señor.*" The Mexican ghosted into the shadows.

Landry crossed the lobby through dim light, and a thin-
faced, mustached clerk threw him a shifty look and pushed
the register forward.

As he wrote, Landry became aware that someone had
come up noiselessly behind him. At the same time he noted
the curious crooking of the head that the clerk put upon his
signature. He laid the pen down and said dryly, "The name's
Landry. L-A-N-D-R-Y. Frank Landry. Any comment?"

"Don't have my specs," the man said, coloring. "Can't
see what you wrote there."

"You won't have to, now." Landry turned, knowing
whom he would see, and it was Kirby Steele, a still, cold
look in his eye.

"So it's Landry," Steele said slowly. "I wondered about
you—"

Landry hooked his elbows over the desk and watched the
other levelly, trying to make up his mind about him. "Now,
just what makes you curious about me?" he mused. "Still
think we've met before?"

Steele weighed the arrogance in that speech, and
presently he said, "No. If we had, I should have remembered
you, friend."

"Like I thought." Landry straightened lazily and went in
front of Steele toward the corridor where his room would be.

Half way across the lobby Steele's voice reached out for
him. "In this town it is unwise to turn your back on arrogant
speech."

Landry turned. "Now, if that were true," he said mildly,
"you'd have shot first and explained afterward—if you have
any reason for shooting."

Steele was wondering about him, his pondering reflected

on his face. "Just what is your business here?" he demanded waspishly.

"I'm curious. Like to see the other side of the hill. I've straddled a lot of hills in my time, and the last one was up the way from this town. Maybe you've heard of my kind of people—fiddlefooted. Your foot starts singin' a song, and you've got to travel."

Steele took this with a frown and an angry flush. Still, he chose to ignore the irony. "Darby Wayne tried to line you up," he stated.

"That so?"

"I'm asking you."

"That'd come under the heading of *his* business," Landry said. "Ask *him*."

Steele's slow smile bypassed his eyes. "I'm going to give you a piece of advice," he said finally. "Here it is: if you stay in this place, line up on the right side."

Landry was tired of parrying. "Now, you listen to me," he said. "You and your damn town are like a lot of men and towns I've met and seen before. Nothing here to change my ways. If you've got some reason to work me into a play, go ahead. But I figure you're the kind who does the talkin' and lets the others burn powder." With that he turned away, going toward his room.

The other man's agate-hard gaze stayed on Landry until he disappeared. Then he glanced into the shadows along the wall where a woman sat, beyond the fringe of the lobby's light, watching this exchange. A breeze swung the lantern overhead and a random ray fell across delicate features and awoke dancing lights in her honey-blond hair and in the brownish-black eyes. Kirby stepped toward her and said, "All right, Carolina. What about him?"

The woman stared at him for several long, displeased seconds. Then, slowly, she rose. The corners of her mouth were screwed down in displeasure, and her gaze was full of deep, quiet anger.

"He is completely beyond your depth to handle, Kirby," she said with quiet scorn. She studied him for a moment. "I think it was a mistake to give you power. It has given you a sense of your own stature entirely out of proportion to your real strength. What you really have is a kind of bravado that is neither courage nor real arrogance."

Truth found his weakness and hurt him. "Damn it," he said angrily, "this is not the time to philosophize about your dislike of me. What do you propose to do about this fellow?"

"Nothing—now."

"Do you realize that he might be Steve Landry's next of kin—even his brother? A man with that name is a danger—"

"Shut up!" Now she came close and looked him full in the face. "You were always the small man, Kirby, wanting power and knowing neither how to get it nor what to do with it—until I stiffened your spine and gave you power and showed you how to use it. Now you think that you are big—but you run from shadows. Do you know why?" She paused, then with an ironical smile, "I will tell you: you are a giant stuffed with straw. And we both know that *I* hold you up!"

He glared at this woman, his sister, full of his shame and his weakness, yet daring not to speak his mind—full of hate because she was the stronger, and made him, always, know it.

The woman saw all this in his face, and it brought a laugh from her, a short, victorious laugh. Then she turned away. "Put some of your men to watching him if you feel uneasy," she said with unconcern. "Then, later, if you have to, you may act brave and powerful."

Walking softly, she crossed the lobby and turned down the hallway that Landry had taken. Before the door of his room she stopped, hearing the sound of splashing water on the other side. For a moment she hesitated, her brow wrinkled in thought. Then she went on and entered her own room at the far end of the corridor.

Chapter 2

ALWAYS, Carolina Steele remembered the despairing futility of want; it was a nightmare which rose, terror-filled, out of the past to haunt her. And the remembering was the harsher because the war had come, piling poverty upon penury, and threatening never to let her escape from the thing which had pursued her through childhood.

Even before the war had ended, Carolina knew that her world would never again be the same; the surrender of Lee's armies at Appomattox had been merely a confirmation. When her father and Kirby had gone to join Lee, leaving her alone—her mother had died during Carolina's infancy—she had determined that whatever issues might be decided upon the battlefields, Carolina Steele would come out of the conflict undefeated.

The shabby gentility of their lives had always infuriated her. Her father, an amiable, ineffectual anachronism, had spent his days in gentlemanly tippling and reminiscing of the days when the people of the South were *gentry*; meanwhile, the lands dwindled away under mortgages and the fields abounded in weeds where cotton should have grown. It was only natural that this gentle, pompous dreamer should have been among the first to answer the Confederacy's call to arms, and it was in character for him to die gallantly and a bit madly at Gettysburg, imagining himself an example of the finest flower of Southern chivalry.

Carolina Steele had never been duped by pretense. Rec-

ognizing the emptiness of her father's cherished symbols,
she hated them because of his devotion to and preoccupation
with them: they stood in the way of a better life for her.

Great beauty she had and, therefore, beaux. But her girl
cousins and friends had new gowns and they rode in fine
carriages, while all her scheming ingenuity was needed to
keep her old gowns from appearing downright shabby. And
as she grew older, her feeling of prideful inferiority crystal-
ized into a fierce determination to one day have more than
all the others, to shine in comparison with them. A victim of
her family's soft ineffectuality, she hated it while fires raged
in her breast.

Because she grew to young womanhood beautiful and
slightly disdainful, men swarmed to her, only to be rebuffed
because the interested swains were not sufficiently well off
to buy her ambition along with her body. Her relationship
with Kirby was typical. His sharp, sardonic intelligence recognized the scheming female with her eyes upon the
heights, and long before he left the university to go to war,
a barrier had been raised between them that they were never
quite to lower again.

Perversely, the war years gave her a twisted satisfaction,
for as they drew on, she saw those whom she had envied
lowered to her own level, reduced to shabbiness and want,
even to hunger and a grim, courageous kind of despair
which she hated in them because it came from a feeling of
loyalty to a cause which she did not let herself believe in.
She was her own cause, and her battles would be fought for
that cause alone. Long ago, her father's symbols had cured
her of any sentimental attachment to abstract ideals.

As the defeat of the South loomed, she began to examine
the knowledge that only Kirby was left for her now. Even,
she played with the idea of trying to understand him, should
he return safely. And then, gradually, the prompting of memory convinced her that it would be impossible: Kirby, her father's son; Kirby of the books and the cynical, Olympian
detachment from her whole world: the brother who seemed
to read her, and, as a result, to hold her in contempt because

she was realistic and determined—*grasping* was the word
he used. No, she finally admitted, it would not work. And
yet, as the creeping paralysis of Emancipation, with its
growing tempo of poverty and slow starvation, crept over
the country, she knew that she was waiting only for the day
when he would come back. As defeat became a sickly current in the very air of living, Carolina Steele was planning
feverishly for the future, waiting for Kirby's return to see
how he would fit into her projected scheme of things to
come.

She read of the war in the faces of her neighbors and
friends, heard of it from their lips. And frequently a warped
and secret satisfaction came to her as she viewed the slow
and dreadful humbling of those whom she had envied in better times. Their talk of losses, personal and material, was
empty words, swept by her on strong winds, for she neither
sympathized nor understood. There was too much of harsh
reality about her: holding to her two remaining servants;
seeing that the crops were worked, the meager tax money
gotten together; the specter of starvation kept at arm's
length. Her own escape from an undesirable world lay in the
plans she doggedly framed and discarded; in the fantastic,
imagined lengths to which she went to gain the wealth and
security which would forever shut her off from the hated
world that lived in and about her. And so she closed her
mind to the stern things which touched her, bore them, and
told herself that this was only temporary—a long, black
night before the day in which she would *make* things different.

Almost, she did not notice that the war had ended, for its
ending changed nothing in her life. Only, now, the roads became filled with returning soldiers: men on foot and on bony
travesties of horses—ragged, wounded and sick, most of
them half starved and suffering from dysentery. Some
of them came to beg for food, and when she had it she fed
them, grudgingly, for she resented their having participated
in the war for what the war had brought to her. Then, one
day, Kirby rode up to the house, an unshaven, sick scare-

crow in faded butternut upon a scarecrow horse. At first she
thought him another coming to beg a bite. Then came recognition, and all her hatred and resentments were forgotten as
she ran to meet him, feeling already the weight lifting from
her shoulders.

His mocking gaze halted her headlong rush. In one chill-
ing moment the wary, distant years of their relationship
flowed back as Kirby smiled thinly and said, "So comes the
warrior home from the wars."

That was all. White-lipped, she murmured, "I'm glad
you're back." Then she turned toward the house, and did not
see the wavering, lost thing which played through his gaze
for a moment. He got down, then, and came up the steps to
her.

For an instant their eyes met squarely, but the thing
which might have broken there did not. They had their moment of strained embarrassment, before Carolina said, "I'll
get you something to eat—what there is."

"I have grown unaccustomed to fine things," he said
wryly, "and I foresee no future in which I will ever know
them again."

So came Kirby Steele home from the wars—the man
upon whom she should have been able to lean.

They did not quite starve. It was the slow, dulling attri-
tion of never enough to eat, which blurs the mind and brings
gauntness to the limbs and spirit, leaving one sustained
chiefly by the desire to once again fill the belly until it is re-
plete and bulging with food. But Carolina knew, as the days
dragged into months, that Kirby was sick of a thing that
could never be cured. This she knew when she saw him
touching the books in the library with halting, unsure fingers, opening a page, passing on, smiling his slow, bitter and
lost smile, and closing the pages again. Rarely did they
speak to one another; their reticences grew in despair, forc-
ing them further and further apart.

At times, when she could bear it no longer, she would fly
at him, goading him, taunting him into doing something
which would bring food for them to eat. And then he would

smile that ironical smile and mutter, "Why? To prolong an existence already insupportable?" Inevitably, as he lost himself in miasmatic dreams of the past, Carolina's disdain and her determination hardened.

Reconstruction gave her her opportunity. The land was swarming with carpet baggers and scalawags—Northern administrators of the military government of occupation, and their renegade Southern accomplices. These waxed fat and rich, living in luxury as they bled the South white with taxes and claimed as tribute every tangible value that remained in the wake of war.

Perhaps Kirby was unaware of the tax collector who drove out to the Steele mansion that raw October day. Undoubtedly, he did not see what passed between this well-groomed man and Carolina, for he remained in the library while the man was there. But Carolina had noted the fat team of bays, the fine carriage and the expensive garments, as well as the obvious diamond solitaire and the pearl cravat pin. When the tax collector returned to his carriage, Carolina Steele had an engagement to dine with him at the hotel in town. And she had something more: the strength to get what she wanted, together with the wile not to price herself out of the market.

Kirby became aware, slowly, of a great shame in the weeks that followed. But he was able to submerge it in the cynical rationalization which had now become his chief spiritual resource. Hating her fine clothes, the rich foods and the mellow whiskies that were now in the house, he ate those foods and drank those liquors, and told himself that they were no less palatable. Only occasionally did remembrance of the past bring him that dark kind of shame reserved for men who live from the marketing of a woman's honor.

This mood was on him the December evening when Carolina came into the library, where he stood before the fire. He looked at her, slim, beautiful, noting how good living had filled out her splendid body, and hating her for that. He came slowly toward her and said in a low voice, "I should kill you, Cãrolina. My father would have done that."

Hate leaped from her eyes at him. Then she struck him in the face.

He staggered back with an oath. Standing straight and still and cold, she said, "Kirby, if you ever mention this to me again, I shall kill *you*. When you think of what *should* have been, remember that *I* picked up the broken pieces. Some of those pieces were sharp. And *you* got only a scratch!"

His glance wavered away. Sheepishly, he turned back to the fire, saying nothing, looking at the flames.

Carolina studied him. "We are going away," she said finally. "You will find a bag and clothes in your room. Go get dressed."

He spun around, surprise all over his whiskey-loose face. "Are you mad?"

"This man is rich," she said composedly. "I have told him that I will marry him if he will take us away from this country. Tonight he is coming to do that."

"Go away yourself," he said darkly. "I'll get along some other way."

She came a step nearer. "I need you in my plans, Kirby. He is not going with us."

Kirby saw her flushed excitement, the hard brightness of her eyes.

"He will have fifty thousand Yankee dollars with him— the funds of his office," Carolina went on swiftly. "Also, tickets from New Orleans." She paused a moment; then, "There is a pistol in your bag. I will bring him here, to the library. You will know what to do. He is an enemy. Remember that—if you have to."

He looked at her, slack-jawed. "Carolina," he muttered, "we could hang—"

"Damn you!" she flared at him. "Damn your weakness, your cowardice! His money was taken from our people— from *us!* Is it wrong to take back money stolen by an enemy?"

A crafty light crept into his eyes. Slowly, he nodded. "That's so. But the servants—"

"Gone. I sent them away this morning."

Now a reluctant, sly admiration for her competence came over him. At last, "We could bury him in the cellar," he said musingly. "By morning we would be half way to New Orleans in his carriage."

"They will think he skipped the country," she agreed swiftly. "Why not? Half of them do. Now, go get dressed."

At the doorway he turned. "By the way," he said ironically. "Any objection to telling me where we're going?"

She looked at him, then away, her eyes seeing far spaces and a new life with all the unbroken vistas of things still unknown. "To Texas," she said quietly. "We will make our new beginning there."

It was toward midnight when Kirby Steele finished the work with the shovel in the cellar. He washed up then and went to the library where Carolina, warmly dressed for the road, waited for him. He nodded and neither spoke. Then she turned away, indicating the bags with a glance. One bag she carried with her, and it was the small one the man had brought when he came.

When the luggage was stowed in the carriage, Kirby turned back to the house. "In a moment," he muttered to Carolina, and then ran back through the darkness. Into the library he went, and looked long at the book-filled shelves, and the chair where he had sat in other days, reading those books. Then, grim-faced, he went to the fireplace, and, taking a burning brand in the tongs, went swiftly through the house, firing bedclothes, curtains, draperies. By the time he returned to the library, fire had eaten into the ceiling and had started along the`walls. He took one last look, then went quickly through the smoke-filled hallway and out of the Steele house forever.

He heard Carolina's gasp as he climbed to the seat beside her, but said nothing. A moment later he clucked to the bays and headed out the lane, bound for the back roads on the way to New Orleans and Texas. As he drove into the night, he knew that he had sold himself to his sister, and would never again be his own man.

It was toward the misty dawn before she spoke. Then, quietly, she said, "It was just as well, Kirby, your burning the house."

He tried for a long while to fashion the right reply, but when he found it, he knew that it would mean nothing to her, so he simply said, "Why not? There was nothing worthwhile left there."

Chapter 3

LANDRY lit the lamp and put his things away. In his war bag he found a clean shirt, and after he had scrubbed down and changed, the tenseness had gone from his muscles and from that corner of his mind which formed his thoughts. A prying uneasiness, growing from the happenings of the afternoon, lay just under his consciousness, but he pushed it aside and made his way to the dining room.

He found a corner table, ate his food absently, and afterward rolled a cigarette. With his coffee, ease returned, and then he sent a slow glance around the room.

The scattering of diners aroused no interest in him. Then, at a far table, he saw a woman, and this woman was watching him in a strange, speculative way. She was partly screened by diners, but he could see that she was not yet past being young, with honey-blond hair full of sultry light, and that her dark brown eyes had the bright, liquid overtones of women who are quick in their passions and angers. She had a dainty, pointed chin, delicate nostrils and the full, lush mouth of a woman who knows what may be said in a kiss. Watching her, he saw, too, that another thing lay about her mouth, and that it was dormant hardness and implacability.

He had caught her gaze full upon him, and his instant readings of the currents within her emboldened him to brush aside distance and tell her with his gaze that he appreciated the things in her that were feminine. She met this look with-

out resentment, even with a half-concealed curiosity, and
then she turned indifferently away.

It was brief, but heady and climactic: that moment had
left him shaken. Even as he made this secret admission, the
woman rose and, without a glance in his direction, went toward the door.

He saw, now, that she was of medium height, with full
breasts, a slim waist, and high, well-rounded hips. As she
went from the room, he was keenly conscious of the easy
churning of long legs and the gentle undulation of her hips.

Landry kept that vision of her as long as he dared. And a
restless fever burned up within him, opening his memory to
small things out of the past: the song of wind in the tree tops
outside a fire-lighted cabin at night, the feel of a woman's
soft, lithe back through satin; the loneliness stirred up by
stars hanging over a moon-bathed desert; and the powerful
alchemy set in motion by the scent of a woman's hair with
whom he had once danced and never seen again. He let
these images make their momentary conflict with the
harsher things lying within him; and then, as the vision of
Mary Wayne rose before his mind's eye, fresh as a breath of
mountain air, he knew that all this told him merely that this
was a hard and lonely land. With that, he got quickly to his
feet, feeling unease and irritation.

Leaving the dining room, he cruised through the lobby
and stepped into the street, pausing to let his glance feel for
the texture of things in the night of this small town.

A pair of men stood at the corner of an alley below the
hotel, watching him. He let them have their look; then,
blowing smoke into the darkness, he drifted over the dust to
the Longhorn. Men passed him, darker shadows in the darkness. A brief voice said, "Hell, yes, it's a frame-up. What's
the matter with that?" and the gruff, complaining reply was
lost to Landry's ears. Closing a compartment in his mind on
those half-heard words, he crossed the street, and as he came
to the swing doors a rising clatter of hoofs toward the town's
edge caught and held him. After a moment he saw them
coming on at a trot, a dozen riders cutting their silhouettes

briefly through the dust-murky light which filtered into the street from houses and stores.

As they passed the Longhorn they reined down to a walk and Landry noted at their front the heavy-headed gunman who had been with Steele this afternoon. This one caught sight of Landry and watched him until they had trooped past.

At the Casino some of the riders dropped out. The rest rode on to the hotel and got down. The blond gunman moved into the light from the hotel's doorway, spoke briefly with the others, then went inside.

Landry watched this bunch of men. A pair of them moved downstreet into the shadows, while three leisurely crossed the way, merging into the blackness further down. Those who had alighted at the Casino had gone into the night, but the bright winking of a cigarette's burning end said that one or more of them had taken up a stand farther down the way.

Landry's interest in this scene had risen, and now, knowing that a trap had been set, he stepped into the Longhorn and went to the bar, where he hooked an elbow on the wood and pondered what he had seen. The bartender came forward with a deliberate drag to his feet, and Landry said, "Whiskey."

The barkeep looked at him sourly and said, "You're in the wrong place."

"This a saloon?"

"You rode in with Hagberg and the Corralitos crowd. Go to your own water hole."

Impatience with the snarling suspicion loose in this place hit Landry. "Who in hell drinks here? You've got no sign out."

Two other men were standing near the front of the saloon, watching the street. One of these now turned and said, "He came in alone, Grady. Earlier."

Grady shot the man a quick look, then turned to Landry. "What you doin' in town?" he asked suspiciously.

Almost beyond anger, Landry said tightly, "Do you want my money, fellow?"

Grady's glance fell slowly away, and he brought bottle and glass and put them before Landry. Still he stood there, his hands on the bar, doggedly eying this newcomer. "Maybe you just came on in ahead of the Swede," he insisted. "Wiser that way."

"You heard what that fellow said." Landry jerked his head toward the front.

"Only one kind of business in this town," Grady growled. "What's yours?"

"Whiskey salesman," Landry said, pouring a drink. "That way, I never go dry when dumb barslops like you keep hold of the bottle."

Grady colored. He let Landry have his drink. "Maybe you're to hold things down here when they bust loose—" He hung on that, fitting it into his mind, then turned toward the front. "Will, what about this fellow?"

Will, stirred up by Grady's uneasiness, came forward. He was a solid, thick man with a burly jaw and red hair. "Yes." He glowered at Landry. "What about you, stranger?"

Landry made a half turn, facing Will. "I've seen some nosy places," he said, "but this is the worst."

"You could be one of the gunmen Steele's bringin' in."

"More than that. I could be Christ Almighty, and it'd still be none of your business."

Suspicion shot up in Will's gaze. "No fancy talk. What brought you here?"

"Just keep puttin' your dib in," Landry said. "You'll find out."

Will's face hardened. He took a slow, decisive step forward, and Landry said, "That's far enough, Will—"

Outside there grew up the loose commotion of running horses, and Will was caught and held by the sound. The man near the window said crisply, "Ardoin's comin'."

Will showed Landry his teeth in a wolfish smile. "Now we'll see where you stand, hard boy." He edged toward the front, holding Landry in his line of vision.

But Landry had now forgotten Will. The name spoken by

the man at the window had riveted all his thoughts and attention elsewhere.

Outside, the bunch of riders reined in with a nervous clatter and a creaking of leather. A moment later a tall man, thin-hipped and heavy through the chest, shouldered through the swing doors, shooting a quick look about the room and catching Landry on its point. He stepped aside as Will spoke to him, and through the door spilled eight or ten other riders, heading for the bar, fast.

Presently the big man looked up and said loudly, "Have your drinks and stay put unless I tell you. If there's trouble, they've got to start it."

A man's voice rose querulously, "Why in hell do we run for a hole? Just let 'em swing out!"

"Do as I say." The tall man now stepped away from Will and came toward Landry. He was a still-faced man with a kind of taciturn melancholy sitting about his lips and pulling lines down into his tanned cheeks. Landry caught his gaze and saw that his dark eyes were filled with speculation, lying behind a thin, hard mask of wariness. Then he looked away and came on, taking a place at the bar beside Landry.

The barkeeper brought bottle and glass, said, "Hello, Ed." He cocked a brow in Landry's direction. Ed nodded, poured a drink and took it fast. Then, still keeping his gaze off Landry, he rolled a cigarette, crimped the end and stuck it in his mouth. With that, he turned. "Match?"

Landry struck a match and held it to the cigarette. In the burst-up of flame, Landry saw the other's eyes, a not-bad humor in them now. The man drew back, blew out smoke and said, "Thanks." His glance went over Landry appraisingly. "You the fellow that stopped at the Wayne ranch this afternoon?"

"Before I answer that, are you Ed Ardoin, owner of Pitch-fork?"

Ardoin nodded, his eyes watchful.

"All right," Landry said. "I'm the one that stopped at Wayne's. Frank Landry. That mean anything to you?"

"Maybe."

Landry made his judgment. "It ought to. You knew my brother, Steve."

Ardoin had been leaning an elbow on the bar. Now he slowly drew erect. "How do you know that?"

"I got a letter from Steve. It said that, if anything went wrong, to look up Ed Ardoin of the Pitchfork outfit." He paused. "That was his last word. Four months ago."

Ardoin's gaze swung slowly around the saloon. Then he said, "Come with me."

They went toward the rear of the place, through a door and went up a pair of stairs in the darkness. Another door opened, and Ardoin struck a match and lighted a lamp on a table in this room, which was a kitchen.

"We can talk here," he said.

As they faced one another across the table, there was a blankness in Ardoin's countenance that Landry did not like. Ardoin shifted his feet, looked down at the table, and afterward his glance came up again. Slowly he said, "Your brother was killed."

Landry nodded. "I figured that. It was a long time—" He was thinking, now, of the letter.

Everything is going like we thought—it had said—
It's a good tract. Some funny things going on around
here, but nothing to really worry about, after you get
here. Just in case anything happens, get in touch with
Ed Ardoin, owner of the Pitchfork outfit. He's our
neighbor.

There had been a worry in Steve's mind when that was written. It had nagged Landry all the way from Montana to this place.

Ardoin now said, "I don't reckon Steele was too pleased to find you here."

"Why not?"

"Want it from the beginning?"

"From the beginning."

Ardoin stubbed out his cigarette in a saucer. "You boys

bought smack into trouble," he said with slow bitterness, "and the trouble is Corralitos—Kirby Steele and his sister, Carolina."

"I know *him*."

"Carolina's the one that counts—tougher than any ten men in this country, and twice as dangerous. But pretty as hell with it, which—" he hesitated, searching to voice a thought.

"Brown eyes, light hair," Landry said, guessing. "Strong features, but fine—"

Ardoin nodded. "You've seen the best of her."

"What's shaping up in this place? Enough guns out there in the street to defeat Grant."

"Like I said, it begins with Corralitos."

Landry waited, and presently, Ardoin continued, "The line between Frio and Jackson counties cuts east-west about four miles north of town. My outfit and Darby Wayne's— Pitchfork and Circle Running W—are the two biggest in Frio. Carolina's Corralitos brand covers damn near all of north Jackson County, just below us. This desert lies between the two big range areas."

"What's the reason for trouble in that?"

"Carolina's for fencing and breeding up her herds. Way it is, you turn good bulls loose, they breed on anybody's stock. Then the increase of a good herd is cut up by maverickers and cow thieves, until some years it's just plain hell to make a living."

"She sounds smart," Landry said.

"Sure," Ardoin agreed. "But now, with every outfit represented at roundups, and the Association letting a man take a commission on all strange brands in a herd he sells, things ain't so bad."

"Still don't improve the stock," Landry said.

"Well," Ardoin said grimly, "Carolina's hell-bent on getting fences. And because Darby Wayne and I wouldn't fence, she tried to buy us out. We wouldn't sell."

He stopped, thinking of that, and Landry said, "So?"

Ardoin went on. "Winter times, storms come down out of

the Buckhorns where Pitchfork and Running W cows range. Sometimes two, three thousand head drift over the County line. We used to cut and drive 'em back. But that," his lips twisted bitterly, "was before Carolina decided she wanted all hell's creation."

Landry waited a moment. "Now?"

"Since we refused to sell out to Corralitos, we can't cut herds unless we fight her gunmen." Ardoin's voice rose sharply, "Not only that. She works our brush for mavericks and rustles the ranges on stormy nights, to make it look like a drift."

Landry puzzled with this thing a moment. "County line, hell! A drift is a drift and a brand is a brand. You cut your brand out, that's all there is to it."

Ardoin laughed shortly. "Sure, it's easy to say. But listen, friend. Carolina's got a Pitchfork brand in the name of one of her men right south of me, and a Circle Running W brand down below Darby Wayne's line. Now"—his eyes glittered venomously—"what in hell's so simple about that?"

"There's the law! You can't duplicate brands—"

Ardoin snorted. "Mister," he said, "you're not used to a big place like Texas. Brands in this country are by *counties*. Carolina Steele has a perfect damn legal right to our Pitchfork and Running W brands, if she's the first to register 'em in Jackson County. She can throw our cows in with her stuff, and who's going' to say it's stealin'?"

For a moment Landry tried to put this audacity together with the soft voluptuousness of the woman he had seen earlier in the hotel. At last he agreed, "She *is* smart."

"Tomorrow," Ardoin said, "there'll be a court decision on the brands. But it's her county, her court, her judge, her sheriff. That's why all the guns in town."

"What does the law do when you boys start burning powder?"

Ardoin shrugged. "Lon Wilson is Carolina's sheriff. He just fills the office, nothing more. In this town you still kill your man on the street and ride away."

Landry understood, now. Hate was loose in this place,

and people had staked their lives against it. Law existed only to serve lawlessness; and into this, Steve had come and been drawn under by the dark, hidden currents.

"We started talking about Steve," he pointed out.

Ardoin nodded. "The ranch your brother bought—the 2 Bar L—lies right up against mine, but in Jackson County. It was the only thing near the line that Carolina didn't have her hands on. She needed it, because Jim McCanless used the Paso Ventana there to run Mexican cattle over the border for her."

"Who's McCanless?"

"One of the Corralitos crowd. He wants to marry Carolina, and Kirby hates his guts. Was wanted all over Texas until Carolina took him up and sent him to Mexico. Now he rustles Mexican beef and brings it across for her herds without paying duty. Nice, eh?"

"Come back to Steve," Landry said.

"McCanless was after Steve because Steve drove him off the 2 Bar L with about three hundred head he'd brought over for Corralitos. And"—he leaned over the table—"Carolina Steele tried to buy Steve off his place. No luck."

Landry had his mind full of new and disturbing facts, and he needed time to sort them out. He built a cigarette while Ardoin watched him, pulled silently on it for a moment, then said, "Now, I suppose he'll be after me when I take over the place."

"You won't."

"Why not?"

"It was sold for taxes. Three weeks ago."

Landry said, "That's impossible. A property has to be derelict—"

"It was declared derelict after Steve's death. Somebody bought it. Give you three guesses."

"Listen, Ardoin," Landry said impatiently. "Do you know who—"

"Hell no. You think Carolina'd let her pen pushers open the books for the public?"

"I see." Landry sat back, thinking his deep and turbulent

thoughts, making his judgments and filling in empty spaces in his whole frame of knowledge. "All right," he said at last. "Who do you *think* killed Steve?"

The other man shifted his weight on the chair. His fingers tapped a tattoo on the table top for some seconds. "I don't like guesses," he said. "But"—his glance came up sharply to Landry's—"it'd be damned interesting to get a look at the register of deeds—just to see whose name that property's in right now!"

Landry watched Ardoin thoughtfully. "I didn't ask you anything about Carolina Steele's fight with you and Darby Wayne."

Ardoin was a not-fast man, with his deep currents of melancholy, and now he eyed Landry morosely and said, "What happened to your brother can happen to all of us unless this is stopped. I want your gun on our side." Then he waited.

Landry soaked this up, taking the logic, finding the flaws in it. "How about your people?"

"They top us," Ardoin said grimly. "Carolina's bought the hire of a lot like McCanless: Swede Hagberg, Bill Coulter, others. If they'd cut loose tonight, they'd own this country tomorrow."

"What makes you so sure there's going to be a war?"

"This last winter," Ardoin said, "better than two thousand head of Pitchfork and Running W cows drifted across the county line. Steele's settin' 'em up in a trail herd." He waited a moment. "We're going to cut that herd—my bunch and Darby Wayne. We're just waitin' for the trial. Then—"

"You mentioned gunmen. Think it'd be safe to cut?"

"There's only a holding crew with 'em," Ardoin said. "But when we cut 'em, this country will go up in smoke."

Landry was about to reply, when outside a shot split the air and the drumming of oncoming horses rolled up in the street. Ardoin lurched to his feet and went into the dark front room. Landry followed him to the window overlooking the street.

Up from the south rolled a dozen horsemen, burning

powder into the air and splitting the night with shrill yells.
Landry saw the flash of wide-brimmed sombreros and of
concha-studded vests as they swept on, and he knew that
they were Mexican *vacqueros*. A heavy-shouldered man,
tough-faced and thick in the chest, rode at their head, and as
they came abreast of the hotel and pulled up in a boiling up
of dust, this one let out a piercing war whoop that went ring-
ing through the street. Before the hotel he dropped from his
saddle, loosed a crackling of Spanish epithets at his wiry,
dark-faced riders, then wheeled and strode into the hotel.
With him went a sense of departing wildness.

Ardoin looked at Landry. "McCanless," he murmured.

Landry left the window, walking slowly back to the
lighted room. Here he faced Ardoin.

"I'm on your side of this thing," he said quietly, "but I
won't line up."

"How do you mean that?" Ardoin frowned.

"I'll play the game my way."

Ardoin's gaze clouded ever so slightly. "You the kind that
don't like company?"

"You fellows haven't done so well your way," Landry
pointed out. "Maybe mine will be better."

Ardoin made an impatient gesture. "You stood up to
Steele's gunmen this afternoon. Our side needs men like
that. Now, just why in hell have you got to play a lone
hand?"

The querulous note in his voice impressed Landry
strangely. "I didn't say that. But if I'm going to be any good
to you, I can't advertise who I am to the Steele crowd. Steele
suspects me. Darby Wayne thinks I'm a distant relative of
Steve Landry. Let it stay that way. Then I can do some
good."

Ardoin pondered over it and finally said, "All right. You
and I work together?"

"We'll see." Landry turned toward the door leading
downstairs. "There a back way out of this place?"

"I'll show you." Ardoin bent over and blew out the light.
Then he led the way through the darkness down the stairs.

Landry heard him shuffling about in the gloom, and presently the fresh coolness of night air hit him. "Here," Ardoin said softly, and then the lighter shadows of night showed through the blackness as Ardoin held the door open.

On the threshold, Landry paused. "One more thing," he said. "How was Steve killed?"

"He was sitting at the table, with his back to an open window," Ardoin said. "There were two cups of coffee on the table. He had a knife in his back when I found him."

"What kind of a knife?"

"A Mexican blade. The kind the *vaqueros* use."

After a moment, Landry stepped into the darkness. He had gone three steps when Ardoin's low voice caught at his boot heels. "Landry."

"Well?"

"Jim McCanless is just as handy with a knife as he is with a gun." Then Landry heard the soft closing of the door. He stood there in the darkness for some moments, sorting out his feelings, and laying his plan of action. Then he headed for the faint light of an alley down which he would find Broken Wheel's main street.

Chapter 4

KIRBY STEELE caught the onrushing commotion of McCanless' crew of *vaqueros* as they swept into town. From the window of his room, fronting the hotel's second story, he watched their rowdy arrival, the lamplight making sharp patterns of distaste along the bold angles of his face. After a while he turned away, a distant kind of dislike in his eyes as he glanced at the man seated at the room's round table.

"McCanless," he said shortly.

The other man watched as Steele came and sat down. He was a thick man with long arms and huge hands, whose fingers were deceptively slim and soft. An oversize head, square and heavily chiseled, seemed to weigh down the upper part of his body, giving him a top-heavy appearance. He had the light, fair countenance of the northern races—out of place in this land of sun-darkened men—and thin, blond hair. His eyes were round, dead and inert with the inertia of those whose thoughts come slowly and are hard to shake loose.

"Want me to stay around, Kirby?"

Steele poured a drink of whiskey, took it fast, and made a face. "It's all right, Swede. You can go."

Swede Hagberg hesitated, trying to move his ideas past dead center. "I don't trust McCanless. I'd better stay."

"Now, that is strange," Steele mused, knowing the irony would be lost. "Imagine not trusting McCanless. What has he ever done but commit an odd murder or two?"

"He'd knife you in a minute."

"Yes." Steele pursed his lips thoughtfully. "I believe he would."

"He'd do more than that. He'd put a word in Carolina's ear if he could—"

"What do you mean?" Steele swung about.

The Swede waited. "You're too far away from the talk," he said finally. "But I pick it up. McCanless would like to see you out of the way, and Carolina holdin' everything."

"Would he, Swede?" Steele asked softly, "Why would he want that?"

Hagberg shuffled his feet uneasily. "I—well, Kirby—" he began.

Steele rose out of his chair, his face angry and dark. "Keep your damned mouth shut," he rasped. "And stay away from gossip. Understand?"

"I only meant to warn you." Hagberg backed away. "You know what I'd do to anybody that ever tried to double-cross you—"

It came over Steele that this dolt was offering him tribute. Instantly he regretted that he had shown anger, knowing that this man, of all those about him, was the only one who felt loyalty toward him.

"I know," he murmured, sinking into his chair. "Perhaps you are right." But the thing that had been hinted at was still there between them, like a great, ragged hole in his pride.

"You don't have to be smart to know what's going on here," Hagberg said presently. "McCanless figures if you were out of the way he'd marry Carolina—maybe—and get his own paws on the works."

"Swede—" Menace rose in Steele's voice.

But Hagberg was not to be stopped now. "Kirby," he pushed on, "you're in a lonely spot. Everybody stands to gain by getting you out of the way!"

Steele was thinking, now, under the impact of the big man's words, of what Carolina had told him this evening. And the whiskey was like a catalyst to the boiling compound of emotions which Hagberg's charges had stirred up in him. Knowing that Hagberg spoke from loyalty, he heeded his words and drained truth from them. Presently he got up. "Thanks, Swede. I think you mean well for me."

"I'd gun down anybody who ever tried to cross you," the big man said flatly.

The sound of heavy footsteps now echoed along the corridor. Jim McCanless pushed the door open and stepped into the room.

He said in a robust voice, "Hello, Kirby." Afterward he glanced at Hagberg and said airly, "Old Squarehead again. How's Kirby's gun artist?" Then he laughed, not unpleasantly.

"Want to find out?"

McCanless was a tall man, thick through the shoulders and solidly built, with tough, rugged features. Curly black hair hung down over his forehead, and he had a wide mouth that would have been generous except for the tightness at the corners. He laughed a lot, not always with good humor; he smiled a lot, and some of his smiles were used in place of a curse. Arrogance was all through him and boldness with it. On top of his dark-eyed glance was a leaping and darting alertness, and beneath this a reservoir of sly, hard cunning.

Now he looked at Hagberg and waved the challenge aside. "Go shoot up tin cans on the dump," he said with a lopsided grin. "You're not ready for me yet." Then he came to the table and sat down.

Steele waved a hand at Hagberg. "Be here when Ardoin and Wayne come over."

Hagberg went out, and Steele sat down facing McCanless. He shoved the bottle and a glass across the table and watched the big man have his drink.

McCanless put the glass down and wiped his mouth. "Never seen this damn town so full of people. You really draw 'em in."

"Yes." Steele watched him distantly. "After tomorrow we'll be sitting on top of a very big thing."

McCanless' eyes turned shrewd, but he grinned. "Get away with it?"

"Why not? My outfit, yours—who can stand up to that?"

McCanless nodded. "The Mexican beef go out of the picture pretty soon?"

"What makes you think so?"

"Well," McCanless said easily, "it's just a question of time until we break the back of Running W and Pitchfork. Why fool around with Mexican beef when there's a job for everybody up here?"

Steele poured another drink and put the glass down. "Don't start making plans, McCanless. Whatever we say, you just do it."

The bluntness of this speech tore aside the mask of McCanless' geniality. "Who in hell do you think you are?" he snarled. "I do business with your sister, not you."

This had been a test, and Steele had made it for his own reasons. Now, his quick-rising wrath was drowned in a colder, more deliberate need for caution.

"We both do," he said evenly. "And you will find that I am right." He hated McCanless with the abiding hate of a dishonorable man who feels that he is being further dishonored. That hate made him say, "Remember, Carolina's plans may not be yours."

"I'll worry about that."

"Do so," said Steele. "And while you are worrying, here's another thing to preoccupy you: a man came to town tonight. A man by the name of Landry."

McCanless sobered. He leaned back, staring dubiously at Steele. "What the hell is this?"

"A man by the name of Landry. A competent, hard kind of individual."

A man came to the door, held it half open and spoke to Steele. "That fellow went into the Longhorn, Kirby. Later, he disappeared with Ed. What next?"

"Keep looking," Steele said waspishly. "When you find him, take him over to the jail and have Lon Wilson lock him up on suspicion."

The man went out. MaCanless asked, "That him?"

"The same."

The big man nodded. "It *could* be just the name—"

"On the other hand, it could be something else."

Unexpectedly, McCanless laughed, a reckless laugh, which tossed aside unpleasant contingencies. "To hell with it. The other one wasn't so tough—"

The door opened and Hagberg said, "Wayne's coming in. Any orders?"

"Tell Darby and Ardoin to come up here. You and Coulter come along."

Hagberg left. McCanless said, musingly, "Well, this is the showdown. Wonder what they've got?"

"Nothing," Steele said. "Nothing will be changed."

McCanless got up and walked to the window, as outside the sound of trotting horses swung toward them, rose to a crescendo, and came to a slow-dying halt before the hotel. "They're here," he said. "Now we'll see how big their medicine is."

It struck Steele that he spoke as though everything at stake at this moment were of direct and personal concern to him. Feeling the nudging of hate that this big man had placed in him, he frowned.

"Yes," he said dryly, "from now on we'll see what happens."

Landry came into the main street below the Longhorn. Standing in the shadow of a building, he felt out for the temper of things in the street and, after a while, had found it in the sum of the horses racked along the walks and the men coming and going or lounging with apparent idleness along the plank walks. Then he stepped out and turned his nose south, drifting easily along through the shadows in the direction of the Courthouse.

Beyond the post office, he caught the brief gleam of a cigarette deep in an alley's furrow. He went on, lengthening his stride, and halted in the middle of the next block, listening back down the way he had come. He caught a slight shuffling sound, and with that he stepped into the darkness

of a nearby doorway and waited. Presently two men ghosted
out of the shadows, passing near him in the doorway.

A few feet beyond they stopped. One said dubiously,
"Sure he came this way?"

"Dead sure. You heard what Wayne said, up the street."

"Well," the other replied, "we'll look a ways farther."

They went on into the darkness.

Landry was still thinking about the name they had spoken, when the two drifted back, faded into the blackness and
disappeared. He eased out of his hiding place, then cut
across the dust toward a pair of frame houses that sat beyond
the street's light.

Halfway over, the growing sound of trotting horses came
to him. Turning, he saw a group of riders coming on through
the intermittent slashes of light upstreet, and he recognized
at their head Darby Wayne, lank, proud and stern-faced. At
the hotel they scattered for the hitch racks, and after a word
to another who rode beside him, Darby Wayne spurred down
the street toward Landry.

Landry quickly went on. He hit the boardwalk and turned
south just as Darby Wayne pulled up. Then, as Landry
looked around, Mary Wayne came off the steps of a porch
ahead of him.

Landry tipped his hat and would have passed on. But
Darby Wayne called after him, "Landry. Wait there."

He turned. The girl was looking at him, and in the dim
light coming from a window in the house's front, he saw a
questioning, thoughtful look in her eyes, and saw, too, that
the light did strange and pulse-warming things to her hair.

He came back and lifted his hat again. "Evening, Miss
Wayne." He nodded to her father.

Darby Wayne said, "Just a word of warning. Night like
this, a fellow like you ought to stay close to the bright
lights."

"I'm used to the dark," Landry said laconically. "Don't
scare me any more."

From atop his horse Wayne stared at him disapprovingly.

"For your own good," he said shortly. Then, he asked the girl, "Where's Harry?"

"He went up the street an hour ago. He was going to wait for you to come in."

The old man grunted. "I've got to go back with the crew. You'll be all right here with Harry?"

"Of course. Don't worry."

"All right." He hesitated. "You say a little prayer that things go right at the meeting—"

"Maybe a show of force—" she began.

Darby Wayne made an impatient sound, wheeled his horse, and spurred away.

Landry turned and found the girl's gaze on him. There were lights deep in her eyes, and a softness about her mouth that the day's hard light had blotted out. She saw him watching her mouth, and looked away with quick embarrassment.

She went to the steps and there she faced him. "Can't you come up a little while?" she asked. "I have something to tell you."

Landry said musingly, "You, too?"

She gave him a small frown. "What's that?"

"Ever since I came to this town," he said resignedly, "people have been telling me things: get out of town; stay here and fight; this one is a crook, the other a saint—" He shrugged.

"Well," she said quickly, "you don't have to listen to *me!* I just thought that—" Then, quickly, she stepped up on the porch. He followed.

He had been needlessly rude, and regretting that, he came close and looked down at her. For a little while the immediate things in each other's mind were forgotten, and Landry looked at her as he had that afternoon, and found her answer in kind.

Gently he said, "Now don't get mad when I say this, but right at this minute you could tell me anything, and I'd believe it."

A slow smile crinkled her eyes. "So there *is* another side to you, Mr. Landry," she said lightly. "I wondered about that. You're not all steel and rawhide and gunsmoke after all!"

"Who could be?" Landry grinned. "Who could be, if a red headed woman thought he was something else—"

Mary Wayne laughed, a gay, comradely laugh, as wholesome as rain-washed air and the smell of pine. "Come up here, Sir Galahad," she said easily, taking his hand and drawing him up on the porch. "I *do* want to tell you something."

She led him in the darkness to a side porch and then into a room lighted by a lamp burning on a table in the room's center. There she let go his hand and faced him.

Her open, candid gaze went over his face, taking in every detail of his features and lighting at last upon his own level, gray-eyed gaze.

"Perhaps I shouldn't tell you this," she said after a moment. "But men are not always the best judges of such matters." She saw his faint smile, and went on, "You said this afternoon that you came here to work for a cousin. Did you mean Steve Landry?"

"Yes."

Slowly she shook her head. "You are too late," she said gently. "Steve Landry is—he was killed—"

Her glance widened to catch his reaction. But he merely nodded gravely. "I know that."

"You—how did you find that out?" Then she colored.

"It's apparently not a secret," he said wryly.

She nodded. "I'm sorry. I suppose he—meant something to you."

"A great deal."

Landry was watching her steadily, summing her up, finding in her the lost delights of women whom he had known, long ago, the knowledge of whom had been replaced by another kind: those of the cow towns and the fast-growing camps, of the honky-tonks and the gambling halls. He had a moment of secret shame while making this contrast. But the sum of all things that were her reached out wistfully for him in this moment, as he asked, "Why did you tell me this, Mary Wayne?"

She turned her face away, confused. "I—you stood up to Kirby Steele's gunmen this afternoon," she said. "Men here do not do that—"

"And you thought that I might fight on your father's side in this war?"

"No," she said finally, "it wasn't that. It was that—well—" She hesitated, then turned quickly to face him, her chin up. Almost defiantly, she said, "I wanted to know what you would do, now that there is no job for you. Will you leave this place—ride on—or will you stay here?"

The naivete of it moved him strangely, for he knew that she had paid him the tribute of frankness as would a trusting child. He stepped close to her, a lean, tall man full of wild hungers and hard urges, yet one who knew where lines must be drawn. She would have turned her gaze away, but he cupped her chin in his hand and bought her face gently around.

There was a dogged kind of shame in her eyes, and, lying side by side with it, interest and an alive, pushing want that stirred him deeply. Softly he asked, "Does it make a difference to you what I do?"

The bluntness of his query pointed up for her the foolhardiness of her having asked him here at all. With that knowledge she grew crimson, and suddenly he saw tears well into her eyes. He knew then what loneliness could mean to a girl in this place, peopled by rough men whose passions were stark and unbridled, whose knowledge of women was that gained in the sink holes of the hell towns. Understanding her loneliness, he said, "I'd stay here all the rest of my life—just for the chance to look at you sometimes."

Then he took her face between his hands and kissed her on the mouth, so gently, hearing her soft sigh as time stood still for a little while.

Presently, as though physically unable to bear it longer, the girl jerked away and turned her back to him. He could see the quick rise and fall of her bosom, the flush that had spread over her face, coloring even the soft skin of her neck.

She stood looking down at the table. Then she started to say something, choked over it, and was silent.

"Mary Wayne," Landry said gently, "I know what you are thinking. You are saying to yourself, 'I only saw him this afternoon for the first time.' And you find that hard to face, and are trying to hate yourself."

She half turned. "I've never let any man kiss me the first time," she said, almost savagely. "You must think that I'm like these—these—"

"Don't say it," Landry murmured. "You're sweet, Mary Wayne. No, don't turn around. If you do, maybe I won't be able to tell you either. But remember: there's no time limit on things like that. They happen, like a flash of lightning from a clear sky. And maybe it's nicer than if you'd waited six years—who knows?"

The girl was listening, and he saw her slow half smile. Shyly she said, "Then you don't think I—"

"I told you," he insisted softly. "At this moment you're like a dream of something I've lost. Maybe it'll change, but we're interested only in this moment. You don't have to tell me what kind of a woman you are. The trouble with you, Mary Wayne"—he paused, thinking how to say it—"is that you haven't been kissed enough!"

Then he turned and left the room, striding quickly across the porch and down into the street. A voice kept telling him that he acted like a fool, but his step was light and his heart was singing.

Behind him, Mary Wayne stood watching the door through which he had gone, her eyes full of luminous lights. After a while she smiled, a slow, secret smile, and then, humming softly to herself, she went to her room.

Chapter 5

DARBY WAYNE glanced across the table at Kirby Steele, then at the men behind Steele: Swede Hagberg, dull, leonine, dangerous; Jim McCanless, smiling easily, with the threat of swift-cutting steel and its same cold treachery behind that bland, brash gaze; Bill Coulter, wild and tough, showing concern for nothing, feeling for nothing. In these faces, Wayne read the future, and it was dark and ominous.

Flanking Wayne were his son, Harry, weathered, glum old Drav McLain and Ed Ardoin. Until now, Ardoin had said little, and it nettled Darby Wayne to realize that he alone was doing all the talking against the thing that was piling up against them here.

"You can't talk around it, Steele," he said flatly. "The fact remains: you take the Runnin' W and Pitchfork drifts in the winter. It's plain stealin'."

Steele ran his hand over his mouth before he said, "Two years ago we began asking you people to build fence. What have you done about it?"

"Fences! You rob us blind and then want us to find money for wire. That's the damnedest gall I ever saw or hope to see!"

Steele shrugged. "You had your chance."

Ardoin now said, "We came here to settle this thing of brands. Any other talk is a waste of time."

Steele shot Ardoin a quick look. He poured a drink and

took it in one brief swallow. "My own feeling is that *any* talk now is a waste of time."

There was a small silence. Darby Wayne growled softly, "Your fake Runnin' W south of the Frio line is a drift trap. You've even got the same smooth right-ear crop and under-half left-ear crop. You've done the same thing with Ed. What kind of skunk's business do you call that?"

"Perfectly legal," Steele replied coolly. "You'll see that in the morning." Then, before Wayne could reply, he added, "You have no proof that your cows are mixed with mine."

Old Drav McLain shuffled forward. "Our herds get smaller," he rasped. "Your get bigger—not by the natural increase. With *grown critters!*"

"That's what *you* say!"

McLain swore, and Steele's face hardened. Behind him, Coulter shifted his feet. He was watching McLain with a cold, still look.

Now Darby Wayne rose, slow wrath burning up into his face. "You damn polecat," he said softly. "You stink up the air of this whole country."

There was a swift motion behind Steele. He turned quickly, alarm on his face. "Hold it!" he snapped. Then he faced the others. "Bad judgment, Wayne. This is no place to start a fight."

"No place to run? You'd think of that!"

Hagberg's dull voice broke the silence. "Kirby, you don't have to take that. Say the word—"

"Oh, for Christ's sake, shut up!" McCanless cut in. He glared at Hagberg, who had gone ashen-faced. Then, to Wayne, he said, "Darby, I just work for Corralitos. But why don't you boys use some sense? Maybe this thing can be worked out—"

"Ah," said Steele. "The fine, silken hand of diplomacy!" Then he said deliberately to McCanless, "Jim, keep your damned mouth shut."

McCanless uttered a low sound and colored. Steele insisted, "Stay out of this until you're asked for an opinion."

Here, now, was a sense of disruption, and it made itself

felt in the abashed glances of the Steele men and in the grim smiles of the others. Seeing this, Ardoin said, "Well. Didn't you fellows take a vote on how you'd finish us off?"

Steele rose, closing the momentary rift. "Get this straight," he said, hard-faced. "I let you come here because every condemned man has a right to say a few last worlds. But you're done. Unless you sell, we force you out."

For long seconds that ultimatum hung there, working a slow readiness into Steele's men and raising the vague, half-forming desire for conflict in the others. Inaction held them, stealthy, barely balanced inaction, and then Wayne let go a harsh breath.

"All right," he said slowly. "We won't sell. We won't get out. That's the way you want it. By God, you'll have it! Now"—his angry glance beat against all of them—"we'll wait and see what the law says tomorrow. If they vacate your brands, well and good. If they don't"—he paused—"we'll fence. We'll do more than that." His voice rose now, hoarse and wrathful. "We'll build a wall that'll hold our cattle on our own range. A wall, Steele, you hear? And it'll be one you won't like. *It'll be a wall of guns!*"

For a moment he glared at Steele, his dislike and resentment beating through his gaze like hammers. Then, abruptly, he turned on his heel and stalked toward the door. The others followed.

As the sound of footsteps faded, Swede Hagberg waited, then stepped into the hall, closing the door. "Ed," he called. "Wait, Ed."

They all stopped. Ardoin spoke a low word and the others went on and down the stairs, while Ardoin waited watching the blond gunman with obvious dislike.

Hagberg's bulk loomed through the half-light. Near Ardoin he halted. "Listen, Ed—" he began.

Ardoin said crisply, "Don't want to talk to you. Get that through your head, you dumb Swede."

Now, surprisingly, Hagberg grinned. "Sounds like old times," there was a half-wistful note in his voice. "Like when we was ridin' for the Santo Domingo outfit in Sonora. You cussing' me, callin' me a dumb Swede—an' me likin' it."

Ardoin's sigh was soft in the darkness. "Yeah. Nothin's changed—except you got too good with your guns."

Silence. "Kirby treats me right," the Swede said heavily. "Fellow has to remember things like that."

Ardoin shook his head hopelessly. "You always needed me around to explain things."

"Now listen, Ed—"

"You're loyal to Kirby. That's enough for me."

"He gave me a job," Hagberg said defensively. "Not punchin' cows for forty a month—somethin' better. You think I liked to see you and all the other boys gettin' ahead, and me there, still twining' a lasso and handlin' an iron? I got as much right to get ahead as anybody, Ed. I got—"

"You got no damned sense," Ardoin said flatly. He was thinking of the time the Swede had come to Pitchfork seeking a job as foreman, of the necessity for refusing him that job, and of the dumb hurt in the smoke-dull eyes as Hagberg had nodded and slowly ridden away. Hagberg had come as a friend, and had been turned away, not understanding why friendship had failed to get him the place he wanted. Yet, conscious of these things, Ardoin said, "He gave you a job. Sure. Hired gunman. He speaks and you shoot. He hates and you kill. To hell with that!"

Hagberg mumbled, "Bodyguard, Ed. That's all—"

This thing which lay between them was impossible of solution or of understanding. Ardoin shook his head. "He couldn't have made a better choice," he murmured. "You don't even know the difference between right and wrong." Then he turned and went rapidly down the stairs.

The Swede watched him go, a dull, lightly pained expression in his eyes. "So long," he said in a low voice. "Be seein' you, Ed."

This caught the other in midstride. A lost, pleading note in that voice told him of failure to understand, and of dumb misery and confusion. It hurt Ardoin, and it angered him that it should be so. "I'll see you in hell!" he blurted. Then he ran down the steps.

Coming to the street, he spied Darby Wayne and McLain going into the Longhorn. He hesitated, reviewing the events which had transpired upstairs, and after a moment his glance shifted down the street toward Darby Wayne's house. He stiffened as he saw a man come off the porch and fade into the southward darkness. Something familiar about the man's walk prodded at him, and he eased along down the way until he could be sure. The man passed through a slash of light from a house's window, and he saw that it was Landry.

Ardoin stopped short. He watched Landry's figure merge into the blackness of the night and a frown grew and deepened on his brow. Then, his mouth a little grim, he went on quickly downstreet.

Kirby Steele raised a brooding glance as Hagberg came glumly into the room. "Stay away from that fellow. He's on the other side of the fence now."

"I know," Hagberg murmured unhappily. "I know."

"You and Coulter go down and pass the word around to the boys that there'll be no rough stuff tonight. Then come back."

Hagberg nodded and the two gunmen went out.

McCanless and Steele sat looking at one another. The big man's countenance wore a patronizing kind of disapproval, half amusement, half anger, and it made Kirby Steele feel for the moment like a precocious child, and McCanless meant that it should. Presently, Steele's glance fell away and he reached for the bottle, poured a stiff peg, and drank it. Then, with new assurance, he looked again at the other. "Well?" he said insolently.

"Like I thought," McCanless said contemptuously. "You don't have the cut for it."

"For what?"

"Being Napoleon. You're full of wind and large ideas."

Before Steele could reply, the door opened. A man

stepped inside and said shortly, "We lost him again, down toward Mex town."

Steele swore. "Get Coulter. He'll bring him in!" The man nodded and left.

"That's what I mean," McCanless said in a low voice. "You're all right pushin' that kind around, but you're out of your class with me."

With the whiskey in him, Steele again knew that he was McCanless' master. All kinds of games must be played, for the moment or with the long view, where human beings were concerned. He understood this; the others did not. And because he was their superior mentally, he could beat them or use them as he wished. "Yes," he said enigmatically, "perhaps I am. Further out of your class than you would think, Jim."

He had another heavy drink, then, and with it he raised his glance to the other, narrowed, thoughtful, obscure.

"Don't ever tramp on my toes again when others are around," McCanless growled. "I'll tip your hole card."

Steele was thinking of what Hagberg had said about McCanless and Carolina. He did not believe that this great barbarian loved Carolina, save for what she might possess in her own right, if Kirby were eliminated from the picture. That idea caught on a corner of his mind and hung there. Then, enjoying his position of superior knowledge, he said, "Jim, you are a competent person for the kind of work that has to be done in this place."

McCanless said nothing, but a hard slyness grew up in his gaze.

"I wonder if it has ever occurred to you that a greater share of the good things could be yours?"

McCanless slowly shifted his weight. After a moment, "Maybe it has," he said craftily. "What have you got in mind?"

His tone told Steele: *Anybody can buy him. I could get him to sell out Carolina, if the price were right!* The impact of this knowledge filled him with an elation which he must hide. He bent over, reached for the bottle and poured another stiff drink of whiskey, somewhat unsteadily this time. He took half the glass, grimaced as the sharp, sour odor of it rolled up through his nostrils, and then he lowered the glass and grinned crookedly at McCanless.

"Perhaps you have noticed," he said carefully, "that Carolina has been playing a rather high hand lately. For instance, in the case of this man Landry—"

The door opened and Carolina Steele stepped into the room, followed by Swede Hagberg. The drained whiteness of her face told them that she had heard.

Kirby Steele saw this instantly, and he set his glass down. Before he could rise, she crossed the room and swung her fist into his face, rocking him back against his chair and bringing a broad, red, welt to his cheek.

"You damned traitor," her voice shook with fury. "Plotting against me, like some disgruntled cowhand!"

Steele grew livid. Shame and pride goaded him to stand up to her in this moment of humiliation. For an instant he glared, then he lunged out of his chair. "That's the end," he said thickly. "Not even you can do that—"

Again she hit him in the face, catching him off balance. He reeled, cursing, and once more she struck him, laying names to him that left scars on his pride. He tried to retreat and regain his balance. But now he was dizzy with the effect of the whiskey, too, and his boot caught in the nailed-down matting rug and he fell, his head striking the hard wall with an audible thud. Momentarily stunned, he sat there, and the woman came to him and kicked him hard in the ribs, bringing a groan. He fell over on the floor, moaning.

Carolina Steele looked down at him, her eyes agate hard.

"The next time it will be a gun," she said in a low voice. "Brother or no brother." Then she turned to McCanless.

"Come with me," she snapped, and after a moment, he rose and followed her.

From the doorway, Hagberg had watched this. As Carolina passed, he rumbled, "I don't like it. By God, you're too hard."

She swung on him like a wildcat. "Watch your tongue! When I want advice, I'll ask for it."

Unblinkingly Hagberg said, "Push these others around, if you want to. But don't get funny with me."

A matter-of-fact threat in his voice reached her. She bit back her retort and glared at him, not quite knowing what stimulus would make him react. Then, quickly, she wheeled and went out the door. McCanless followed.

Hagberg went over to Steele and helped him upright. Steele groaned.

"She bust a rib, Kirby?"

Steele sat against the wall and ran his hand loosely over his mouth. "Give me a drink."

Hagberg brought a glass of whiskey and Steele drank it. Afterward, with Swede's help, he got to his feet and sat down at the table.

Head hanging, half numbed by liquor, Steele was seethingly conscious of the momentous thing that had happed here: pride and arrogance had gone from his world, and in this moment it seemed that it might never return.

Presently Hagberg said, "I never liked a woman headin' an outfit."

His words filtered into the whirling chaos of Steele's consciousness. He took another drink. Then, slowly, he raised his eyes to the Swede.

"I wonder if you would understand," he muttered thickly, "if I were to tell you why I think the devil must be a woman?"

Hagberg said nothing. "There was a time," Steele went on, "when two worlds were open before me. This one of force and violence and lawless things. And another of"—he paused, looking long at the glass in his hand—"of, well, it does not matter."

Hagberg uncomfortably shuffled his feet. "Kirby, I'll take you to your room. Better look at that rib."

Steele glanced up at him owlishly, his face gone slack and beaten, with spit oozing down from the corners of his mouth. "The rib," he said. "That's the trouble: *Adam's* rib,

Swede." He leaned forward confidentially. "Listen. Here is a secret, a most profound truth: *money* is not the root of all evil. That root is women!" He hesitated, his eyes wandering loosely and with a glassy stare over space, as he tried to regain contact with a thought which he had lost a moment ago.

"Two worlds," he mumbled. "Two worlds—" He fell silent. "Two ways to go, and I chose the easy one—"

Chapter 6

THE GIRL'S gaze upon him through the darkness was neutral and waiting. Here in the vine-screened side porch, the air was cool and full of night's sweet smells, and it hit Ed Ardoin suddenly that he had, perhaps, waited too long.

"There was an understanding, Mary," he said presently. "It is still good?"

He heard her soft sigh. He could see only the dim outline of her face, and wished that he might know what was on it. "Ed," she said gently, "there is still as much between us as there ever was. No more, no less."

"Now, just what does that mean?" he demanded testily.

"We grew up together, Ed. I've never really known another boy but you, and you—well, there are not too many girls in this country. I suppose it was natural that we should take it for granted that we would someday—" She hesitated, then was silent.

"Get married," he finished.

"Yes, I suppose so."

"And now we should not take that for granted. Is that it?"

She made a small, impatient gesture. "Why do you bring this to such a press tonight? What is behind all this, Ed?"

Ardoin weighed the question. Around them, all through the town, was the play of wild currents riding the soft night wind. Out there was his future, and here, beside him, was the woman who must share that future if it was to be a good one. Ed Ardoin knew this with an unshakable certainty. His swift jealousy told him that that future was threatened, and this knowledge shaped his words.

"What was that Landry fellow doing here?" he asked suspiciously. "Has that anything to do with this new attitude of yours?"

"So. You were spying on me, weren't you?"

"I saw him sneaking down this way. I followed, because this town is full of men tonight, and I knew Darby wasn't here." He left an accusation hanging there, waiting for her reply.

It was a long time in coming. "Yes, he was here. My father spoke to him, before he went to the meeting."

"That meeting lasted a good while," Ardoin said quickly. "Did it?"

He had the feeling that she was hiding something. For a time he wallowed among ugly thoughts, and then his judgment rode out on top, and he said, "You don't want to tell me anything?"

"I have already told you all that concerns us. It really does not matter that he kissed me—"

Wrath surged hotly up in him, and he grasped her arms, hard. "It doesn't? It doesn't matter that he kissed you?" He could not see her face and the anger there, and he shook her, venting his mad jealousy.

"That trail runner!" The feel of her beneath his hands and the thought of another man kissing her was a searing pain all through him, and he flailed out at it. "And you! Letting him kiss you like some little tramp, some dance hall girl—"

She slapped him in the face. He recoiled, with an angry exclamation.

"You fool!" Mary Wayne stepped after him, trembling with rage. "How can you talk to me like that!"

It was very still for a moment; then Ardoin turned away. "I'm sorry," he muttered. "I shouldn't have done that."

He had taken three steps, when she called out to him. She came forward, hesitated momentarily, then her hand went out to touch his cheek, briefly, but it was a truce and a tender of her relenting. "Let's not fight, Ed," she said. "That sort of thing is not for us."

"What is there for us, Mary? Anything?"

"There's a long future ahead to see what—what happens."

"All right," he said stubbornly. "But I'll know what to do about that fellow Landry, now."

"Be careful," she said sharply. "He is not to blame in this."

"Not to blame? Kissing you and—"

"I wanted him to kiss me." She waited, then, working with her thoughts. "I—I made him do so. Now"—she threw back her head defiantly—"do you want to shoot me down for that?"

It was more than he could understand. "Mary," he murmured. "Mary, what in the name—"

The girl came close to him. "Don't ask me why I did this thing tonight," she said gently. "I felt cheap, foolish, for a moment"—she paused, and looked away from him—"and then, when I had kissed him, I was glad—" Her glance swung quickly back. "I didn't have to tell you this, Ed. But I want to be honest with you—"

Her obvious sincerity helped a little. Still, he said, "What made you do it? *Why?*"

"I really don't know," she said after a long time. "Perhaps it was a thing in his voice, the way he walked—the fact that he stood up to Kirby Steele this afternoon—"

"That impressed you," he said acridly. "You think that one man's bravado can solve the whole problem. Well," he said, his voice sharpening, "remember this: one little slug from a gun can end all that courage."

"No. It is something that goes on to make men proud after the guns are still and the smoke and shouting have cleared away."

"That mean that the rest of us lack courage?" he asked thinly.

"I did not say that."

"You said—"

"I said that courage cannot be killed. It cannot be talked about and analyzed. When you try to take it apart, it disappears into thin air."

Ardoin took condemnation from this speech, for it rankled within him that he was unable to stand up to the forces that were bearing them all down. Now he said, hoping to hurt her, "You seem to know a lot about Landry. He give you these lessons?"

"I talked to him and heard him talk. That is all a woman needs."

Ardoin studied her. "Something has changed you, Mary. Was it—him?"

"I don't think so—I don't know."

For long seconds he was silent. "There was a nice thing between us," he finally said. "I meant it to be just a beginning. I'll not let it go."

"You know," she replied, "I have never wanted that changed, either. But now I wonder about a thing. How can you hold it? How do you chain love to you? How high do you build the wall to keep it prisoner?"

A strange emptiness took his speech for a moment. Then, "We'll see about that!" he blurted, and went quickly down off the porch.

She stood looking after him. Presently she murmured, "How many small things are there that can set it free? Can just the way a man holds his head do that?"

Carolina Steele cast a swift glance about the lobby and saw only the night clerk dozing in his tilted-back chair behind the desk. She wheeled and faced McCanless.

"You would be wise"—her eyes were stone hard—"to walk away from such talk as Kirby was starting up there."

McCanless fumbled in his vest pocket for the makings, built a smoke and lighted it, and still he did not reply. Nettled by his slow insolence, she said sharply, "Or, again, perhaps you *were* interested in it."

His dark eyes crinkled slowly. "Could it be that you are afraid?" he murmured.

"Is that your answer?"

He was a big man, full of the hungers that ride men. Looking at this woman who had been his when she wished it so, wildly hot memories rose up in him, clashing with a half-fear and a greedy envy of her strength and the material things which she controlled. He admired her and wanted her; yet he had a basic dislike of her because she had wealth and power to command.

"Damn you, Carolina," he muttered sardonically, "you get more beautiful every day. And uglier inside with it."

"Answer me!"

McCanless laughed, a brash laugh, full of irony for them both. "It strikes me Kirby might have a point," he said.

She paled. "You too. You—along with Kirby."

"I said he has a point. What's the idea of goin' easy on this fellow Landry?"

Now she understood, and a fear fell away. "There is a time to handle him later—if he should be dangerous," she said pointedly. "Meanwhile, remember that I know what is best for all of us. It could cost you something if you were to forget."

"Money?"

"Yes."

"That all you think about, Carolina?"

"What else is worth thinking of?"

There was a disdainful beauty about her, now, that excited him. He took a deliberate step close to her. "A hell of a lot more," he said huskily. "You know that."

"No." She shook her head. "You can forget that. It never happened."

"Some things can't be talked to death, Carolina. Why do you think I came up here tonight?"

"Because I sent you orders."

Again McCanless laughed. "A clever woman!" he said. "A clever woman in a country that is not clever! Listen, Carolina. This town is full of Corralitos guns tonight. But think—half of them burn powder on *my* say-so."

"So you *were* listening to Kirby! All right"—she stepped

back, her eyes blazing—"you will get what you are asking for, but—"

"Come here!" He grasped her wrist, pulling her to him. His face was hard now, with a deep-lying ugliness that threatened. "You'd better think things over before you start playing free and easy with me. Remember that I helped make you what you are, and I can spoil your little game anytime. Now. Tomorrow."

Realizing instantly that he spoke the truth, she turned to the one weapon with which she could fight him. "I know that." She let her gaze soften and the hardness go out of her body. "But what can a woman do, when she finds disloyalty on every side, even from the—the man who—" She let a break come into her voice as her glance fell away.

"You know why I threw in with you from the start," Mc-Canless said, softening. "I'd sell my soul for you. I already have. You know—"

"Don't!" She turned her head quickly, away, biting her lip. "Don't, Jim—"

"You know," he drove on, "that every move I've made, every breath I've drawn, every step I've taken, was because you told me to do it, and said how and when and where it would be done. It wasn't always easy, but I did that, Carolina—"

She faced him, knowing that he was again in her power. "I know," she said softly, "I know, Jim."

He looked at her for a long hungry moment. Then he said tightly, "Let's not stand here talkin' all night—"

A movement at the doorway caught their attention. They turned just as Landry came into the lobby. Without a glance in their direction he went to the desk. The clerk looked up drowsily and then got to his feet.

Landry said clearly, "I'm lookin' for a fellow same name as mine. Steve Landry. He been around here lately?"

Upon leaving Mary Wayne's house, Landry had drifted farther down through the darkness until he came to the end of the buildings on that side of the street. Here, now, set back off the street was the two-story frame building that was the Courthouse, fronted by a scrabbly lawn of sand and caliche, in which occasional patches of bunch grass struggled to maintain itself.

At the corner of the alleyway Landry halted, scenting carefully through the shadows for what might lie hidden about this place.

Through a window on the ground floor a dim light shone faintly into the night. Thinking of what Ardoin had said about the secrecy surrounding the public registers, he knew that there would be a watchman, and after some moments he discerned a dark figure riding a back-tilted chair near the front door. Even as Landry watched, the shape moved and a match flared up, then died.

After some moments, he made up his mind. Starting up a low, carefree whistling, he stepped across the alleyway, scuffing his boots unconcernedly in the dust.

As he turned up the walk, he heard the legs of the watchman's chair hit the ground.

"Stop there!"

Landry went on, whistling his jig-time tune.

"You hear? Stop right there!"

Landry halted. "Well." He gave a short, ironic laugh. "Kirby didn't tell me that! What's the matter with *you?* Nervous?"

He sensed the man's wavering determination, but saw, too, that he held a gun in his hand. The watchman said suspiciously, "Kirby who? And who in hell are you?"

"Now, there's a question!" Landry jeered. "*Kirby who?* Are there eight or ten Kirbys around here?" He took another slow step.

"All right," the man said presently. "Maybe we know who Kirby is. That don't explain *you*, mister."

"You want to keep your job, friend, you'd better let anybody do his work when he uses Kirby Steele's name." Landry advanced, carrying with him an air of assurance.

"Well—" the man said doubtfully. "What's your business here?"

Landry went past him. "Come in here. Kirby sent me for some information." As he went up the steps, he heard the man coming along behind, grumbling low to himself.

At the door Landry turned facing the man. "Kirby wants to know—" he began, and then he struck him a short, mauling blow above the temple. The watchman moaned softly, and the gun clattered on the steps. Landry caught him as he fell, and he dragged him inside.

Landry took the man's keys, trussed and gagged him with belt and kerchief, then went up the half-dark stairway in the rear. Here on the second floor there was no light, and he groped his way along the walls until he came to a door and then lit a match to read the signs on the paneling. The third door he tried was the Recorder's office. He blew out the light, and after trying the keys, he found the right one and entered.

The lightness of the night sky was opposite him, and he went to the windows and drew the blinds, pulling them down to the sill. Afterward, he struck a match and looked around. There were three or four tables with chairs, and a lamp which he lit, keeping the flame low. With that, he saw a heavy wooden closet at one side of the room near the windows, locked with a padlock. He rapped the wood, and the sound told him that it was heavy, and his judgment said that it would be walnut or oak.

A serape lay under the lamp and he took it up, drew his gun and put the muzzle against the lock, wrapping both lock and gun in a heavy muffling of the serape's folds. Then he pulled the trigger, and the lock shattered. A moment later he had found the three heavy ledgers titled Deeds, and was scanning the index for the name of Landry, Steve.

Shortly he found it, the description of that tract which had been in Steve's name. He read it through, then turned to the next page, and here his attention narrowed. It was merely a court order, declaring the property derelict and subject to public sale by the proper authorities. He read the order through, and then his eye found a note penciled on the page's margin, and he bent over to decipher this note. Finally he made it out: "see page 102." As he turned the page, he knew that here he would find an important answer.

That certainty was on him as he scanned the first few words of assignment in a Sheriff's Deed of Sale, and the words meant nothing to his mind for a moment.

In consideration of one dollar and other good and valuable considerations, the receipt of which is hereby acknowledged, I hereby Grant, Bargain, Sell and Convey to Harry Wayne, his heirs and assigns forever, the following real estate—

This was followed by a quit-claim deed, whereby Harry Wayne assigned the same property to Carolina Steele!

Landry drew a long breath, went back and reread it again. But his mind felt numb, and he went over it still once more, comparing the descriptions of the properties. He had to bring the words out, boldface, into his mind in order to comprehend that Harry Wayne had bought the property which had been Steve's, and then had transferred it to the mistress of Corralitos.

For a long time he stared at this record of violence and greed and sordidness. Then he closed the book and replaced it. Moments later he cut the bonds holding the still-unconscious watchman and headed into the street.

The coolness was like a wash of clean water over his mind as he came outside. In the shelter of the building where he had waited before, he paused to build a cigarette, and the tangy smoke sharpened his senses, and made him realize that this thing went deeper than he had thought. He recalled Harry Wayne's attitude before Steele this afternoon, and a certain disapproval in the elder Wayne's gaze as he had looked at his son; he remembered, too, Mary Wayne's tenderness and the sudden rush of passion in her kiss. All these things were in his moment of summation. But the final factor of Harry Wayne's true color would not fit into place, and after a while he turned toward the center of the town, walking fast.

A block northward, a man eased out of the shadows of an alley ahead, and waved him down. "Got a match, mister?" the man asked in a low voice.

Two things hit Landry instantly. First, the fact that it was a play for him, and then, resentment that it should be so obvious. "Sure," he said, stepping forward, his left hand feinting at his shirt pocket.

His right uncoiled and swung a rushing blow at the pit of the man's stomach, and he gave a retching grunt and went down as Landry whirled low and met the rush of the one who came up behind him. He caught the charge with his shoulder at this one's waist, and sent his right arm snaking about the man's middle, while his left hand shot up and caught the upraised arm. For an instant he braced against the momentum of the attack; then he threw up his knee in a driving sweep to the man's groin. It hit, bringing a sharp cry of pain, and Landry felt the fight go out of this fellow in a quick convulsion, and heard the dull thud as a heavy object hit in the dust of the street. They fell, and Landry landed on top with his hands reaching for the throat. As his hands closed over the other's wind, the man clawed wildly but weakly at Landry's relentless fingers. His knees flew up and hit Landry in the back, once, then the strength oozed from him. After a while he quit struggling and lay still.

Landry sat astride the man until his wind came back to him and then he got down on his hunkers and felt through the dust until he found the gun with which this man had intended to club him. He slipped it into his belt. Afterward, he made himself cool and wary, and stepped back into the street.

He headed toward the hotel, past lighted houses and stores, wondering how he would play the thing when he got there. Through all his thoughts about this town and its deep-running currents of conflict was an elusive whispering to his consciousness which nagged him. He could not get it to come through in definite form. He had the feeling that it was important to the way he should walk into the hotel, but was not sure. Then a man detached himself from the darkness across the street and angled over the dust towards him, walking with long strides.

"Landry." He turned, and Ardoin was there, and he halted, wondering at a new note in the man's voice.

Near him, Ardoin stopped. "I don't like to stampede a man," he said sparely, "but how about workin' with me and Wayne?"

"I told you," Landry said carefully, "I'm with you. But don't ask me to throw a gun yet."

Ardoin hesitated. "After all the reputation you built for yourself by standin' up to Steele?"

The light irony was not lost. "I don't give a damn about reputations," Landry said deliberately. "Besides, most men hit me about alike in certain matters—Steele or another."

A light current of animosity ran between them now, and suddenly it had widened in the silence following Landry's speech.

"Your neck bows easily," Ardoin murmured. "A thing I don't like in many men."

The faint challenge was uncalled for, and it surprised Landry. "What you like is of no importance to me," he said, starting up the street.

Ardoin kept thinking, *This man kissed her tonight,* and a small hatred was in him which Mary Wayne's explanation could not erase. Yet, withal, his judgment told him that he had no basis for action against Landry, even while he kept feinting out at him, wishing to fan the friction of his dislike with words.

"Landry." His voice was taut.

Landry turned, and something in the motionless, waiting figure sent impatience through him.

"Get it over with, Ardoin," he said. "What is it?"

The other laughed mirthlessly. "You press. Just stand hitched and I'll have my say."

"Say it."

The memory of Mary Wayne's confession came roiling darkly up in Ardoin, and he took a deliberate step forward. "Nothing like a clear understanding," he said meagerly.

"Right from the start. You're to understand about . . ." His voice trailed off, then, as he looked at Landry, and suddenly it came over him that he could not finish it.

"Sure you understand it yourself?" Landry waited a moment longer, then turned away.

Behind him, Ed Ardoin cursed himself for a fool, remembering, now, the way she had said, "How high do you build the wall to keep it prisoner?"

Landry came to the hotel's doorway, and with his foot on the first step he saw Carolina Steele talking to Jim McCanless—a man who was handy with a knife. He stopped short, eased to the door's side, and his ears reached out to catch what McCanless was saying.

"Every move I've made, every breath I've drawn, every step I've taken, was because you told me to do it, and said how and when and where it would be done—"

Then he heard the woman's low-voiced reply, "I know. I know, Jim."

That speech struck deep into Landry's consciousness, and almost instantly he put it together with what he already knew, to form a pattern in his mind. Now he remembered, too, a thing that Ardoin had said in the room above the Longhorn: "Carolina's the one that counts. She's tougher than any ten men in this country, and twice as dangerous—"

With that an elusive factor in his thinking about this place and its problems took shape. Knowing what he must do, he stepped into the hotel.

Chapter 7

LANDRY was instantly conscious of the hovering silence behind him. The clerk's glance shifted to a point over Landry's shoulder, and then he passed his tongue over his lips and said, "Never heard of Steve Landry."

"Funny. He wrote me to come down here and help take a herd up the trail."

The man said nothing. Landry grumbled, "You're like all the rest: 'never heard of him.' What is all this?"

The clerk shrugged. Landry heard a step behind him, and he turned.

Jim McCanless stood watching him with a still, narrow look, and three paces behind him was Carolina Steele, her face quietly alert. Presently McCanless said, "Maybe I can help you. I knew the man you mentioned—Steve Landry."

"Thanks. He was a cousin of mine. Wrote me he had a trail job for me."

McCanless said slowly, "You seem to think people around here don't want to talk about Steve Landry." He waited a while. "They never like to talk to strangers about a fellow who's been killed."

"Killed?" Landry said incredulously. "You're crazy."

"Knifed," McCanless said steadily. "You'll have to look for another job, friend."

Landry was thinking about two cups of coffee on a table and a knife in Steve's back. "*You* don't seem to mind talkin' about him."

"Just my way." McCanless smiled frostily. "I'm different."

"Well then," Landry said easily, "maybe you'd tell me this: who killed Steve?"

A slow grin came over the big man's face, by-passing his eyes. "I'm not a law officer. One man more or less killed in this place is no novelty. Why should *I* bother?"

"That's right, why should you?" Landry pushed away from the desk and made as if to leave. "Well, thanks for the information, anyhow."

"Wait a minute. That job. Anything to hold you here now?"

"No," said Landry coolly, "nor anything to take me away."

McCanless was about to reply when steps sounded heavily on the stairs, and Swede Hagberg came lumbering down into the lobby. Here he paused, his gaze settling on Landry. Then he looked at Carolina and pointed to the six gun in Landry's belt.

"Coulter's gun," he said. "I'd know it anywhere."

"Swede, shut up!" the woman said sharply.

Landry said, "Whoever *he* is! Coulter one of your little playmates?"

"Kirby wanted this fellow taken care of," the Swede still watched Landry. "Coulter couldn't do it, but—"

"Be still, you fool!" Carolina's voice was furious.

"I'll just do it myself." Hagberg backed off a pace. "Kirby's word goes as far as I'm concerned—"

Now Landry swung about facing Hagberg. "All right, Buster," he said softly, "whatever your orders are, cut loose when you're ready. But before you do, how about an explanation of this little party?"

It stopped Hagberg, for explanations always left him at a loss. Carolina Steele stepped forward, her eyes flashing. "Kirby was drunk," she shot at Hagberg. "Now, get out of here!"

Hagberg muttered, "He went into the Longhorn. He was talkin' to Ardoin. That makes him one of their guns—"

She swung a hard, speculative glance to Landry.

"Damn it," Landry said with hard impatience, "I take my drinks where I find 'em, and talk to any man who speaks my language. If this squarehead wants to make something of that, let him come on."

She watched him, settling her judgment, and afterward she turned to Hagberg. "All right, Swede," she said placatingly. "A stranger can ride into this town and make a mistake. I'll take care of this."

Hagberg stared a bleak moment at Landry, then stepped around the woman and shuffled out into the street.

"So," McCanless said softly. "Coulter's iron."

"Where did you get that gun?" the woman asked suspiciously.

Landry made a gesture of impatience. "From a fellow who stepped out of an alley and tried it on my head for size. If you want him, you'll find him lyin' at the mouth of the same alley, down the street."

After a moment McCanless chuckled. "Let me have that iron. I'll give it back to Coulter."

Landry handed over the gun. "Just in case I stay around, what's the chances of callin' off your dogs?"

"This was a mistake," the woman said slowly, watching him. "I'm sorry it happened."

"All right," he said, starting toward his room. "I just wouldn't want to be lined up against you, if you play that way."

"Wait." McCanless' voice came after him. "You *did* talk to Ardoin. How about that?"

Landry turned. "I talk to anybody as long as the talkin' holds out." He let the words hang there a little while, then went on to his room.

Watching him go, McCanless said, "Well, that's that. Kirby got his tail up about nothing."

Carolina Steele was thinking of another moment this evening, when this tall stranger had walked into the hotel lobby, and she was putting that moment side by side with the one just past and finding a disharmony which awakened her wily awareness. Earlier he had shown arrogance and a hard, contained drive such as few in this place had ever shown; and just for that moment in which Swede Hagberg had challenged him, his crouching, cold competence had again come through. The rest of it, his talk with the clerk, his conversation with McCanless, did not, somehow, fit into the original picture he had drawn of himself, which, she felt, was the right one. Why, then, had he chosen to let the other side of the picture appear?

"There's another thing," McCanless interrupted her thoughts. "How about Kirby, Carolina?"

She turned to face him, her glance cautious. "What about him, Jim?"

"You'll have to watch him. You heard what he started up there tonight."

She nodded. "Was there—was there anything behind it, Jim?" She waited a moment. "Tell me, truthfully. Do you believe that he is seriously plotting against me?"

"He'd like nothing better than to get you out of the way and have his hands on the whole thing."

She showed alarm and disbelief. Wide-eyed, she searched his face as though for a denial of those words, and all the while she was saying, "This great fool! This blind, greedy fool!"

Finally she said, "I can't believe that. Kirby hates me. But not for those reasons—"

"Don't kid yourself," McCanless said harshly. "If I didn't have my eye on him all the time, your neck wouldn't be worth a nickel."

She drew back from him, sobered. She was thinking, now, that she hated McCanless no less than she hated Kirby, perhaps more. And knowing that his demands on her would be repeated, it was a new kind of hate, to be added to her knowledge that he had become dangerous. She read him easily, and what she saw was menace arising from his greed, greater than his fleshy lusts. He could, as he had said, ruin everything for her. In this moment it came over her forcibly that he, too, had played out his usefulness to her, even as had Kirby.

In a small voice she said, "Jim, is this true?"

He nodded. "We can stop that worry, if you say the word—"

She turned her face away, feigning shock. And she was thinking: *Now it is certain.* With Kirby out of the way, Mc-Canless would feel very near, indeed, to control of Corralitos; he would be sure that he could dominate her, control her through the power of the deeds that he had committed in her name.

After a long time she faced him, showing a thoughtful and apprehensive countenance. "You must stick with me, Jim. I must have someone I can trust—"

He smiled with expansive confidence. "Worry about something else. You'll always have me."

"I know. I know that, Jim." Then, with a lingering tenderness, she went across the lobby toward her room.

Wrath bubbled up hotly in her as she left McCanless. She was thinking, "Two who are dangerous to my plans—two who would ruin it all." It occurred to her, as she walked past Landry's door, that her great need was for someone capable of meeting these two men and besting them. She saw Landry in her mind's eye once more: hard, and easily defiant, and she remembered, too, the strange rising up within her of a mood to match his own. As she lit the light, she found herself wondering what his eyes would look like in sunlight, and how his voice would sound, speaking not in anger. A moment later, she knew that she would find out these things, even while discovering if he were the one to free her of the two who now had lost their usefulness to her.

Her reflections were interrupted by a quick, soft rapping on the door of her room which faced the hotel's rear. Quickly she stepped to the windows and pulled the shades low. Afterward, she went to the door, opened it slightly, then swung it wide as Harry Wayne stepped inside. Quickly she shut the door behind him.

Wayne stood a moment, looking at her, devouring her with his gaze, before he took her in his arms. She gave him her lips, and as he kissed her, his eyes closed but hers did not.

When, finally, he let her go, he held her at a distance and said huskily, "A long time. It's been a long time—"

She nodded quickly, then an alertness came into her eyes and spread over her face. "Tell me, Harry," an urgent note cut along her voice. "Is there any news for me? What have you found out?"

The men who returned to Texas after the War Between the States found their herds dispersed and running wild. Multitudes of unbranded cattle roamed the throny brush of the *brasada* and grazed over the swales and draws of the plains country. It was the chaos of a great industry which had gone without management during the bloody years when more potent issues were being decided. Yet the uncontrolled natural increase of these herds proved to be the foundation upon which the cattle industry was to grow to its later gigantic proportions. Too, the great number of unbranded range animals was the root of many of the evils which stalked the industry through those boisterous years when Texas cattle went up the trail to the railroads, and later swept over and beyond the tracks to stock the ranges of the North. When no man could lay claim to cattle, they were any man's. Thus, license grew up in branding, and with license came rustling, brand-jumping and brand doctoring.

The most pressing problem of the Texas cattlemen of this time was the establishing of brands and the burning of that mark on wild-range beef. With rope and running iron, with fast-breaking brush horses and dogs, they plunged into the *monte* and began to carve order out of chaos. By 1867 the great herds had begun to form and to draw upon the backlog of cattle still running wild. In that year, more than a quarter of a million head went up the long trail to the railroad. It was a haphazard business, this first northering of the trail herds, a catch-as-catch-can search for markets for the only thing that Texans had to sell—meat, hide and horn. On the way, the drovers battled drought, swollen rivers, stampeders, Indians, bushwhackers, and Texas fever. If and when they

found a market for their cattle, there was little or no profit
left after their trail crews were paid off.

These hazards had their restraining effect. The following
year, less than a fifth of the previous year's number of cattle
went north from Texas. It was a year of failure and a year of
triumph, for that year the Chisholm Trail was routed, and
Abilene, Kansas, became the funnel through which, in succeeding years, a half of the range animals in Texas eventually flowed on their way to market.

The enormous size of the Texas herds made it impossible
at first for the Kansas market alone to absorb them. This
draining off had yet to await the opening of the far northern
ranges, which drew their first stocker cattle from the Lone
Star State. Meanwhile, there developed on the Texas Gulf
Coast a temporarily avid demand for cattle to be slaughtered
for their hides and tallow at reducing factories strung along
the coast from Matagorda Bay to Corpus Christi.

At these factories, carcasses were thrown into the bay or
left to the buzzards, the coyotes or the sun. A certain per-
centage of the meat was packed and shipped in brine. But,
on the whole, the industry was as odoriferous as it was
wasteful. To such establishments thousands of mossyhorns
were brought annually. Prices were low: five to seven dollars around might be the average, and payment as question-
able as the practice itself. Yet, since there was little money
anywhere during this period of Reconstruction, and cattle
were plentiful for the taking, it provided a living until better
times might come.

Into this phase of the cattle business came Carolina
Steele and her brother Kirby, on a steamer out of New Orleans carrying a cargo of Florida lumber. Her determination
to wrest riches and power from this new world had been
strengthened by shipboard contacts with Texas cattlemen returning from New Orleans, sharpened by their accounts of
endless range and unlimited supply of cattle and by their expansive talk of free land and the making of an empire by the
strong.

At Providencias, a stinking port on the Gulf near the

mouth of the Colorado, they left the ship. For two weeks
Carolina prowled the hot, dusty streets, going unfastidi-
ously into the slaughter pens and the tallow factories, riding
out to see with her own eyes the long, slowly arriving herds
and the hard-bitten men of the brush country who trailed
them in. And always she talked to men as a man, prying
into their secrets, blotting up information, stealing their
minds, looking for the key to this new game, conscious all
the while that she was a desirable woman and using the
hunger of men to open them up to her. At last, she felt that
she had found the answer.

She went, then, to Kirby, who had been drinking himself
into a semicomatose state. "You will quit drinking now," she
told him firmly. "Where we are going, there will be no time
for your mooning self-pity."

He glared. "Anything will be better than this little
nosegay of a town."

She said with sobering intensity, "I have been busy looking to the future while you tried to drink this place dry. Listen to me!"

"I'm listening. Is there anything else I can do where you
are concerned?"

Carolina choked back a sharp reply. With forced patience
she said, "I have talked to a man who has been to Kansas.
The herds that these Texas men drove up the trail this year
found the tracks at Abilene. Do you know what that means?
Shipment to the Eastern markets! Before long, cows will
mean more than just hide and tallow. Not even the Texans
themselves fully understand what is coming. I tell you, in
five years from now, millions of cattle will be put on the
trains in Kansas. And . . . thousands of them will be ours!"

As she finished on a note of triumph, he watched wonderingly. "Dreams," he mused presently. "Delusions of
grandeur! And where, my dear sister, are we going to get
those cows?"

"We have them now—some of them. I have bought a
ranch near the line between Jackson and Frio counties."

"And where is *that?*"

For only an instant she hesitated. Then she waved an arm
grandly. "To the northwest. Near a small town called Broken
Wheel—"

"Appropriate," he said softly.

"Perhaps. At any rate, we leave tomorrow."

He marveled at her, hating her for the forceful qualities
that he lacked. Finally he said, "I am not going, Carolina. I
intend to return East. I'm through with you—forever!"

She studied him narrowly. "Remember, Kirby, I need not
go back East to turn you over to the Reconstruction authorities. They are here, too!"

Steele colored, and suddenly he lurched to his feet. "Do
so! You will drop the noose about your own pretty neck at
the same time." Then he turned toward the door.

Her voice halted him. "I would tell them that you killed
him and forced me to flee with you. That you hated him as
an enemy. That defeat had twisted your mind. They like to
hear such things about us Confederates, now."

It struck Kirby Steele that her crafty mind had gone
straight to the core of the matter. Still, he said, "Not when I
tell them that you tricked the poor fool, and are as guilty as
I."

"Ah! But they would not believe that I had done that to
my husband." She watched this reflect in his face. "I forgot
to tell you, Kirby—we were married the day before *you
killed him!*"

Speech left him. After a long while he shook his head and
said in a thin, weary voice, "Someday you will make a great
mistake, Carolina. Someday you will be tripped up by your
drive and arrogance. And when that moment comes, there
will be no one to lend you a helping hand, or even to pity
you, for you will have only enemies about you."

She gave him a thin, malicious smile. "Be ready in the
morning." Then she turned her back, and after a moment he
went out the door.

Three years later a Corralitos herd went up the trail. And
Corralitos was Carolina Steele's brand. It had been set up by
hard-bitten crews who put their irons on every maverick

they could find on the Corralitos range or hunt down on the
ranges adjoining. With the proceeds of that drive, Carolina
Steele bought two neighboring herds at range delivery, and
in the rounding up of the animals comprising them, her men
swept up other brands, too, burning over the old ones and
searing into their hides the two small boxes, side by side,
which were making her name the greatest—and the most
hated—in the country.

The year 1873 brought panic in the cities. In Kansas City,
the Wall Street of the rangeland, banks closed their doors.
Kansas housewives bought Texas beef over the counter for
three cents a pound, and the panic reached out to the south
and the west and settled over the ranching country. The big
herds no longer trailed out toward the Dipper. Land prices
plummeted, cattle were next to valueless, money was almost
nonexistent.

Carolina Steele was at the forefront of these changes.
With the beginning of the break in Kansas City, she guessed
what was about to happen. She threw together two herds,
trailing one out for New Orleans, the other for Rockport on
the Gulf. The herd at New Orleans sold for a nice profit, the
market not yet having reacted to the Kansas City situation.
The other, made up of culls and old cows, went into the hide
and tallow factories. Then she waited, her money in hard
cash, until the crash came. Within six months she had
bought two adjoining properties and her cattle were taking
on prime condition, waiting for the strengthening of prices,
while other herds plodded wearily northward toward a market that might not exist.

In Rockport, she met Jim McCanless, who returned to the
West with her as her sometime lover. Shortly afterward, he
established himself in Mexico, just across the border from
Corralitos range, and thereafter a steady stream of Spanish
cattle, rustled from the northern Mexican ranges, began to
flow into the Corralitos herds. Now she encountered the
dangers of overgrazing, a problem which was solved by the
acquisition of two more small ranches whose owners had
presumably been killed by bandits. Local officials did not

push their investigation. By now Carolina Steele had determined that she must have the greatest ranch, the largest herds, and finest house, the richest things, of any person in the country. The means to this end steadily became more and more incidental.

With rising markets and the resumption of the drives to Kansas, she knew that she had been wise. The long, steel finger of the railroad, probing out for the heart of the West, was now exploring both to the north and the south. Carolina rightly foresaw the end of the trail drives. Soon, now, ranching would become purely a matter of the best prices for the best beef. This meant better bulls and selective breeding, which, in turn, would require the building of fence and controlled grazing. She saw this become a certainty as stocker herds went on past the railroad's east-west line, funneling thousands of Texas cattle into Montana and Wyoming, where the plains were being swept free of marauding Indians. The longhorns wintered well in the rigorous northern climate, and they could be held on northern ranges for months, putting on tallow, until the owner found the price he wanted. Texas cattlemen now had their choice of going slowly to the wall or of raising better beef.

The reluctance of Darby Wayne, Ed Ardoin and her other neighbors to recognize these changes had infuriated Carolina Steele, had burned down her determination into a hard, cutting edge of ruthlessness. She had seen the vigor and blood of a hundred good bulls dissipated on the scrub stock of the free-ranging cattle in her own herds and her neighbors'. And between her determination and her neighbors' reluctance to change with changing times there was no chance of reconciliation. They must go.

Carolina Steele stood at the very peak of her power this night when Harry Wayne had come to her room. And as she looked at young Wayne, she knew that she would overstep, with her courage and her intelligence, all obstacles as she had before. . . .

"What did you find out, Harry?" she repeated. "Is there anything I should know?"

He sank frowning into a chair and eyed her. "Always business," he grumbled. "Can't you wait for even a minute, Carolina?"

She smiled. "I'm sorry, Harry. But you know what this means to us—"

He watched her, then said, "A man by the name of Landry came to town today. Did Kirby tell you?"

"Yes."

There was a slightly uneasy silence. "He claimed to be a cousin of Steve Landry," Wayne said. "But I don't know." His glance was worried.

The woman said presently, "Is that all? What is the feeling in the other camp—your father and Ed Ardoin?"

Here in this room, Harry Wayne would betray his father and his friends, and it would not be a new experience. But it was a thing he did not do easily, and therefore he needed the anesthesia of her flesh to dull his sensibilities against the feeling of dishonor. Now he rose and came near her, letting his eyes drink in the full promise of her body, her warm, soft curves, the curving, red line of her lips.

The woman read his thoughts and swayed close to him. "Tell me, Harry," she said in throaty voice.

He waited, and as the hot flood of his desire quenched his reluctance, a stubborn corner of his mind framed his words, "You play a deep game, Carolina. I've sold myself out for you. And yet every time I mention getting married, you dance away from the idea."

She drew back with a little frown of perplexity. "You are not fair, Harry," she said in a wronged voice. "You know that we agreed that it would be better to wait until we can run the Running W and Corralitos together. Why do you say that I am putting you off? After tomorrow—" Then, suddenly, she smiled and swayed against him, and her arms went over his shoulders, pulling his head down.

Wayne felt her mouth, wet and hot, on his, and for an instant, the gentle suggestive bite of her teeth on his lips. With that his reserve left him and he strained her to him, hard. This woman of fire and warm flesh, of tempestuously passionate moods, was worth everything—even honor.

When they drew apart, flushed and breathless, Carolina went quickly to the table where the lamp burned and turned it down to a faint, dim glow. Afterward, she raised a slow glance to Harry Wayne. "Tell me," she said.

He waited only a moment before he said, "If the trial goes against them, they'll ride over to that herd you're holding in the Putumayo Draws. They'll take enough guns to handle the crew you've got there, and cut the herd."

Her gaze slowly hardened. "This will ruin our plans, Harry, it will spoil everything!"

"You'll have to pile up guns over there. Enough so they won't try it."

"Yes"—she watched him closely—"I could do that."

"No gunmen—Hagberg or those others. Just enough hands to make it look big and discourage them. After all, my father will be with them—"

"Of course, Harry. Someday, he will thank you for doing this." Then she smiled at him. "I'm glad that *you* made the decision. It is hard sometimes, and I—well, I think that a man's judgment is best—"

Believing again that she leaned on him, he took her hungrily in his arms. She came to him without restraint, for now she knew what she must know, and it was a weapon in her hands.

A cool breeze had sprung up, pouring down the funnel of the alley on which Landry's window opened, pushing the curtains aside and bringing freshness into the room. He sat down on the bed, staring into the darkness, and finding it better suited to his mood than lamplight. After a while his gaze turned pensively to the window, and with that he came alert as he caught movement in the shadows past his window. Someone had gone stealthily down the way, careful not to disturb the balance of things there in the darkness.

Landry rose and catfooted to the window. After a while he heard a shuffling step in the dust farther down the alley, and he pushed the curtains aside and eased over the sill, standing for a moment to make sure that no one had come from the street behind the other. Then he went noiselessly down the building's side.

After a moment he paused to listen. Ahead of him a darker shadow moved among the shadows, disappearing around a corner of the hotel's wing. He crossed the alley and ghosted along the side of the harness shop, and presently he saw a lighted window whose blind had been drawn. A moment later came a gentle rapping, and seconds afterward a door opened and he saw Carolina Steele speak to a man who stood on the small outer porch, silhouetted against the room's light. Then the man stepped inside, and just as the door closed, he recognized Harry Wayne.

The shock hit him hard, and he stood there for a long time, thinking of Steve and of Mary Wayne and her father. Then, with a sick feeling, he turned back to his room.

He undressed in darkness and lay back on the bed. It occurred to him, after a while, that there was no winning, now, for Darby Wayne and Ed Ardoin. Phrasing it thus, he asked himself if that mattered, if anything—other than avenging Steve and helping Mary Wayne to survive this ordeal—was important to him. Then he knew that the problem reached him only insofar as it might be a part of his own, or as a thing which involved the girl who had kissed him tonight, sweetly and hungrily.

He lay long mulling these thoughts over, and gradually revulsion and a sober kind of hate came over him as he summed up the diabolical and heartless craft of Carolina Steele, who had made Harry Wayne a spy in his father's camp—Suddenly it hit him: one who could match wits with the woman, might, conceivably, even the odds. It would be dangerous, it could be fatal. But it would be better than one lone gun, however capable, added to the relatively few pitted against the Corralitos horde.

He thought of that a long time, and then he lay back and

closed his eyes. Just before he went to sleep it came over him that he had not considered the adverse reaction. He knew, then, that Mary Wayne's opinion of him was important in all his calculations. For a brief moment he felt the stirring up of a conflict, then he forced it from his mind and went to sleep.

Chapter 8

THE DAY came up sultry out of a gray-red dawn, bringing with it a promise of heat that roused Landry early. He got up, washed and dressed and made his way to the dining room. By the time he finished eating, other diners had begun to drift in for breakfast. Most of them he had seen the night before: the town had not emptied during the night.

Horses had already begun to line the racks along the street as he came outside. Sober knots of men stood about in subdued conversation. It crossed his mind that here was a foreshadowing of the fate of this country, and that these men sensed it.

He turned north and went into the livery stable. A pair of riders stepped out of an empty stall, coming toward him, and they stopped and turned and watched him for a moment wordlessly, then moved out toward the street. These details made their impress upon his consciousness. Currying the black, he let them slide along the edge of his thoughts, finding their place in the pattern that was shaping up in his mind. To them he added new faces—long, sober ones—as he returned to the street and went across to the Longhorn.

He found Ed Ardoin there, talking to the sour-faced, sleepy-eyed Grady. Ardoin muttered, "Morning." He did not seemed pleased. Grady glowered and stood his ground.

Landry looked at the bartender with distaste. "Go sweep up," he said briefly. "I want to talk to Ardoin."

Grady colored, and his eyes hardened, then wavered

away. Afterward he shuffled off toward the rear of the saloon.

Landry turned to meet Ardoin's stiff, neutral gaze. For some seconds they stared at one another, and finally Landry said, "I wish I knew about you."

"Just what I was thinkin'."

Landry nodded. "I guess we'll both find out. I'm going to throw in with you."

Ardoin watched him. "How?"

Landry said carefully, "Someone has to get in with that bunch. Spoil every play they start and set up some that will backfire in their faces."

Interest now came up in Ardoin's glance. "So?" he said finally. "Who does that?"

"I do."

A thing in Ardoin's glance wavered for a moment. He pursed his lips thoughtfully, spat at the sawdust, then raised his gaze. "It could be a double play," he said meagerly. "I don't trust you too far."

"To hell with what you think," Landry said flatly. "If you want my help it'll have to be on that basis."

For three seconds Ardoin stared at him. "All right," he said finally. "What else?"

"You figure this trial will go against you people?"

"She owns the judge," Ardoin pointed out.

"Just so. When the trial is over, you get to the street fast. When the Steeles and their crowd come out, act like you're starting a play for Kirby. I'll stop that play. Now, what will her sheriff do in that case?"

"He'll probably fade," Ardoin said. "But remember: a word could blow this town sky-high. All these boys are nervous and ready for trouble."

In the pinched whiteness about Ardoin's nostrils, Landry saw that he was doubtful, perhaps afraid. He said, after a little while, "Well, if you don't want to—"

Ardoin drew up. "Now I know what it is," he said tightly. "It's your damned cocksureness: as though everybody but you was afraid of his shadow!"

"Cool off," Landry said sharply. "We're not through yet."

Ardoin glared at him, and then drew a long breath. "All right," he said. "What's the rest of it?"

"You're not to say a damn word to anyone about my working with you."

Ardoin's eyes grew calculating and shrewd. "Not even Wayne?"

"Especially Wayne."

It occurred to Ardoin that here was a weapon in his hand where Mary Wayne and her feelings for this man were concerned. But he hid his thoughts from his face and said casually, "Whatever you say. But you're taking some risks."

Landry looked at him squarely. "Not if I know who's for me and who's against me." Then he turned away toward the street. Ardoin watched him go, a thoughtful look in his eye.

The town had begun to fill with a leisurely stream of people flowing toward the Courthouse. Even as he watched, Darby Wayne and Drav McLain rode into the other end of the street at the head of the Running W crew. Before the Courthouse they dismounted, and for a moment, as they hit the dust, there was waiting all through the street. Then Wayne led the way into the Courthouse.

Landry cruised down the boardwalk, his glance restless and reaching. Halfway to the Courthouse he leaned his shoulder against a store front and built a cigarette. A thin, sad-faced man with a bitter mouth beneath heavy mustaches, and wearing a star on his vest, came from a store below Landry, looked uneasily about the street, glanced unhappily at Landry and shuffled over toward the Courthouse, disappearing down the alley at its side. Landry remembered Ardoin's summation of the sheriff: "He just fills the office, nothing more."

Above, now, Landry saw Carolina Steele and McCanless leaving the hotel and come quickly down the way without looking at him. Landry recalled last night and Harry Wayne, and the thought tore away the woman's beauty as he remembered. Afterward, Kirby Steele, Hagberg and another came out and stood talking before the hotel. Hagberg's gaze found Landry, and he said something that brought the glances of the others around. After a while they came down the boardwalk, but did not look over the street as they passed.

Now Ed Ardoin came down the walk. Landry said quietly, "Remember." Ardoin nodded imperceptibly and went on, and then Landry eased off the building and sauntered down the way in his wake. He watched as Ardoin crossed to Mary Wayne's house, and presently she came out with Ardoin. Spying Landry, she gave him a nod and a smile. As he tipped his hat, Ardoin scowled in his direction and then faced ahead, saying something that caused her to turn and look at him in vexation.

The street was almost empty now, and he watched the last of the hurrying pedestrians go up the Courthouse steps, then settled down to wait. He found himself wondering if Ardoin could be trusted to play his role; and then he remembered the strange look that had come into the man's eyes when he had learned that Wayne must not know of Landry's plan. As time dragged, he found himself pondering that look, and trying, unsuccessfully, to analyze Ardoin's satisfaction in the fact that Wayne should be kept in the dark.

Somehow, the picture of the sheriff, slinking down the alley beside the Courthouse, hung in his mind, along with the certainty, left in him by Ardoin, that the decision to be pronounced across the way had already been arrived at. There had been shame in the man's step, and indecision. He thought: *This reaches clear down into men's souls.*

It was over sooner than he had expected. He heard the banging of a gavel, the muffled monotone of a man speaking, and afterward the rising clamor of angry voices. The next moment Ed Ardoin came down the steps, tight-lipped and hurried. Landry stepped into the doorway of the store behind him and waited.

Ardoin crossed and took up his stand at the boardwalk's edge, his boots planted in the dust of the street. Even as he faced across the way the crowd began to spill from the Courthouse, and in their midst strode Darby Wayne, tight-faced and grim. Beside him stalked Drav McLain, and the Running W riders closed them in, sullen, sober and ready for trouble. Darby Wayne shot a look of surprise at Ed Ardoin and the latter jerked his head sharply, after which Wayne spoke a word and he and his crew moved downstreet and swung into leather. They pulled slowly away from the racks into the street, not hurrying to leave town.

Carolina Steele came out with McCanless, who sent a quick look about, polling the situation, expecting trouble and watchful of it; Kirby Steele, Coulter and Hagberg followed, and these three fanned out and came down the steps abreast. Now on the sidewalk before the Courthouse was another dozen Corralitos riders, and through the street was a scattering of *vaqueros* and other partisans. Only the Running W bunch was in the saddle. Somewhere, in a place where they could do some good in a pinch, Ardoin's Pitchfork riders had their eyes on this scene.

They had reached the last step, and McCanless had turned to speak to Kirby Steele, when Ardoin's voice rose over the clamor. "Steele! Listen to me, Steele!"

A frozen silence instantly blanketed the street, catching motion and holding it.

"It was a dirty deal!" Ardoin's voice ripped the stillness. "A blessing on thievery."

McCanless and Hagberg moved up to Steele's side, while Coulter edged out on a flank. Kirby Steele said, thinly, "Don't try to buck the law, Ardoin."

"Your law! Corralitos law!" Ardoin drifted toward the street's center. "There's another way to settle this thing, Steele—"

From down the way, Darby Wayne's voice rose angrily. "The best way, by God!"

And Drav McLain shouted, "Cut loose the wolf. We can ride a few of 'em down."

Steele spoke quickly to Hagberg, and the Swede looked at him and then at Ardoin, and afterward moved deliberately into the street.

"Not him, Kirby," Ardoin jeered. "Damn you, come out yourself!"

Hagberg stopped, with something like relief. Steele said, querulously, "Get back on the sidewalk, Ed. This is no time for gunplay."

"Yellow! You've filled this country with big talk and rough actions. Now let's see how hard a man you are."

There was a moment of waiting now. Landry, watching, caught a movement at the side of the Courthouse, back of the crowd. Lon Wilson, the sheriff, stood there, his weak face lighted momentarily by a kind of eagerness as he watched Kirby Steele. Then, in the street, Darby Wayne began edging the Running W crew up the way, and at that moment Wilson turned quickly and disappeared from sight.

The move of Wayne's bunch brought the moment to near explosion. Now Carolina Steele moved forward and said to Ardoin, "A lot of people would be killed if you started this thing, Ed. Clear the street and go home."

Still watching Kirby, Ardoin replied, "You declared this war. You can watch it start."

The woman looked doubtfully at Ardoin, then at Kirby. McCanless shoved to the front and let his hard eye run over Ardoin and Wayne. "Pull out of here, Darby," he warned, "or there'll be empty saddles in a minute."

"There'll be that anyhow." Then he demanded, "Bring him out, Ed! Damn him. I'll count it out for you. One—"

"Ardoin," Steele said meagerly, "you must be crazy."

"Two!" Wayne's riders began to spread across the street.

At that instant, McCanless' voice rose sharp and loud, "*Al socorro, muchachos! Los a caballo primero!*" And then Landry saw the *vaqueros* filter into the street from vantage points where they had been hidden, and the group of Running W riders, though mounted, was under their guns.

In the split second before Darby Wayne shouted the count that would open firing, Landry stepped into the street with drawn gun.

"*Turn slow, Ardoin.*"

All eyes swung to him. Coolly, he stepped across the

boardwalk as Ardoin turned. "Head for your horse. Get out of town."

"So," Ardoin snarled. "Like I thought—one of Steele's gunmen."

"No matter what you thought. Breeze!" And then Landry heard Darby Wayne's round, angry oaths, and Wayne pushed his horse toward him.

"Stand back, Wayne."

"You played it smart, damn you! You and your mealy-mouthed talk about your own business. For two cents, I'd—" his face was tight with rage as he leaned out of the saddle toward Landry.

Landry said, "You, too. I'll shoot down the first three men to go for their guns, and somebody'll take it from there."

The moment of stillness drew out. Landry watched, tense and poised, feeling the beat of hate through their glances. Then, easily, Kirby Steele stepped into the street with drawn gun, and Coulter and Hagberg were with him.

"Go on," Landry said. Ardoin threw an angry glance over his shoulder, then moved down the street, going toward his mount. "Let it ride, Darby," he said to Wayne. "Our day will come."

Darby Wayne had had overmuch of defeat. Suddenly unable to contain his anger and chagrin, he rose stiffly in his stirrups, shaking a gnarled fist at the Steele faction. "Damn you all!" he cried hoarsely. "You think you can beat us with a crooked law, think again. The next time we meet, we shoot! And the next time after that, until this thing is settled. Take that home with you. Sleep on it tonight. Remember it tomorrow. Because we'll never let you forget it, night or day!" Then, past speech, he threw himself back on the leather, jabbed home the spurs and raced down the street, followed by his crew. Their high, angry shouts racketed through the streets' cayon, and as they passed out the north end of town, Darby Wayne's voice came back on the air, loud, wrathful, clear. "Next time, powder smoke!"

Landry holstered his gun and turned toward the board-

walk. Now, with the breaking of tension, normal movement
came back into the street's flow, and he took out his makings
and curled up a cigarette as Jim McCanless and Carolina
Steele came across the dust toward him. Landry raised his
hat to the woman. McCanless gave him a brief, white smile,
and the woman said, "I want to thank you. This could have
been unpleasant."

Landry said, "It struck me as a poor place to start anybody's war."

"This is not *anybody's* war," she replied sharply.

"All right, *your* war, then."

He turned away, but McCanless said, "You're not going
to be popular with certain people after this. Better decide
which way to go and go that way."

"I may do that," he said indifferently, and went on up the
street toward the hotel, his mind already turning toward the
next move in the game and how it would come.

He became aware, with a chill feeling, that he was nearing Mary Wayne's house, and he raised his eyes, sending a
glance over the street in that direction. She was standing on
the lower step, watching him, and Landry saw the mixture
of shock and anger on her face. There was an instant colli-
sion of drives with him, and his stride broke as he looked at
her. The girl, thinking that he was coming across to her,
drew up, and in a significant gesture, cleansed her lips with
her handkerchief. Then, quickly, she ran up the steps and
into the house.

It cut in a way that Landry would not have believed possible. Smarting, he pushed on toward the hotel and as he
came up, he saw Coulter, Hagberg and Kirby Steele standing before the doorway.

Grudgingly, they opened a way for him, and Steele said
softly, "What's your game, Landry?"

"You'll never get it," Landry answered. "You'll just keep
on askin' questions." He started to brush past, and Hagberg
said to Coulter, "This is what he looks like in daylight, Bill."

The thin-faced, wiry man stepped close, favoring Landry
with a still, wicked look. "I'm goin' to cut you down if you

stay around," he said. "No man can do to me what you did last night and enjoy good health for long."

In that wild, tough face Landry saw that this man was one who killed for his own distorted, childish reasons. For an instant he was tempted; then he turned to Steele and said, "They'll do it every time. Chain up poodles like these and tell 'em they're watchdogs, first thing you know, they begin to act like curly wolves. But they can't stand raw meat."

As he went into the hotel he heard Coulter curse, and something from Kirby Steele that he believed might have been a chuckle.

He lay down and reviewed the past hour. Above every other thought rose the discomfiting knowledge that Mary Wayne now believed him a traitor and an enemy. Nor did it help to know that he could not explain to her, if his wild gamble were to pay off for the good of everyone concerned.

The morning grew as he waited, and he had drowsed off when he heard the knocking. Instantly alert, he got up and opened the door. Carolina Steele stood there, giving him an enigmatical smile from darkly liquid brown eyes. "May I come in?"

Landry stepped aside. As she swept past him, he caught the scent of a subtle, exciting perfume. Then he closed the door and faced her.

She stood near the window, the light livening her hair. A waist of yellow silk, tight-clinging, gave breathless outline to the rounded perfection of her torso, the smooth shoulders, the full, symmetrical mounds of her breasts. She stood looking at him with a frankly appraising glance that he knew was not brashness but open, feminine curiosity. Seeing her thus, and finding this mood, Landry felt a sudden quickening of interest, and knew that she had planned on precisely that reaction.

Finally she smiled. "I came to see you on business. I suppose you know who I am?"

"Yes," Landry mused. "Carolina Steele. The terror of West Texas."

"Why do you say it that way?"

"That's the way they all tell me."

"I see." After a moment, "Do you believe that, Mr. Landry?"

"Well," he said, "I expected something different."

"I know. You had trouble with my brother, Kirby. You probably have heard—things—about me. But do not make swift and faulty judgments. I want your help. Will you listen to me?"

He was thinking of all that Ardoin had told him about this woman. He was thinking, too, of the delicate balance which he must maintain between her drives and the purpose of his deception. "Your brother dug a hole for me last night," he said gruffly. "How does that fit in?"

She made a grimace. "Kirby could dig a hole for me, too."

"Now, just what do you mean by that?"

With candor all over her face, she replied, "I have a reputation for playing a deep game, but there are currents all about me that are beyond my depth. I only know enough of them to—to be a little afraid. . . ." She let her voice fall low.

Landry told himself, *Ardoin underrated her. She even convinces herself, in these moods.* "That may be," he said. "But why tell me about it?"

The abruptness of his tone surprised her, and she weighed him carefully with her glance before replying. She knew now that if he were to do her will, she must have time to study him.

"I was impressed by what you did at the Courthouse," she said finally. "Why did you do it?"

"I told you: too many people around who had nothing in the fight." He waited a moment. "Besides, I have no great love of Ed Ardoin."

"Why?"

"Let's just say he's not the kind I admire."

"You have no great love for anyone," the woman mused. "I wonder what you would be like if ever you did?" Then, before he could reply, she said, "I do need your help."

He cocked an eyebrow. "So Carolina Steele needs my

help. With all Texas to draw from she needs Frank Landry, a drifter from Montana." His lips twisted ironically. "Now, just what is so special about me?"

She colored slightly. "I dislike sarcasm," she said bitingly. "But I have my own liking for arrogance. Furthermore, I need a man who is sure of himself, and who is not afraid of odds."

"I understood that you held all the odds."

She frowned, but ignored his words. "I want you to ramrod Corralitos."

"Hagberg. Isn't that his job?"

"Hagberg is *Kirby's* man."

"You'd better explain that," Landry said.

Now she came close. The day's heat was in the room, and the woman's presence, the perfume of her, was all through the place, lightly, provocatively. Landry felt its subtle, insinuating tugging at him as she held him with her warm, open gaze.

"I am at my wit's end," she said at last. "I do not know where to turn unless it be to a man like you, a stranger who is not afraid, and who is not yet involved in this thing on one side or the other."

Landry waited. Presently she continued. "My brother and I own Corralitos, but"—a change came into her voice—"he would do anything—*anything*, you understand—to get full control. He is working with Jim McCanless—"

"I've heard of him."

"What did you hear?" she said quickly.

"Nothing much."

She laughed a short, dry laugh. "McCanless is in love with me. I hate him. He and Kirby are planning on taking all Corralitos, somehow. Perhaps"—her eyes grew slowly wide—"they are planning to get rid of me. I do not know. But this I know: everyone at Corralitos is on Kirby's side. I need someone whom *I* can trust. Will you come?"

Landry hid his surprise. "What makes you think that you can trust me?"

"I will make it worth your while to be loyal to me."

"How about Kirby? Will he like my being there?"

After four seconds she said deliberately, "He may have no great choice in the matter, if you take this job. Understand?"

Landry saw instantly that here was the opportunity he needed. Perhaps she did not fear either her brother or McCanless. It did not matter, for within her were such drives as would impell her to take drastic action, should the basis for fear ever appear to be real. The relationship of the woman and the two men had its disruptive wedges of doubt and suspicion.

"I understand," Landry said evenly. "Make it worth my while, and I'm your man."

As she watched him, she was thinking, *I have played it right. Good-bye, Jim McCanless. Good-bye, Kirby.* And she had a swift vision of herself, alone and powerful, mistress of this country and its ranges, with their vast wealth and prestige. Thinking that, she looked at this man and found him good as a man, and for an instant another, warmer, more secret idea crossed her mind.

"It will be worth your while," she said in a low voice. "Perhaps in ways that you do not now imagine." Then, with a slow smile, she turned toward the door. Here she again faced him. "When can I expect you?"

"Maybe today, maybe tomorrow."

She nodded and went out, leaving him with the picture of her half-secret smile and the curving fullness of her body.

When she had gone, Landry lit a smoke and sat down on the bed, and it was a long while before the idea came to him that she might have been playing with him, that she had read him. But he pushed this thought aside, knowing that in the days that were to come it would be a nagging worry following him along the dangerous path that he must follow.

Chapter 9

DARBY WAYNE was ready, his crew saddled and idling near the corrals, when Ed Ardoin and six riders came in about noon. They set off toward the southeast, pointing their horses for a spot some ten miles away, where the Buckhorns sent a broken flank of draws and canyons south of the Frio line into the very lap of the desert—the Putumayo Draws. Here, in certain of the main canyons funneling back into the hills, there was water and grass, and here, Drav McLain had said, was the Corralitos herd which they were going to cut.

It was entirely clear to Darby Wayne that the last peaceful recourse had been exhausted, and even as he recognized this hard fact, he felt the piling up of his years and an oldness in his spirit that was a new thing for him.

He had come to this country with the first wagon trains west; he had built his life largely as had the others. And with the passing of good years and bad, he had retained a blind faith in his ultimate destiny, a destiny small and strictly circumscribed, but bounded by a code of honor both personal and universal to the land. A man raised cows and sold them for a profit when possible; he married and had his children and watched them grow up and marry and become with their families a part of the land. In this, a man might find peace of a kind, honor and contentment, and what more mattered?

It had been the advent of Carolina Steele, and the pushing drive of Corralitos, which had upset the balance of the country and destroyed the fine, precise gearing of his own

life. And because he was a blunt, honest man who wanted
only to be left alone and perform the acts prescribed by his
code, he was both outraged and discouraged, now, as he realized that the past, with its certainties and its fixed unfolding, was gone.

Some things he knew with a leaden certainty. Peace
could never be achieved between the factions now. Trust
would not be possible between them, no middle road of san-
ity which either could follow, after today. It would be war,
relentless and unyielding. He did not like to think of that. He
glanced guardedly aside at his son, riding on his right, and
afterward let his gaze slip to his left, to Ardoin. And the sight
of these two filled him with an uneasiness about the future
that was both unexplainable and unreasonable.

The smell of the hills began to flow down to them now,
for they had cut an angle across the arid wastes and were approaching the broken rises leading up to wooded slopes. The
sounds of their passage—the complaining friction of leather,
the jangle of bridle metal, the loose and unrhythmic beating
of the horses' hoofs made for Darby Wayne a known and familiar sound, and it occurred to him that in this moment, surrounded by family, Running W riders and friends, he could
be riding alone, because there was only one answer to the
problem facing them and he had it and could not make it
good.

He looked at Ardoin. "It was a damn-fool play this morning, Ed," he said. "Things like that, once started, have to be
finished with fire."

Ardoin kept his gaze on the distance. "I didn't count on
Landry."

"Just so. But you needn't count on him much longer. Not
after the next time we meet—" And Wayne fell silent, remembering the surprise of the morning, and filled with a
helpless anger that he had been taken in by another of
Steele's gunmen.

Wayne now turned into a trail leading up the stone-
cluttered flank of a canyon topped out in timber. Single
file, they rode in silence with the heavier blowing of the

horses on their ears until they came out high in a grove of pines. Through this the trail passed, eventually taking them down into another canyon where an almost dry creek bed was a blur of dampness among rocks and boulders.

He found a clear way up and now the horses labored, and when the climb was over they were once more in timber, and the wind had cooled, coming down off the crests with the smell of greenery and of pine. For half an hour they wound their way along the flank of a hill, cutting eastward with the sun at their backs making intermittent patterns of light and shade among the trees. Then, after a brief descent, they were at the lip of another canyon where a well defined trail led into the valley below. They pulled up.

Before them stretched grass and a running stream, and here cattle grazed, tightly herded by four riders to prevent them from reaching timber or from drifting away into the rocky defiles bordering the valley.

Ardoin presently said, "Damned clever. We're standing just about on the county line now."

"We'll go down without a show of force," Wayne said. "I don't figure they'll want trouble."

Ardoin turned his gaze toward the wagon, half a mile down the valley, and standing at the edge of timber. There was an air of peace and repose over the scene that raised his spirits. "No," he said. "I make it four riders. Must be two or three at the wagon, snoozing'. Not enough for trouble."

With a wave of his hand, Darby Wayne turned his horse into the downward trail. In ten minutes they were at the bottom, fording the small stream and turning the horses over grass toward the wagon. The nearest rider was on the fringe of the herd, two hundred yards away. He saw them and circled back, in order to round the herd away from them.

They rode on steadily, bunched up a little, and scattering with their passage bunches of cows wearing the Running W and Pitchfork brands as well as the twin boxes of Corralitos. Then, as the wagon stood only a hundred yards away, three riders reined out from behind it and rode toward them twenty-five yards, where they stopped and let their indolence show by cupping their hands over the horn as they waited.

Darby Wayne took warning from that cold, indifferent waiting. He said, "That Coulter with those other two?"

"Yes," Ardoin said, low and thick. "It's Coulter."

Harry Wayne said quickly, "Doesn't mean a thing. He probably just rode out—"

And Darby Wayne growled, "Shut up, Harry."

They rode to within twenty feet of the three, and here Darby Wayne threw up a hand. He shifted in his saddle, and now his face had grown tight and his dark eyes had an uneasy look in them. Something was wrong here, a smell of waiting and of hidden threat. Almost, he could catch it on the wind, and he saw it in the faces of the three men as he faced them. But it was the still-faced Coulter who broke the silence.

"You're late for dinner and early for supper," he said without interest. "I can't ask you to get down."

His voice said, _Move along,_ and it cut Darby Wayne across the grain. Color flared into his cheekbones, but he tugged at his mustache a moment before he said firmly, "We've got no time for that. Just came to cut this herd."

"That's too bad," Coulter murmured. "You can't cut it . . . today."

Ardoin spoke up. "We'll just ride through quiet, and see if there's any Running W or Pitchfork stuff. If not, all right. If there is—"

"You won't cut it at all," Coulter said, so soft, so low. "This herd is set up for the trail. Steele doesn't want any of the tallow worked off them. If any of your stuff's in there, they'll be cut back before we trail out."

There was a wall here. Darby Wayne knew it, and he knew that something had gone wrong.

They were fifty feet from the wagon, and a dozen feet beyond the wagon was a finger of timber. He looked at that, and thought there was a movement behind the screen of greenery, but he could not be sure. Then he looked out across the meadow and saw Running W cows there, and his resentment burst. He was tired of being played for a dupe, and dog weary of turning back in the face of threats. He stiffened in his stirrups, and knew that now was the time, regardless of what lay behind this Corralitos arrogance.

"You damned gun hawk," he ground out at Coulter, anger reddening his face. "Half of this gather belongs to me and Ardoin, and you know it! To hell with what your crooked law says! I told you we aim to cut this herd, and we're going to do it. You can make up your mind quick as to whether we do it peaceful or—"

Coulter clawed at his gun. Before it cleared the leather the long, angry whine of a bullet passed over them and afterward the slap of a rifle shot cut though the silence. Coulter's horse shied and his shot went high, and behind Wayne came the booming of two quick shots as one of the men with Coulter clutched at the horn, opened his eyes wide and staring, and slowly toppled from the saddle.

These things happened in an instant, and then Darby Wayne heard the singing and whining of lead coming at them from the timber, and saw the fingers of flame jabbing toward them from hidden guns in the wagon's box.

"Mow 'em down! Goddamn it. It's an ambush!" Then his own guns were out and bellowing, and the horses had gone into a frenzied dancing and skittering as the battle rolled on upon them.

Coulter had swung from the saddle, pulling his horse in front of him. As Darby Wayne slammed fire in his direction, a burst came across the saddle horn and Wayne rocked in the leather and coughed. It had not reached a vital spot. But the hidden fire coming both from the wagon and the screen of trees had thrown the advantage over to Corralitos. Ardoin shouted, "Get to hell out of here. Find cover!"

"Stand your ground!" Darby Wayne's voice was strained, but he kept up fire.

Suddenly a couple of riders wheeled their horses and broke away from this punishing fire. A third started to follow, slipped sideways in the saddle, rode for a distance hanging on with failing hands, then hit the ground, rolled over and lay still.

Harry Wayne, shooting at random into the trees, worked his horse over to Darby Wayne's side and shouted, "Our boys didn't come to fight. They came for cattle. Let's go!"

Simultaneously, Ed Ardoin yelled, "Come on, Darby," and spurred away. In a moment they all had turned and were galloping out of range.

Darby Wayne *had* come for his cattle. He had come prepared to fight for them. And the resentment in him was matched by the outrage of having ridden into an ambush. He saw the fleeing riders, and he saw Ardoin running away from this fight, and he heard his son counseling him to retreat. It was too much.

"Go on, damn you!" His voice was strident and rich with defiance. "Run now, and you'll run the rest of your lives!" And suddenly he hit his horse with the spurs and opened fire at the wagons.

Two slugs hit him at once, and Harry Wayne heard them thud into him. He heard the breath slam out of his father in a hard grunt and saw him topple backward. By the time he reached him, lying on the ground, Darby Wayne was dead, his guns still in his hands.

The firing quit now, except for the occasional flat slap of a rifle, potting at the distant riders from the cover of the woods.

Wayne got down, knelt by his father and looked at him for a long time. Then he turned a thin white look toward the wagon as Swede Hagberg climbed over the wheel and dropped to the ground. The Swede stared at him expressionlessly, and afterward three more came out of the wagon, holding guns. Others now sauntered deliberately over from the edge of timber, and Harry Wayne counted a dozen men and knew that there were more.

It was the thing that he saw in Coulter's eyes, as the still-faced man looked at him, that made Harry Wayne sick. For a moment he stared at the gunman, then, shifting his gaze, he got up.

"Don't start anything," a man said. "We'll cut you down. About your old man—it was the way the cards fell, that's all."

Numbly, Harry Wayne went to where his father's horse was grazing, and as he turned back Ed Ardoin rode up, under the covering guns of Corralitos men.

Silently he got down. Swede Hagberg said, "Ed, you get to hell out of here. We don't want to wipe you boys out."

Ardoin faced him. "It was pretty neat," he said thinly. "But we'll have our say yet. Someday you'll eat our lead."

Coulter took a step forward. "You talk too damn much," he said.

Swede Hagberg lumbered up to Coulter. "That's enough, Bill. Or would you like to see if you can beat *me?*" Coulter looked at him for a moment, and there was a flicker of some deep interest in his glance. Then, without a word, he turned and walked away toward the wagon.

Ardoin and Harry Wayne tied Darby Wayne's body over the saddle. Then, silently, they mounted and reined away toward where the others waited. Three men had been hit, one of them bleeding profusely from a thigh wound. Ardoin sent two men back to pick up the body of the other, who had been killed in flight. While they waited, glum, unhappy and beaten, they smoked and sat with their dark, secret thoughts. Then the others came up with the dead rider and they took the trail back the way they had come.

There was one thought at the bottom of all these men's minds: how had this ride turned into an ambush, and who had engineered it that way? One man among them knew this guilty secret, and it was a knife in his own heart.

They had reached the Running W and taken Darby Wayne into his house, when Ardoin said, "I'll bring Mary from town."

Harry Wayne looked at him, started to blurt out something, then said, "She'll be along this evening with Drav."

"I'll just go in anyhow. There's something I've got to do." He was thinking of his talk with Landry last night; he was remembering now, that Landry, an outsider whose game was deep and obscure, knew of their plans. He, himself, had told Landry of their intentions. Who else could have betrayed them? As he rode across the wastelands in the late afternoon sun, he remembered how Landry had said, "You mentioned gunmen. Think it would be safe to cut?"

When Darby Wayne led his cutting crew into the Putumayo Draws, Mary Wayne was having her moment of bitter self-reproach. She had been more deeply moved by the moment in Landry's arms than she had cared to admit, even to herself; and out of the long hours of remembering, after he had left her and gone into the night, she had built up a whole fantasy of hopes and borning dreams. They had died too suddenly and too hard this morning as she had witnessed the tableau before the Courthouse.

During the brief instant when she had looked across the street at Landry, she had wanted to run to him and make him deny the apparent truth; to force him to offer some—any—justification for the act which branded him a spy and Correlitos partisan. Then the enormity of it had risen before her mind, and she had fled into the house, shaken.

The morning had dragged with the weight of lead on her spirit. Then, as the stark reality of the day in Broken Wheel began to flow about her, she consciously set about destroying the last of the magic that the night before had brought her. Noon came and went, leaving her with an empty feeling.

Mechanically, she went about preparing early supper for herself and Drav McLain, with whom, later, she would ride back to the Running W. She heard the town's customary noises, the movement of horses and wagons through the street, and slow, occasional snatches and drone of conversation, and the not infrequent, expressive silences. It was a known, a real and a tangible thing. She told herself that last night had not happened, that only this day was true, but in this she found only cold comfort.

At four, Drav McLain came in and sat at the kitchen table

with her, and somehow, in the grim, dark lines of the old man's face, she found a solid, familiar comfort.

"Any news, Drav?" she asked.

He looked at the girl for a moment, squared his shoulders and said, "This is a bad thing, Mary. Your paw is in a whip-saw now."

"What are they saying?"

"It's war. It beats hell, but it could just about mean the end of things for us."

She thought this over, and a stubborn anger, born of the blood in her that was Darby Wayne's, rose up and gave her words. "Not by any means. There's always a last battle to every war!"

"So there is." He nodded briefly. "But who's going to say which one is the last?"

"Did the Corralitos bunch leave town?"

"McCanless and his crowd about an hour ago. Kirby, this morning after the trial. Coulter and Hagberg and most of the gun artists about the same time."

The girl mused, "Carolina. Still here. And—" Then she stopped, and as Drav McLain looked at her quickly, she colored.

"Landry," he said softly. "Mr. Big—"

Quickly she rose. "I'll wash up these things. It's time to go."

He was about to say something, when there came a sharp knock at the front of the house. They looked a one another and McLain's face grew tight. Mary Wayne saw this and shook her head. "No. They wouldn't come here." Then, re-assuringly, she said, "Wait. I'll see who it is."

Halfway down the hall she recognized the tall form of the man waiting there, and her heart leaped. Then, remembering all that had happened this morning, she drew a deep breath, squared her shoulders and went forward. When she faced Landry, he saw a woman beautiful and a woman angry, with the hot, seething wrath of a woman who has been deceived.

Seeing her thus, he knew not quite how to begin. "Mary

Wayne," he said after a moment, "I want to tell you something—"

"Get off this porch," she said coldly. "Drav McLain is here. Unless you go, he will drive you away with his gun."

"You've got to listen to me."

Landry took a step forward, and at that moment Drav McLain bulked into the doorway. He said heavily, "Keep your damned foot out of a Wayne doorway, or I'll chop you down."

Landry said, "What I have to say is for this girl alone. Suppose you go back to the kitchen."

McLain rumbled a deep, angry sound and looked at the girl. Still watching Landry, she said, "Go on, Drav. If I want you, I'll call." McLain hesitated, then went reluctantly toward the house's interior.

Landry took the condemnation from Mary Wayne's glance before he said, "This morning was the hardest job I ever had to do—because I kissed you last night. Does that mean anything to you?"

Color flamed into her cheeks. Between tight lips she said, "You came here with lies last night, and you add lies to them today. Did you think that I was so taken by you that I would immediately open my arms to you after what you did this morning? You are a fool. Now, get out of here." With that, she turned away.

His hand shot out and caught her wrist. She spun, fury all over her face and outrage making her voice tremble. "Let me go! You—"

"Think what you want to," Landry said, "for I can't explain. But I didn't lie to you last night. You have to believe that."

He saw the wish to believe work over her countenance and into the blue eyes. She opened her lips to reply, and before she could, the sound of a running horse broke down the street, drawing their attention. A moment later Ed Ardoin pulled up in a rising of dust before the house, dropped from the saddle and came across the boardwalk. He was a still-faced man at all times, and hard to read. But now Landry saw something in his countenance that put him sharply on guard.

Ardoin came stiffly over the plank walk and up the steps, his gaze holding Landry's. Then he glanced aside at the girl, and said, "What's this fellow doing here, Mary?"

"He is here through no choice of mine. Run him off, if you wish."

"Maybe you'll want to do it yourself," Ardoin said quietly, "after I've told you."

Something in his voice swung her about, facing him. *What is it Ed?"*

He waited a little while before he said, "Mary, your father—"

He stopped as he saw her stiffen and grow pale. Then, gently, he said, "You'd better come along with me, Mary. Darby's been shot."

Landry took the quick shock of this news and then he looked at the girl's white face. Finally she drew a long, ragged breath. "Is he—is he . . . ?"

Ardoin nodded solemnly. "They killed him when we tried to cut that herd over in the Draws."

The girl leaned back weakly against the doorframe, her eyes dry, her gaze empty, and seeing her, Ardoin turned a hard, venomous gaze again upon Landry.

A quick step sounded and Drav McLain came into the doorway. "What's this about Darby?"

"They gunned him. When we rode in for the cut, they opened up with guns in the wagon and in the timber behind it."

Landry saw the paleness come under Drav McLain's burnt-dark skin. Then the old man's gaze turned on Landry. "Your damned crowd," he breathed. "Darby Wayne was a friend, all my life!" Suddenly he stepped back, his hands lowering toward his guns.

The girl saw this and whirled. "Drav! More shooting will not bring him back. This man had nothing to do with—"

"I'm not so sure," Ardoin said softly.

Landry looked at Ardoin, taking inventory of the situation. He remembered, now, the night meeting of Harry Wayne and Carolina Steele. The smell of young Wayne's treachery was all through this thing, and in his mind was the knowledge that it was a secret which he could never divulge. Not after the blow which had already fallen upon Mary Wayne. It came to him, too, that Ardoin might be expected to doubt him, since he had confided the cutting plans to him during their talk over at the Longhorn. He stood here in an impossible situation, one which left him neither credence nor understanding from these people whose fight he was fighting.

"Maybe you'd better explain that," he said stiffly.

"Only four people—outside of Mary—knew that we were going to cut that herd," Ardoin replied. "Darby, Harry, Drav, myself. That is, until I told *you!*"

He heard the girl's quick intake of breath. With a kind of desperation, he said, "I had nothing to do with it. For that matter, what makes you so sure that *anyone* told Corralitos? It would be natural to send men out there, after what happened this morning."

"No," Drav McLain said angrily. "That was planned. And, damn you, you had a hand in it!" Suddenly he went for his gun, and then Landry drew, covering both Ardoin and McLain.

"All right," he said sharply. "We'll talk like this. Listen to me: I had nothing to do with Darby Wayne's death. As for that play I stepped into this morning—it was plain foolish." He looked meaningfully at Ardoin. "I think even Ardoin would agree to that."

Ardoin knew what he was called upon for in this moment. But there was, in addition to his pact with Landry, a broad base of doubt in him, and it had widened, now, with the death of Darby Wayne; there was, moreover, his abiding jealousy of this man whom he had again surprised with Mary Wayne. He said, "Can't see why in hell you say that. If *you* didn't tip off Corralitos, who did?"

He's putting me in a hole, Landry told himself, *and he's digging it deep*. He said gruffly, "Ardoin, you know better than that."

Ardoin shook his head. The situation was somehow to his liking. He glanced at Mary Wayne and the hurt in her eyes as she looked at Landry goaded him further. "No. What else would a fellow do if he was going to *line up with the Corralitos crowd?*"

It was very still for a moment, and then Mary Wayne came slowly forward and stopped before Landry. "Is that true? Are you joining Corralitos?" It was almost a whisper.

The effectiveness of his bargain with Ardoin depended upon these people believing that Landry was a Steele partisan. He had stipulated that it be so. Yet in this moment when such partisanship was identified in Mary Wayne's mind with her father's death, Landry found it hard to bear. For a moment he wanted to blurt out the truth, and then he thought of Harry Wayne and of the girl's troubles, and knew that he must keep the secret.

"Yes," he said meagerly. "I'm joining Corralitos."

She slapped him in the face. Then, before anyone spoke, she turned and ran into the house. After a moment Ardoin said, "Drav, go see if she's all right." The old foreman looked his hate at Landry, then went in.

Landry holstered his gun. "Well, you did a good job," he said coldly.

Ardoin still eyed him narrowly. "I don't trust you. I had my heart in this."

"I said nothing to Corralitos, and you know it."

"Who did?"

"How in hell do I know?"

"You think any of us would spill the beans, you're crazy!"

"I don't think anything," Landry said. "If you want to keep our bargain, well and good. If you don't, you can go to hell." He went down the steps, not caring what Ardoin's reply would be. He climbed aboard and was pulling away from the rack when Ardoin motioned to him.

He came to the edge of the boardwalk and stood there,

studying Landry. "All right," he said finally. "It still goes. But the next funny thing that happens, it'll be you and me for it."

"Necessity makes strange bed fellows," Landry mused, returning Ardoin's half-hostile stare. "Maybe it'll be you and me for it in the end, anyhow."

Then he rode down the street, heading south. For a long time Ardoin stood watching him, and later he turned and went thoughtfully across the boardwalk and into the house where Mary Wayne was already learning to face a new kind of future.

Chapter 10

IT WAS, Landry remembered, about ten miles to Corralitos, across the desert wastes below Broken Wheel and thence up into the foothills of the Santisimas. Riding at a walk, he left the town and held southward with the dying sun on his right. He had no desire to push the black, for haste was not at his heels. He wanted time to evaluate the things that had happened, and to project his mind into the future of this strange game into which he had been drawn.

Now, as he rode with the breeze off the desert cooling slightly in his face, it seemed odd that Steve Landry's fate should have been so inextricably bound up with the destiny of these other people. When he had first approached the problem, finding Steve's murderer had been the paramount objective. It was still his chief mission; and yet, he admitted that there were areas in his deeper considerations where it ovelapped other problems which were becoming of prime importance to him.

Darby Wayne's death had moved him as an indication of the ruthlessness of the forces with which he now must contend if his mission were to succeed. There was no doubt in his mind that Harry Wayne had informed Carolina Steele of the cutting plans. It was, furthermore, apparent to him that the woman's cruelty was deep and boundless. Through Harry Wayne, she had murdered his father. The hidden gunmen in the wagon and in the timber, if Ardoin's story were true, was proof that Carolina had hoped to slaughter by surprise, rather than warn away by a show of force.

It occurred to him, suddenly, that perhaps even Mary Wayne might be in danger now, and the thought left him momentarily chilled, for the slender, copper-haired girl had an appeal whose depths he was only just beginning to understand. He thought of that for a while, and then he admitted to himself that much of his fight was for her. Foolish, quixotic, perhaps, but there it was: a reality to be faced.

He had no illusions about Carolina Steele's reasons for hiring him. As the instrument of her harsh will, he knew that once she might have used him, or had begun to suspect him, she would remove him from the scene with as little compunction as she had used Harry Wayne to plot his father's death.

These things hung along the edge of Landry's thoughts for a long time, and as he pushed on, with the foothills coming over nearer, a plan slowly became apparent to him. The solution to this problem must be found in Carolina Steele's own drives toward power and wealth, in the jealousies existing between Kirby Steele and McCanless, and between these two men and the woman. The organization itself was too powerful to fight in the open. Others had learned that this afternoon, and now Darby Wayne would be buried because of the learning. No, he must make Corralitos destroy itself by playing upon the greed, the lusts, the pride and the hates of the people who formed it. It would involve the application of small pressures at weak points, and their multiplication until something broke; the baiting of a snare and patient waiting until someone entered it, driven by uncontrollable urges; the sowing of doubts and distrust; the spreading of the corrosive acid of suspicion; the dissolution of those loyalties which held the group together as a unit. Carolina Steele must be isolated by doubts and weakened by fear of the others, until they were destroyed by their own conflicting desires and she, the evil genius of them all, would be pulled down with them.

Such was Landry's train of thought as he pushed on toward the hills, with the sun now sinking behind the western ranges and the cool wind beginning to flow down off the heights ahead into his face. He sat easily on the leather, his senses coming alive, and his mind now free because the hardest break of all was behind him: the moment in which tragedy had been in Mary Wayne's eyes as she looked at him and then struck him. He pushed that thought aside as the black turned off the desert's flatness and followed a road upward into the first rise of the hills.

For half an hour he climbed, with the darkness deepening as the road curved between heavy stands of pine. Here in the uplands, the winds sweeping off the summits of the Santisimas were chill, and presently he took his jacket from under the cantle and slipped it on. Stars came out, cold and brilliant in the sky, and the smell of night about him was fresh and cool and rich with pine and the sweetness of mountain waters.

Farther along in the night and higher above the desert floor, he caught the lingering odor of woodsmoke on the wind, and knew that he was coming to habitations. Five minutes later he saw winking lights through the trees, and then he came into a small square where three or four houses tried to hide in the pines, showing only their faces to a large general store and saloon. He rode toward this.

There was a lone horse at the rack before the place, and Landry rode on past at a walk and got down on the building's dark side, where he looped the reins and stood peering into the half-darkness. Ahead of him were the shapes of corrals, and he walked that way and saw that in back of this place were a number of cattle pens. He surveyed them thoughtfully, then stepped across a lowered bar and scuffed the dirt with his boot toe. The droppings were old, but the smell of cattle was strong about the place, and it occurred to him vagrantly that it was a strange site for cattle pens. With that he went around to the front, through the long rectangles of dim light from the saloon's dust-covered windows, and stood for a moment looking at the horse tied at the rack. It was too dark to make out the brand, and he waited and built a smoke, listening to the dry rustle of leaves in a big cotton-wood nearby, and afterward he turned and shouldered through the swing doors.

As he entered, talk between the bartender and a customer ended abruptly. The big man standing before the bar turned slowly, and he recognized Jim McCanless, not without a kind of surprise.

It was a small barroom, merely one side of the general building with a pine-slab bar and some bottles in back. A lamp swung from a stringer overhead and the smell of whiskey and of kerosene and dried fruits mingled in the air.

Under McCanless' questioning stare, Landry came up to the bar and ordered whiskey. The thin bartender brought a bottle and a glass and put them before him, and Landry filled his glass and pushed the bottle toward McCanless.

"Thanks." McCanless took the bottle and poured a drink.

They raised their glasses and looked at one another. *"Salud,"* murmured McCanless.

"Con pesetas y tiempo para gastarlas," Landry finished it.

The silence of the night settled over the saloon. The bartender, blank-eyed, stared to the door. In the stillness the rasping of the cottonwood's leaves could be plainly heard here in the bar.

"Off your range, aren't you?" McCanless finally asked.

"I'm on my way to Corralitos. They gave me a job this morning."

McCanless nodded, watching Landry narrowly. "I thought they would," he said after a while. "You ought to get along well with Coulter and Hagberg."

Landry knew then that Carolina Steele had said nothing of this to McCanless.

"Won't have much to do with those boys," he said pouring another drink. "Carolina Steele wants me to ramrod the outfit."

Out of the corner of his gaze Landry saw McCanless stiffen. "Well," he murmured, "you get along fast, friend."

Landry faced him. There was a look of mild displeasure

on the big man's heavy, wild face. Landry said, "Now, how do you mean that?"

"A day after you get here, you're foreman of Corralitos!" He waited. Then, suddenly, he laughed. "Kirby will be very happy."

"The woman hired me."

"Of course. That will merely add to Kirby's joy."

Landry knew that his hand lay close to his vest. He raised his shoulders in a slow shrug. "Their business. As long as she pays the money, what in hell do I care?" Then, looking straight at McCanless, he said, "Or you, either."

A thing moved behind McCanless' gaze. Then a slow smile caught at his lips. "Very true," he mused. "The money is the important thing." He studied Landry for a long moment, then said gently, "It strikes me, friend, that you are much smarter than you appear. Now, between the two of us, did it really matter a damn to you this morning if Ed Ardoin shot up Kirby or not?"

Something came awake in Landry. He saw the sly, remote working of hidden thoughts behind McCanless' gaze, and he said, deliberately, "Not a damn."

After a moment, McCanless chuckled. "Like I thought. Well, that's where the money is in this country. You'd be blind not to see it."

"Yes," said Landry, studying his glass. "It's a damn good setup for Kirby Steele. And it's too bad for the girl, with a weak-spined brother like that sittin' in with half the chips in front of him."

He heard a low rumble of assent. Then, "Strange talk from a new foreman," McCanless said slowly.

"Like I said, I don't give a damn what they do, so long as the money's there." Landry let just a glint of hostility show, and after a while McCanless straightened, picked up the bottle and his glass and said, "Let's go sit and talk. I'm heavy on my feet."

Landry followed the big man to a table well toward the room's back. They sat down facing one another and McCanless poured a drink. Again they raised their glasses. Mc-

Canless said, "You talk a lot about money. Want to talk some more?"

Landry knew that this could be a trap, or that it could be an opening he had tried for. "I hadn't thought about it," he said. "Just interested in my wages."

Up in front, the little bartender picked his teeth absently, uninterested and bored with the night, the silence, the place. McCanless rolled a cigarette, watching Landry closely, and when he had lit it he leaned across the table and said, "A smart man ramrodding that outfit could practically make his own wages."

"I'm not ambitious."

McCanless laughed heartily. "Eveybody's ambitious!"

"You?"

"Why, hell yes! Always ready to pick up a piece of change where I can. And if it would hurt Kirby Steele in the process, that'd be all right, too."

Landry now knew that he had his man. Still, this was not the time nor the place to make his move. He waited a while, then said uneasily, "I can see your point. But the girl hired me."

McCanless said quickly, "Don't get the idea that I'd do anything to hurt her, my friend. Her brother is another thing. He's stealing her blind. You'll find that out when you know your way around." He stopped, sensing that he might have gone too far. Then, "Well, as you say, it's their business." But his crafty gaze was measuring Landry for his reaction.

There was another small silence. Landry said, "I noticed corrals out back."

"Did you?"

"Hell of a funny place for cattle pens, here."

"Maybe not. Maybe there's business in cows up this way, too."

"Well," Landry said pointedly, "it's pretty far from Broken Wheel."

"Just so." McCanless was watching him with a secret kind of amusement. "But it's close to Corralitos. There's always a market for beef in this country. Even Corralitos beef.

You ought to remember that, friend, if you're going to be boss up here." He smiled, and he kept his gaze on Landry with a question in it.

For a time, now, they sat looking at one another. Finally Landry pushed back his chair and rose. "I'll get up the trail," he said, turning. "So long."

"Wait." McCanless rose and came around the table. "I wouldn't want you to get any funny ideas about me, friend," he said gently. "Remember, I work for Corralitos, too."

It was a veiled threat as well as an invitation. "Your ideas seem about right to me," Landry said.

"Good."

Landry hesitated. "I like to know something about the people I work for," he pointed out. "Suppose we meet in Broken Wheel about a week from tonight. Then we can talk about—things."

McCanless' broad grin flashed. "I generally travel with a crew, just in case. Think I ought to bring a few boys along?"

"Up to you." Then Landry went toward the door, leaving McCanless still grinning behind him. As he rode on into the coolness of the night toward Corralitos, Landry knew that business had been transacted. He had started the poison of disunion to work.

Chapter 11

KIRBY STEELE had sent Hagberg and Coulter on to the Putumayo Draws as Carolina had instructed him to do. Afterward, he rode leisurely toward Corralitos, arriving there before noon. The heavy drinking of the night before had left its mark upon him, and after a light lunch he went to his room and slept until the sun began to fall low over the tops of the pines around the house. He came awake with a dark and vicious taste in his dry mouth, and as he rose to the side of the bed, his injured rib set up a sharp throbbing that brought a curse to his lips.

After a while he rose and washed, and then, feeling freshened, he went to his dinner which was customarily served in the patio. The heavy silver, the good linen, and the excellent food of the Mexican *cocinera* restored his humor to a degree. With his coffee he smoked a cigar, and for a while he listened idly to the familiar sounds of the house—the soft, swishing steps of the servants, a snatch of song from the kitchen, the sudden outburst of pithy Spanish as the cook scolded some hapless houseboy.

Carolina, he admitted in this moment, had done well—by both of them. Here were most of the material things a man could want in life, and the cost to himself had been not great, if spiritual values were not computed. For a moment he wondered at the intangible worth of the thing called pride, and then he turned away from this trend of thoughts and its conflicts; it was something that he dared not examine too closely. He sat with this darkening mood as the evening grew to match it. He was there and the *mozo* had brought him liquor, more coffee and fresh cigars, and the stars had begun to punch small, bright holes in the night sky, when he heard a step behind him and Carolina came into the patio and sank into a chair across from him.

He offered her a small glass of liquor. She took it with murmured thanks, then sat back watching him. Finally she said, "Hagberg and Coulter rode in before you were awake."

Kirby Steele sighed, making his adjustment between this moment of relative peace and the harsh realities surrounding it. "And how did we at the wars, dear sister?"

"They killed Darby Wayne," she said quietly.

Steele straightened. It was dark now, and he could not see her face, but the matter-of-fact tone of her voice shocked him. They had had their quarrels with Wayne, and these over deep-lying differences. But this was not the same thing as the killing of hired gunmen by one's own executioners.

"That was a very great mistake, Carolina," he said at last.

"What do you mean?"

"Darby Wayne was something more to this country than you or I could ever be. He was a part of it. Even his enemies respected him. You have destroyed a good deal more than a man who stood in your way."

"I did not intend to kill him!" A troubled note ran along her voice. "I wanted them to drive Wayne's men off without bloodshed."

Steele laughed ironically. "Like throwing a Christian to a lion and telling the lion to bite just enough to pinch the skin!"

"Kirby," she said icily, "I am willing to concede that you were too drunk last night to know what you were saying. But let me warn you: you are becoming too critical."

Steele sighed. He had no illusions about his sister. He recognized that she had become the victim of her lust for power; that vanity had now entered into it, along with covetousness, and that she had, furthermore, reached that state where the mildest criticism is taken for treason. Still, he was

objectively minded, able to see not only Carolina's weak-
nesses, but his own.

"I should point out to you," he said with cold precision,
"that it is your sense of guilt and insecurity which makes
you fear criticism. Would that do any good?"

"None. I leave the philosophy to you."

"Just so."

There was a silence, now. At last Carolina Steele said, "I
suppose that this will mean war."

"No doubt of it."

"Good. It will be an end to waiting."

"And of living—for some," he murmured. "But perhaps
that is not important."

"Damn you, Kirby!" she spat at him. "I will not let you
upset me again. I ask nothing of this country except to be
left alone to carry out my plans. You know that."

Kirby Steele grinned maliciously in the shadows. "Of
course. All the other side must do is lie down and let us ride
roughshod over them. But they take the narrow view and
refuse to do that. They don't realize that we're fighting for
our lives."

Angered, she leaned toward him. "Truer than you think!
One of the riders told me only this afternoon that they found
two more of those big Hereford bulls dead. Those black
Spanish bulls kill them at will, with their long horns and
their catlike agility. How in the name of heaven"—her voice
rose high in outraged complaint—"can we ever improve our
herds unless we can fence and make our neighbors do so,
too? In a year from now the railroad will be coming down
this way. What is the difference between one dollar and
five? I'll tell you: it is the difference between fat cows
shipped directly from pasture to market, and thin cows
driven a thousand miles to the railroad—"

"I know, I *know!*" he protested wearily. "But as usual,
you overlook fundamentals. How did you get most of this
land in the first place?"

"I bought it—some of it. The rest was free for the taking."

"There were other people in it first," he reminded her.

Nettled, she said quickly, "Never mind that. Never mind."

"You've wanted war, really. Why in hell couldn't you get along and be satisfied with enough? We're not going to starve."

"No," she said vehemently. "We are not going to starve! Never *again*." She waited now, and they sat staring at one another through the gloom, not seeing, but conscious of the animosities flowing between them. At last the woman said icily, "Since you insist on being critical, I shall give you another reason. I have hired Frank Landry as foreman."

Steele swore, a round, solid oath. "You *hired* him!"

"I did. What do you say to that?"

"What I've always said," he replied heatedly. "You're as mad as a March hare!"

"Perhaps," she replied sweetly, enjoying his discomfiture. "We shall see." Then, with a short laugh, she said, "I intend to turn some of your work over to him. Then you will have more time for developing those alcoholic philosophies of yours."

At this moment Kirby Steele sensed the shifting balance of his position at Corralitos. Always he had comforted himself with the thought that he served his purpose well, that she needed him for a certain power which he lent the organization. But now it occurred to him that he might have entirely misjudged his place in his sister's schemes.

"Will you give him a position of power?"

"I will put him over every man on Corralitos," she replied defiantly. "And he will be under *my* orders."

He thought of that for a long time. Then he got up and stood looking at her through the darkness. "I see," he said quietly, and went away toward the front of the house.

Night was full upon Landry as he rode into the Corralitos yard. Ahead and to the right he saw light from a long, sprawling bunkhouse, and up a low knoll, surrounded by pines, the Casa Grande. He rode on toward the bunkhouse, stepped down and ground-hitched and went through the bunkhouse doorway.

It was one of a pair of similar structures, but at this moment it alone was occupied. In the front, near the door, were a couple of tables, and at one of these three men were playing cards. The lean, still-faced Coulter was one of them. Ranged on the bunks beyond and running down both sides of the room, other riders lounged or sat smoking. As Landry came in, they turned their full, instant attention upon him. Coulter looked at him and a shadow crossed his face. He laid down his cards and pushed back his chair.

"Well!" Coulter said. "Just look who's here."

Landry gave him a slow glance, then let it pass on around the room. "Where's the foreman's shack?" he asked of no one in particular.

No one spoke. Coulter got deliberately to his feet. "Hagberg's foreman. What did you want to see him about?"

"He *was* foreman," Landry said. "That's my job now."

Coulter looked about the room and then back at Landry. "This outfit has a ramrod. The crew likes him. We won't have him replaced by the first one that drops out of a pilgrim's saddle."

Landry saw that Coulter wore no gun. He said softly, "I did it once, Coulter, and I can do it again. In an alley or a bunkhouse, it makes no difference."

Now, strangely, Coulter smiled. He was still smiling as he rushed at Landry, knocking the table aside in his charge. He hit Landry at the middle, doubled up and furious, and they went down.

Coulter lit on top, and Landry caught two hard blows on his cheek before he could wriggle free. He drove a right to Coulter's midriff, heard him grunt, and then he was on his hands and knees, getting up, as Coulter again came in, swinging. The man was not as heavy as Landry, but he was hard and wiry, and hate was a river of steel flowing through him. He landed two random blows on Landry's ribs, and then Landry swung a stiff one to the man's head and he reeled away, cursing and momentarily groggy. The upright of a bunk stopped him and he hung there for a moment. Landry went in after him, his weight pinning Coulter to the wood, while he drove short jabs at Coulter's head. The gunman swore wildly, shot a knee up to Landry's groin, and that drove Landry backward, nausea and a wild agony grabbing at his vitals.

As he hit the overturned table and fell, Coulter closed upon him. A blow caught him on the head with splitting force and he threw his arms out and found the gunman's waist and they rolled across the floor, kicking, gouging, biting. Landry connected with a short left to Coulter's wind and this slowed him down, and the next one of Landry's connected with the tip of the jaw and he heard the crunching of bone. Coulter groaned and rolled over, and Landry got dizzily to his feet. He waited, getting his wind, and after short seconds Coulter got to one knee, hate beating in a steady flame from his wild, dark eyes. For a moment he crouched, then came at Landry with a swishing blow that he brought up from the floor. Landry sidestepped, swung all his compact weight into a hard right that caught Coulter on the temple and brought him crashing to the floor. He tried to get up and fell back, and Landry went to him, pulled him to his feet and threshed a looping right into the man's face. His fist came away bloody. He felt the strength go out of the other's knees, and he set him up for one more. Then, just as Coulter sagged, Landry struck him full in the face, and the sound was like the thud of a cleaver against meat.

He stood there, waiting for his wind, and then he saw the eyes of the men upon him and knew that it was his move. "I'll ask you once more: where's the foreman's house?"

His gaze beat at them madly, and after a while a man's voice from down the room said, "Over there beyond the corrals, next to the Big House."

"That's better," said Landry. He went to the table near the wall, took a pitcher of water and threw it into Coulter's face. The man stirred and his eyes opened, and Landry prodded him with his boot.

"Get up," he said roughly. "You ride tonight."

"Damn it," a rider grumbled, "that's too hard. A man has a right—"

Landry swung around. "Want to try your luck?"

The man looked at him a moment, then his gaze wavered away. Landry said, "Throw this fellow's war bag out here." He reached down and pulled Coulter to his feet. The gunman swayed a little, then focused on Landry and began to curse him. Landry slapped him in the face. "Ride," he said harshly. "Get off this place. And don't cross my path again."

Hate twisted up Coulter's bruised and battered face. But for the moment he was beaten, and the knowledge brought him close to tears. He let go a sigh, a long one. Then, as a rider brought his war bag and his gun belts to the front, he reached down and strapped on his guns. For only an instant he pondered narrowly, looking first at the guns and then at Landry, and then he shook his head. "No," he murmured. "Later. But make no mistake, our paths will cross." With that he picked up his gear and went out the door.

Even as he passed into the darkness, there was a heavy step outside, and Swede Hagberg came into the room and stood looking at Landry, his face expressionless, his smoke-colored eyes blank. Another moment of waiting spread hard and thin over the room, then, "You're out of it, Hagberg," Landry said. "I'm the new boss. You want to change that, too?"

Hagberg said heavily, "I just want you to know that you can't run anybody off this place but me."

"All right. Now I know."

"I work for Kirby. He tells me to, I'll smoke you out of the country."

Landry was about to reply, when Kirby and Carolina Steele came up on the porch and through the door. "What the hell is this about Coulter?" Steele demanded.

Landry said, "I put him back on the trail."

"You did!" Exasperation thinned Steele's voice. "Well, you can just call him back. Now!"

"If that's the way it is," Landry said evenly, "the job's still open." He started toward the door.

Carolina Steele stopped him. "Stay here." Angrily she wheeled on Kirby. "This is the last time you cross me," she said in a low, furious voice. "From now on, not only the men take Landry's orders, but you as well!"

"Not by a damn sight! You can have your foreman as far as I'm concerned, but since you want an understanding before the whole world, here it is: I take no one's orders—much less this fellow's."

They glared at one another, pale and furious, and Landry said, "It's for you to decide." He stepped past them. As he went out the door, Hagberg growled, "Remember. I work for Kirby. As for the rest of it—well, someday—"

"Sure," said Landry with un-interest. He led the black to a watering trough by the corrals. Then he swung off the gear and threw it over the top rail and turned the animal into the enclosure.

Afterward, he washed his bruised face and rubbed some of the soreness out of his muscles. Then he dried himself with his neck piece and went through the night to the foreman's house. A shadow moved against the blackness and Kirby Steele said, "So. Now I have to face you here. Will you ever show your hand, face up?"

Landry went past Steele into the shack. He struck a match, found a lamp and lit it. Then he faced the other. "I'm here, so let's make the best of it. You were a fool to fight with your sister before all the hands."

It hit Steele, because it was true. "No advice," he said crisply. "I will make my adjustments to you as I have to all the men who have caught Carolina's fancy for whatever reason, from time to time."

"No doubt."

It was still in the room. Presently Steele laughed, an unpleasant laugh. "At least, it will be bad news for McCanless—"

A note in his voice awakened Landry's craft. "No reason why," he said. He looked at Steele, remembering that Steele hated McCanless for what lay between the big man and his sister. "After all, they're going to be married, so—"

"Who told you that?" Steele asked quickly.

"Why," Landry feigned surprise, "McCanless did. Mean to say you didn't know?"

Anger slowly darkened Steele's face. Suddenly he whirled and stalked away into the night. Landry smiled grimly, and as he took tobacco from his vest and curled up a cigarette, he was thinking, *Another fuse lighted. Now to wait for the explosion.*

He turned to his gear, preoccupied with that thought. A step sounded behind him and he whirled. Carolina Steele stood just inside the door, watching him with a strange look. She said coldly, "Why did you tell Kirby that lie?"

Landry eased toward the table and stood watching her. Finally, "You hired me to do something about those two fellows, didn't you?"

"Did you get that impression?"

"Why not? You gave it to me."

Her gaze on him was thoughtful, and Landry knew that her suspicions had been aroused. Before she could speak, he said, "I suppose that you know it was a dumb thing to do—fighting with him in the bunkhouse before your men."

She was an arrogant woman, accustomed to believing that her methods and actions were right. Therefore, his bold criticism disoriented her for a moment.

"I suppose it was," she said finally. "But I came to your assistance there, remember."

"I'm thinking about Kirby. If you really meant that he's through here, why wait until he takes the play from you?"

He saw on her face that she did not understand. "He's not going to like that," he pointed out. "What I told him was another way of making this place unpopular."

"Perhaps. But remember, he owns half this ranch."

Landry said carefully, "You want him to have his share?"

"Not—not necessarily."

"In that case," Landry said slowly, "there's only one thing to do."

Their glances met, and hers did not waver. Finally, "Yes, that's about all. But there is a problem."

"Hagberg?"

"That, and—" She shrugged. "A person cannot just disappear around here, in spite of the free manner of handling such things."

"It's a big world. He could take a trip."

Immediately he saw the shrewd, crafty rise of interest in her gaze. "Where?"

Before replying, Landry pulled on his cigarette, and all the while he was saying to himself, *Now we'll see.* He blew smoke into the air and said carefully. "You have a trail herd going north. Send him with it. It's a long ways to the railroad. Something might happen."

For long seconds she watched him, and he observed the weighing of that thought behind her gaze, and saw its final acceptance. "There would have to be some assurance that he did not return."

Landry said evenly, "I'll give them two, three days on the trail, before I ride after 'em. Then you'll own all of Corralitos."

She nodded slowly, and then a cloud came over her countenance. "He wouldn't go. What pretext could I possibly use to get him away with the herd?"

"Just tell him you want him to go. I'll see that he does."

"How?"

"Does it matter," he asked impatiently, "so long as he goes?"

She colored, displeased with his tone. "No, I suppose not."

"All right. Tell him the herd will leave in three, four days. But listen: he's to leave Hagberg and his other bodyguards behind. Understand?"

"He wouldn't consider it."

"Tell him you need them now for some small raids on Running W and Pitchfork."

She considered this with a pursing of the lips. Finally, "Very well." She turned away, and at the door she faced him again, the odd, speculative look once more in her gaze. "There is something about you that I would like to understand—" Then she paused. "What is there in this for you, that you play my game so easily and so readily?"

"Money."

"Ah. The great common denominator." Then her look changed, and she said musingly, "Are there any other considerations in your life? Could there be, and how far would they take you?"

Landry knew that she had opened a door for him ever so slightly. "I've been told that a woman can be dearer to men than gold," he said. "So far as I'm concerned, it's just a rumor."

She gave him a quizzical look, then after a moment she laughed. "Ungallant, but forthright. Still, you might change your mind." With that she left him.

Mary Wayne had sat alone on the veranda as the day had gone out of the sky in the west and the heavens there had turned cold. How long she had been there did not matter. It really seemed that nothing would ever matter to her again. The last few days had had their piling up of shock and sorrow, and at times she asked herself if she might not really be beyond feeling, now.

Harry had come in after dark, spoken briefly, and after a bite in the kitchen had gone directly to his room where, for a long time, she heard his restless moving about. She wondered about him. Their father's death had hit her with that added shock of the girl who adores her father as the most important male in her life to date; she had not expected the profound reaction which it had brought in Harry.

He had grown haggard and hollow-eyed, but there was no talk of revenge, or reprisal. It was as though her brother were looking upon darker things, remote from the eyes of the world, and beyond the range of ordinary people to feel or comprehend. Seldom did he speak, and then briefly; he had the haunted look of men who battle with the vaporous things of the spirit.

She had had plenty of time to think of Frank Landry and his part in this affair, and now, with the first shock worn away, she realized that there could be no certain blame upon him for her father's death. Loyalty to her clan was in constant conflict with her deeper emotions for this tall stranger. Pride and hatred of her father's enemies told her that she should despise his very name; the remembrance of his kiss and of his strong arms about her made her search for exoneration.

The wind off the desert had grown chill, and she shivered a little with it and with the desolation of her own spirit, and rose and went into the house. Everything here was the same: it was almost as though Darby Wayne had gone to town, and would return in the morning. And then, suddenly, it struck her that he would never again return to fill this house with his hard, bluff and loving presence, and she sat down at the table and wept, pillowing her head in her arms.

She must have slept, eventually, for it was the sound of a running horse in the night that brought her head up, alerted. Even as she rose and turned toward the door, the rider pulled up outside. A moment later, Drav McLain, his face drawn tight and anger reddening his cheeks, stalked into the room.

She read some unpleasant news in his face. "What's happened, Drav?"

"They hit that herd over in the Morales pasture," he said grimly. "Got about forty, fifty head, and one of the boys creased with a bullet."

Harry Wayne entered, looked at them questioningly, and McLain repeated his story, watching young Wayne carefully.

When he had finished, Wayne stared at him absently. Finally, he turned away, but the girl shot at him. "Is that all? Are you going to say nothing?"

"What is there to say?"

She knew her brother pretty well. It was apparent to her that this was no normal reaction for the son of Darby Wayne, who had fought for his rights and the rights of others. "Are you going to lie down before them?" her voice shamed him. "Are you going to offer them the rest of the herds, too?"

"Might as well. They'll get 'em." And then, under her gaze, he colored.

McLain said, "It seems damn near like they got permission to rustle us already."

Wayne shot him a quick look. "How's that?"

"They duplicate brands. They kill Darby. Better pack up, Harry. They'll have the house next."

"Damn it to hell," Wayne exploded, "you'd think it was my fault! I tell you, it was that Landry fellow. Look how he played us for fools that day he came here. Then, at the Courthouse, he showed his true colors. He hasn't been here a week, and things have started to hell on a bobsled. Dad killed, just because—"

"I don't believe that!" The sound of her own voice surprised Mary Wayne, and she found Drav McLain looking at her queerly, while Harry's outraged stare lay against her.

"You don't!" he finally blurted out. "Maybe you think it was *me*. You think *I* told them to lie in wait for Dad—" Suddenly he stopped, his gaze hot, and somehow shifting and unbalanced.

There was a long moment of embarrassed silence. McLain said quietly, "You're the boss. If you don't want to fight, it's your business."

Harry Wayne stared at the foreman. He started to speak, closed his mouth, then suddenly muttered something and turned away. A moment later they heard his door slam.

The girl did not immediately look at the old foreman. It was his voice that brought up her glance. "I'm goin' to town tomorrow," he said gently. "I think I'd better take you in to the house for a couple of days."

She knew that he was giving her this way out, that he would, if the fight came, fight on alone without the help of Harry Wayne because still, to him, Darby Wayne and his principles ran the Running W. These things she knew, and they brought tears to her eyes. "All right, Drav," she said in a still voice. "In the morning."

Later, as she fell asleep, she wondered if, by chance, she would see Landry in town, if something he might say could help to resolve the conflicts within her. Then, hating herself for thinking of him in this way, she fell asleep.

It was the first night of complete rest she had had since her father's death. When morning brought her awake, she rose rested and with a sober resignation that came from her determination to find her way into the future with courage and strength, regardless of the blows which might fall upon her.

Harry's room was vacant, and the covers of his bed had not been turned down. Worried slightly by this fact, she breakfasted and dressed, and when she heard Drav bring up the horses, she went out and greeted him.

"I suppose Harry can get his own breakfast," she said dubiously.

Drav shook his head. "He'll probably eat in town."

"In town?"

"He went in just about with the sun."

She said nothing. But all the way to Broken Wheel she was worried by the knowledge that something had happened to her brother, and that it was a deep and dark and serious thing.

Landry saw the dark flow of bad humor over Kirby Steele's sharp countenance as he came toward the corrals where Landry was rubbing down the black. Before Landry, Steele paused without greeting and stared at him with a narrow kind of dislike in his cold gaze.

"I wonder," he mused, "how much you had to do with this idea of Carolina's?"

Landry ran the brush over the black's withers, knocked the loose hair free and looked at Steele. "What idea?"

"Taking the herd north day after tomorrow. Do you want to reduce me to the status of a drover?"

Landry slapped the currycomb and brush together, laid them aside. "I'm not interested enough in you to bother," he said. "Still, it strikes me"—he looked quickly around, then back at Steele—"that you don't know how lucky you are."

"No," said Steele ironically. "Only you could be expected to know that."

"All right." Landry shrugged.

"How did you mean that?" Steele said with sharp impatience.

Landry studied him. Then he said carefully, "Sometimes an outsider's view is better than a fellow's own."

"Get to the point."

"It doesn't take a genius to see how it'll be after your sister and that McCanless fellow get married." He saw the dark flush on Steele's face, and pressed on. "Maybe you haven't thought about it, but there could be better places for you than Corralitos from now on."

Steele had been watching him with suspicion deep in his gaze. Now he said, "I suppose that I am fated never to know what your game really is. Now, just why are you so interested in getting me out of here, friend?"

Landry looked at him for a long while. Then he took his chance. "Do you think you're the only one who doesn't like McCanless?" he asked softly.

Steele cocked an eyebrow sharply. "Well?"

"You may be tough. I don't know. But I doubt that you could handle McCanless." He waited. "Did it ever occur to you that *I can?*"

"I felt from the beginning that you knew more than you admitted," Steele said. "I'd have bet on it—"

"Don't bet too heavy," Landry said quickly.

Steele waved aside the protest. "I think I see it. You were Steve Landry's—"

"Don't bother," Landry said frigidly. "I'd hate to make you out a liar."

Now Steele nodded his head and a knowing smile came over his thin lips. "You are cleverer than I thought. But since you choose enigmatic speech, let's go a little further with it. Suppose I go north with the herd. Then what?"

"Well," Landry said, "if I were going to marry your sister and knew that there was still your share, I'd move in after you left, and then see to it that you didn't come back."

Steele pondered that. "Go on."

"On the other hand, if you had someone here to take care of me, someone who didn't like me too well, it would save you a lot of trouble. But I would really look foolish if you collected the money for that herd and then took the next train East." He looked at Steele sharply. "Just a hypothetical case, of course."

"Of course." But Steele's face had grown thoughtful.

Landry turned away. "Well, I'll mosey."

Steele let him walk ten paces. Then he called out, "Landry, come here."

"You come here."

Slowly, Steele approached and stood looking at Landry with a critical, weighing stare. "I could tip your hole card," he said softly.

"Why don't you?"

"Maybe I will."

"No, it would cost you too much."

After a moment Steele nodded. "You have the ultimate logic. Now, about this hypothetical question: If I were to go East, I assume that McCanless would not remain at Corralitos."

"Do you?"

Steele frowned. "In the event that I returned. How about that?"

Landry said impatiently, "You're getting all involved. Forget it."

"Answer my question."

"Hell's fire!" Landry exploded. "Can't you figure that out? Your sister would need *someone* she could work with."

"You?"

Landry looked Steele full in the face. "I'll just be here until I can pick up the check for whatever *favors* I do."

With that he turned away, doubtful of how his stratagem had worked. He would know in a very short time. Carolina Steele had left orders for him to ride to town with her that morning.

He went about his work, hounded slightly by uneasiness.

An hour later he brought up his horse and Carolina's, and as he helped her into the saddle, she gave him a smile. Reining out of the yard, he turned to look back. Kirby Steele was leaning against a pillar of the veranda, and as Landry turned, Steele made a slight inclination of his head.

As they pulled down the trail toward the valley floor, Carolina turned to him and said, "You were right. Kirby has agreed to take the herd north. How did you know he would?"

Landry shrugged. "Probably glad to get away after that fracas the other night."

She looked at him closely, but said nothing.

Chapter 12

BROKEN WHEEL lay wrapped in its afternoon torpor as Drav McLain and Mary Wayne rode in. The sun, brassy and bold and free, drummed up a silent symphony of heat from the ankle-deep dust of the street, and thrust its sharp edge at the curling timbers of the bleached frame buildings. Through all the town's length, only a few drowsy ponies, hip-shot and bored, stood before the hitch racks.

McLain watched the street carefully as they came on, for he knew that this was now hostile territory. His quick eye picked out the twin boxes of Corralitos among the brands of some of the horses they passed, and he flipped the reins a bit, urging his horse ahead, not too obviously. He had his business to attend to, but he would get Mary Wayne safely home before he tested the temper of the town.

"I'm going to stop at the General Store," Mary said suddenly, with decision. "They have some new cloth, and I may as well make a dress to keep my mind off—"

McLain interrupted gruffly, "You come up the street later." And there was no arguing with his tone. The girl looked at him quickly and said nothing.

Idly he observed the street. Before the Casino he saw the figure of a man whom he recognized, and that man stepped quickly inside after a look at McLain. The old man felt a tightening inside.

Almost at the same instant he spied a man coming up the street from the direction of the Courthouse, and something in the man's stride prodded at his memory as they came on toward the hotel and the Wayne house below it. A few moments later they pulled up, and he heard the sharp intake of breath from Mary Wayne. With that he recognized the man. It was Frank Landry.

McLain got down into the dust and helped the girl alight. Landry swung up, tipped his hat to the girl, and would have passed on, but McLain said, "You got fifty head last night. Won't be so easy after this. From now on, I'm night ridin'. Do to me what you did to Darby!"

Landry's face had been neutral and distant, but now it hardened. "If the Corralitos crew hit your herds, I know nothing of it."

"You're foreman," McLain said, "and you're a damn liar."

"I'll let that pass," Landry said stiffly. "Age has slowed you down."

In the midst of his rising anger, Drav McLain became aware that Mary Wayne stood very near him, stiff and silent. He saw, too, that a passerby on the other side of the street had suddenly stopped, taken in this scene, and ducked into the doorway of a building. Still watching Landry, he said, "Mary, go in the house."

"I'll stay here."

Landry had been painfully conscious of the girl's stiff whiteness as she faced him. Beyond her, across the street and in back of Drav McLain, he saw Swede Hagberg and Coulter meet, speak a word, and then fan out into the street, going in opposite directions and afterward turning, pincer-like, in toward the street's middle.

Again McLain said sharply, "Get out of here, Mary. Go inside!"

"No."

Hagberg had swung at a rolling walk into the street slightly below them, and Coulter stood twenty-five paces upstreet, near the boardwalk's edge. Trying to figure this thing, Landry knew that the play could be directed against either himself or McLain, but that the heaviest odds lay against the Running W foreman. He wondered, fleetingly, if they had assumed that he was in on it against McLain, and then it hit him with a cold, shocking certainty that McLain was a dead man if he made one move toward the street.

He said evenly, "Stand hitched, McLain, or your next move is the last one."

Then he took a quick step, putting himself between the girl and McLain and the men in the street. He looked at Hagberg. "Two guns," he said softly. "I can beat the best cross-hand draw in Texas."

Hagberg stood in a half-crouch, his hands waiting. He said with stubbornness in his voice, "McLain. That crowd can't come to this town and walk free. What in hell are *you* doin', standin' at his side?"

"Get up the street, Swede," Landry said, and then he shifted his gaze to Coulter. The still-faced man had moved to the street now, ten feet from the walk's edge. Landry turned his head quickly and saw that the girl had moved in back of him, standing in Coulter's possible line of fire. He knew then why the cold-blooded gun hawk hadn't made his move.

He let it stand that way. To Hagberg he said, "Any time you want it. But your business with McLain has to clear through me."

"Orders are to gun those fellows down," Hagberg muttered. "What in hell kind of a boss are you, anyhow?"

Landry had been easing slowly forward. "I told you to get up the street," he said. Then he took three swift steps forward and suddenly he lunged, and his left caught Hagberg on the jaw, swinging the big gunman off balance. Simultaneously, he drew and pivoted and as his gun racketed, its slug tore the gun from Coulter's hands just as it was sweeping up to fire. Coulter staggered back, his jaw dropped and he stood foolishly looking at the revolver lying before him in the dust.

Landry said to Hagberg, "Want to play some more?"

Hagberg stared at him blankly. "This was a foolish play, mister," he said finally. "When the break comes, I'll kill you."

Landry took another step. "Drift," he said thinly.

For a sick, paralyzed moment, Hagberg waited, taking

his choice between pride and humiliation. "I'm tired of waiting," Landry said.

Then Hagberg turned, and his step as he went to the boardwalk was stiff and slow. On the plank walk he faced Landry. "The time keeps gettin' shorter," he said softly. "Shorter all the time." Then he went up the street.

Coulter had stood there, under Drav McLain's gun. Now, as Landry went toward him, he cursed, wildly and with a kind of frenzied frustration.

"You can't be that good! Damn you, you're just lucky."

Landry said, "Next time, I shoot for the bull's-eye. Pick up your popgun and travel."

Coulter's nerve was gone, and he was drowning in a sea of hate and wounded pride. Pale-faced, lost, he suddenly leaned over and picked up his gun, jamming it into the leather. "It was the girl," he said hoarsely. "She was in line and I couldn't open up on you."

"She won't always be there," Landry consoled him.

Coulter watched him with a covetous, hard and hungry look. "No," he said presently. "And you won't always have all the luck." Then, abruptly, he turned and went at a furious lope up the street.

Landry turned back to the boardwalk. "You ought to know better," he told McLain. "Next time, ride in in force."

Drav McLain's dark gaze was filled with speculation. "You're a funny one," he said meagerly. "What made you change your mind?"

Landry's glance slipped momentarily aside to Mary Wayne, who had been watching him with a still, breathless attention. "I haven't changed my mind a bit," he said mildly. Then he tipped his hat and turned away.

Halfway across the street, she called out to him and he turned and slowly came back to her. McLain had gone into the house.

"What is this?" she asked softly, her eyes holding his. "What kind of a man are you?"

He felt the blood crawl up into his face and words left

him. At last he said, "I've never wanted anything in my life so much as I want you to know the answer to that question."

"Then tell me."

Again, now, Landry thought of Harry Wayne and of his treachery, and his hesitation was only momentary. He shook his head. "I can't tell you."

He saw, then, the return of loathing to her eyes. "You could," she said in a voice that cut. "But you aren't man enough to admit that you want to be both Sir Galahad and the Black Knight." Her shoulders went back. "Your true face is a mixture of piety and craft, of sanctimonious goodness and black designs. I shall remember that, now!" Suddenly she wheeled and ran into the house. Landry looked after her a moment, and then he turned and went up the street toward the hotel. He kept thinking that she had moved into Coulter's line of fire, holding up the gunman's play.

At the time Harry Wayne saw Carolina Steele and Landry ride into Broken Wheel, he already had three drinks in him, and they had not helped. Morose and unhappy, he had refused Grady's tender commiseration, for the barkeep's every attempt at sympathy for his father's death merely deepened the many remorseful wounds he was nursing.

He watched them pass down the street; then he stepped outside and saw Carolina get down and enter the hotel while Landry went on with the horses to the livery stable. He viewed this scene darkly, and weighed only momentarily the wisdom of attempting to see her in broad daylight. Then, guilt overcoming his caution, he turned toward the hotel and in a few moments was knocking at the door of her room.

As she opened the door for him, it seemed that for an instant she would block his way. But a wild looseness in his face told her that he had been drinking, and after a brief hesitation she stepped aside for him to enter.

"Have you gone mad?" she demanded sharply, closing the door. "Do you want the world to know about us—about *you?*"

He glowered at her. "It wouldn't matter. How much lower can I sink?"

Feeling a qualm of uneasiness, she softened her mood and said, "Believe me. I am sorry, Harry. It was not meant to be that way."

She saw the quickening of hope in him and pressed on, "It was Kirby who ordered that ambush, after I had told them merely to show force enough to frighten your people off—"

"I'd like to believe that, Carolina."

"You can't believe that I—*planned* it that way—"

He watched her, eager to let her lies still his doubts. In this moment, Harry Wayne needed to believe that his father's death had been completely accidental. Still, he said, "I don't know. I'm not sure about anything, any more. I suppose it's that way when a man loses faith in himself."

Her game with him was about played out. But because he might still be useful, she wished to retain her hold over him yet a while. "Don't say that, Harry. To blame yourself entirely is foolish."

"No," he said slowly. "I don't blame myself entirely. Some of the blame is yours, Carolina."

She paled. "I swear to you that I kept my word," she said earnestly. "I swear that to you on—on our love—" and now she was looking at him with an open gaze, all candor.

It had the desired effect. He uttered an exclamation filled with choked-up misery, and took her in his arms, holding her close, feeling the warmth of her body near him, and letting everything that was feminine about her deaden his sensibilities. "It's been hell," he muttered. "I've needed you to tell me this—"

She let him have his long moment of anesthesia, then stepped back, smiling. "It will not be long," she said reassuringly. "Before a great while this thing will be worked out. Then—"

"Carolina," he said with sudden decision, "we're not going to wait. Not feeling that there was some justification—"

"Hush. You must not even think such things."

The crashing reverberation of a shot rocked through the town's stillness, and its sudden, wild challenge changed everything in the room in an instant. Carolina Steele drew back, a wild surmise in her gaze, her mind suddenly focused on other things.

"You must go," she said abruptly. "I have to find out what has happened."

"There's time for that," he protested. "Other things are more important."

"Don't be a fool!" And she pushed him, not gently, toward the door.

Something that had lain dormant in him a long time rose up in rebellion now, and he threw her hands off. "You damned iron woman! Where in hell is your heart? Don't it mean anything to you that your crew killed my father and that I helped them? Or do you think that this is just another of those things, like your handling Steve Landry—"

He stopped too late, seeing the rage rise into her eyes.

"I didn't mean that," he said quickly. "I didn't—"

Her open palm caught him hard in the face. "Get out! Get out of here and don't come back!"

"Carolina—"

"Before I lose my temper and teach you a lesson, *get out*!"

Half fearfully, he looked at her for a moment, not knowing that this was acting on her part; then he turned and opened the door. "I'm sorry for that," he began humbly. "Carolina, I've got to talk to you—"

She came toward him and he stepped outside, cowed and unhappy. "Then learn how to talk to me before you come back," she snapped and shut the door in his face.

Harry Wayne stood looking at the door for a moment. Then, misery piled upon unhappiness, he turned up the alley toward the street in back of the main street, ashamed to face the day or to look men in the face, and certain in his great misery that he had almost lost her.

As the door closed, Carolina raced for the lobby and the

main street. She found the desk clerk outside, watching the tableau before Mary Wayne's house, and she saw Landry standing in the dust, facing Hagberg and Coulter. She realized that her foreman had fought with Corralitos men to protect McLain, even before the clerk muttered over his shoulder, "Swede went after McLain, and Landry stopped him cold."

A new emotion bubbled up in her as Landry turned to talk to Mary Wayne, and with her woman's instinct she read emotional tension into the girl's abrupt flight into the house. Her face was grave as she turned back into the hotel.

"Tell Landry I want to see him," she said to the clerk, and then went quickly to her room. For a moment she paused before her mirror, looking at her reflection. She touched her hand to her hair, absently, and she was thinking of Mary Wayne and her flight from Landry as his knock sounded at the door.

"Come in."

Landry stepped inside and waited. She said in a neutral tone, "Our agreement was that you work *for* Corralitos, *not against* it."

"Not to the place where I let fellows like Coulter gun me."

"You stopped Hagberg's play against McLain," she said.

"McLain jumped me about a cattle raid last night. That's when those two moved in. Besides, you're forgetting that the girl was there."

"No," she said dryly. "I'm not forgetting that."

"Well," Landry drawled, "if you want me to boss that outfit of yours, you'd better let me know when you raid somebody's herds. It's embarrassing to find out about it from the fellow that's been rustled."

She smiled sardonically, but said nothing. Then she turned away and walked across the room, and he knew that she was weighing another thought that involved him. Suddenly she swung about.

"What did you talk about with that girl?"

"Me. What a low no-account I am."

"Why *you?*"

"Her father was killed by Corralitos. I work for Corralitos."

"It's odd," she murmured, "that she should pick on *you.* Why not Hagberg, Coulter—myself!"

He shrugged. "Perhaps so."

Carolina Steele knew that some emotion other than hate had been behind Mary Wayne's swift flight from Landry. That fact moved her in a strange way, but it was another thing which caused her to say, "It occurs to me that you are too often with Ed Ardoin and those others."

"Does it?"

"Kirby saw you first at the Running W. Hagberg says that you talked to Ardoin that first night in town. Now I find you with Drav McLain and Mary Wayne. What am I to think?"

"Think what you want. If you're not satisfied, you'll have to get another boy."

"You've said that before. Suppose I should?"

"I'll get along."

He had the appearance of being governed by indifference, but some sharper feminine instinct told her that it was not wholly so. He was an easy man to misjudge, and his manner of seeming to care for nothing sent her a challenge and made her want to bind him to a course and to a positive attitude.

"You'll get along," she repeated slowly. "With or without Corralitos. Is that it?"

"That's it." He saw her studying him, and knew that she had not yet made up her mind about him. "But you're making a mountain out of a molehill." Then he turned and went out the door.

After he had gone, she went to the lobby and told the clerk, "Anse, send someone for Bill Coulter. I want to see him."

A half hour later Coulter came to her room. He bore the marks of his fight with Landry, and she noticed them and he saw her survey but remained impassive.

"You are back on the payroll, if you want to be," she said.

Coulter shook his head. "Not as long as *he's* there. Cor-

ralitos is not big enough for him and me. I guess maybe all
Texas pinches in a little on us."

"You don't have to come back to Corralitos. You are to
do a job for me, and tell no one that you are doing it."

Interest quickened in the dark eyes. "What's the job?"

"Watch Landry for me. And tell me what he does."

Coulter watched her, thinking this over. "One condition."

"What?"

"When you don't want him watched anymore, I get a free
hand with him."

She waited a moment before she said, "If I find out that
he *had* to be watched, you will be free to do as you please."

Landry left the hotel and went north to the livery stable
to care for the horses. When he returned to the street, two
things caught at his attention. Coulter came lounging from
the hotel and took up a stand outside, and Ed Ardoin, ac-
companied by three riders, came into the street's north end
and rode down toward the livery stable.

Ardoin hit the dust and the three riders went on down the
street. Landry pulled his makings from his pocket and
turned down toward the hotel. Out of the corner of his
mouth he said to Ardoin. "Meet me over the Longhorn. It's
important." Then he went on.

Coulter kept his gaze on him as he approached, and
Landry favored the gunman with a neutral stare and passed
on down the way. The man's reaction had not been in character, a fact which alerted Landry. When he had walked a
block aimlessly, he looked around. Coulter lounged along in
his wake, too obviously casual. In a moment he stopped to
stare into a store window and out of the corner of his eye, he
saw that Coulter, too, had stopped up the way waiting.

"Thought I heard shootin' a while ago." Landry looked
up into the sad, enigmatical face of Lon Wilson, who had
come from the store and now stood watching him, a remote
questioning behind his gaze. For a moment they looked at
one another. Then Landry said pointedly, "You're a little
late, Sheriff."

Wilson colored, and a kind of stiffness passed over his countenance. He said wearily, "A man can only do so much." Landry said nothing. Wilson's narrowed, bitter gaze went up the way to Coulter, and he watched him a long time. "Right behind you," he murmured. "Go where you're going, and I'll hold him up a while." Before Landry could reply, he turned up the street toward Coulter.

Landry cut across to the post office and went in and asked for mail, knowing there would be none. Leaving the post office, he drifted up the way and stepped into the Casino for a drink. He saw over his shoulder Lon Wilson talking to Coulter, but he knew that he could not wait long. He had a quick drink, went to the saloon's rear, and stepped through a back door into the street back of the saloon. Quickly he cut north until he hit an alley, and he followed the alley's line over the way until he was in the street backing the Longhorn. In a few minutes he was in the saloon's back room, where Ed Ardoin waited for him.

"Upstairs?"

"Yes," said Landry.

"All right," Ardoin said when they were in the upstairs room, "what's so important?"

Landry said, "Kirby Steele is taking that trail herd north day after tomorrow."

"We expected that," Ardoin said sourly. "What's so damned unusual about it?"

Landry quelled his exasperation. "Round up your bunch," he said. "Give Steele three, four days on the trail, and then hit him like the wrath of God! At night, understand. Then you can drive your cows back to your own range. What you do to Kirby is your own business."

Ardoin's face showed a beginning of hope, and then it sobered. "We couldn't get 'em all. One or two would ride back to Corralitos, and that whole damn crowd would run down on us."

"No. Three days from now, you take your crew and lead it against the fake Pitchfork down below you. Chouse the cattle around and burn some powder. Send another bunch the same night to do the same thing with Carolina's Running W outfit. They'll make tracks to report to her. I'll tell her it's war, and split up the main crew and send 'em over to those places for reinforcements. That'll give you time to take care of Steele and his trail crew and to hide the cattle or scatter 'em on your own range."

Now the smile came through. Ardoin said, "Landry, by God! I believe it'll work."

"One more thing. From now on, when I give orders, jump! The timing has to be right, or it'll be no dice."

"How do you mean?"

"Carolina's suspicious of me. She's got Coulter on my tail."

Ardoin nodded. "I'll stick by your plans, and I'll trust you. But if anything goes wrong—well, I'll be around to find out why it did."

"Sure." Landry started down the stairs, and Ardoin followed. At the bottom Landry halted and said casually, "You're not to take Harry Wayne on this trip. You're not even to let him know what's happening."

Ardoin thought immediately of Landry's connection with Mary Wayne, and his first reaction was that Landry was protecting her brother. "Now listen," he growled. "Harry Wayne can—"

"You going to do as I say?"

"Yes. But—"

"Then remember what I tell you, because it's important : if you want this to work, don't let Harry Wayne know about it, and that means, also, *don't let his sister find out.* And don't ask me why!"

Chapter 13

IT WAS around one o'clock in the afternoon when Ed Ardoin got to the Running W. He had put off notifying Drav McLain until last, and now it was the afternoon of the day Landry had scheduled for their feints at the two Corralitos outfits south of the Frio county line.

Luck was with him. He found the foreman by the corrals, saddling for a ride into the Buckhorns to look for strays. They exchanged greetings and the thought uppermost in Ardoin's mind came out. "Where's Harry?"

"In town," McLain said shortly. "Tryin' to drink up all the liquor in Jackson County."

"How come?" But a sense of relief hit Ardoin.

"You tell *me*. Been there, hanging' over Grady's bar for three days." He gave Ardoin a look of disgust. "Guess I'll have to go after him and teach him some sense."

"Let him stay," Ardoin said. "There's another ride you've got to take now. We go against Corralitos."

McLain swung about and looked at him a long time, reading the truth in Ardoin's face. "It's time," he said at last. "Tell me."

Briefly, Ardoin outlined the strategy which Landry had given him. As he talked, McLain nodded his head from time to time. When Ardoin had finished, he spat, clapped his tough hands together, hard. "It'll work. Damn 'em, it'll feel good to be on the other end of the thing for once!"

"All the men north of the line are either comin' or sendin'

their crews. Charlie Buckmelter and Stan Warren will be over here about nine tonight. They ride with you."

McLain nodded. "I'd better gather my boys—" He stopped and his glance went into the distance for a moment. "Darby would have liked this," he muttered at last. "It was what he wanted—"

Then he stepped aboard.

"Drav," Ardoin said. The old man turned facing him. "You're not to say anything about this to Harry or Mary."

McLain looked at him long and narrowly. "Now, that's funny! You'd think that their pop hadn't been killed by them sidewinders. Ardoin, what in hell goes on here?"

Ed Ardoin would have liked to know that answer himself. He was uncomfortable in the knowledge that so much was hidden from him, and resentful of it. "Just do like I told you," he said shortly. Then he reined toward the house, and a moment later, Drav McLain rode away, fast, toward the hills where his crews would be working.

There was a seething, permanent kind of unhappiness in Ed Ardoin these days. It came from his own feeling of inadequacy, and from the fear that Mary Wayne might play no part in the framing of his future. But with the death of her father and the obvious inability of Harry Wayne to take over the reins of the family destiny, Ed Ardoin felt that he could wait no longer to bring matters between himself and Mary to a climax. The Running W needed a guiding hand other than Drav McLain's, while the girl, personally, needed help and protection. Along with his conviction in this regard went all his long years of devotion—the strange, jealous and perhaps unreasonable love that he had for her.

Mary Wayne came to the door as he got down, and looking at her, the marks of worry and of care in her face hurt him. She had aged, somehow, with this thing, and it occurred to Ardoin that Mary Wayne would never again be the carefree, happy girl that he had known. In a way, he told himself, it was good, for she had grown more womanly, more mature, under the weight of events.

He stepped toward the veranda shade and said, "I dropped by to see if everything's all right, Mary."

"Thank you, Ed. Everything is . . . all right."

Her father's death was still recent, and it crossed his mind that now would be the time. As she sank into a chair, he took another beside her.

"You are all alone now, Mary," he said after a while. "Has that made any change in things between us?"

He heard her slow sigh. "Is this your way of asking me to marry you, Ed?"

"I want to care for you. I want to stand between you and whatever may come, from now on." Then he waited.

She took a long while to reply. "You are a good man," she said at last. "You deserve a woman who would return your love, measure for measure. Anything less would eventually make you the most unhappy man in the world, for you are impatient with half measures and greedy for affection as great as your own. I could not give you that. I am sorry, Ed, but I have to tell you this."

The tone of her first word had told him what her answer would be, and his jealousy had fanned up instantly, racing ahead of her logic, her words, her reasons. As she finished, he was thinking back to the first night when Landry had come to town, when she had calmly told him that she had wanted the tall stranger to kiss her. Still, he waited a while before he asked, "Is this final? There can be no changing?"

"No, there cannot," she said regretfully.

"It strikes me," he said suddenly, "that the whole change came between you and me when Frank Landry came to this place."

"That again?"

"Yes! Even that night when last we talked, you gave me some hope. And what has happened in the meantime? He has gone over to Corralitos. He drew a gun against us at the Courthouse. There is a good possibility that he framed Darby when we tried to cut. He has—"

"He stepped before Swede Hagberg's guns in town and saved Drav's life," she said.

Ardoin stared. "He did *what?*"

"The morning Drav and I went to town, Hagberg tried to shoot Drav down. He and Coulter caught us in the street. Landry went before their guns and stopped them." It occurred to her, perversely, that she was not speaking her mind as she had to Landry himself that morning. With that, she knew that Ardoin was right: the change that had come to her with knowing Landry was greater than she wished to admit.

Ardoin knew, guiltily, that he could have explained everything. And the fact that the girl's deeper feelings lay on the side of truth merely angered him.

"You always find some justification for him," he said stiffly. "An enemy." And with that, he rose, knowing that he would never be honest where this girl and her feelings for Landry were concerned.

Mary Wayne got up with him. She then said a thing that hurt in the saying. "Do not misunderstand," she told Ardoin. "He—he has nothing for me, nor ever can. But I owe it to you to tell you that we can never be anything but friends, Ed. I hope that we can always be that."

He looked at her darkly, and then away. "We can," he said at last. As he went down into the yard's dust, she heard his long, hard sigh.

Ardoin rode away into the afternoon's heat, not looking back. Until the very end, now, he would use his position of secret knowledge to do Landry harm. And the end, he knew, could come sooner than he had ever expected.

Landry had had time to think, during the days he had spent in Broken Wheel waiting for Carolina Steele to return to Corralitos. Along with other preoccupations had grown those springing from his evolving relationship with the woman. He had dined with her, ridden with her into the country, discussed with her the various problems of ranching and cattle and railroads, and always, in their talk, he had the sense of her examining him, of her searching for what he was and of probing for hidden motives. And always, when he was away from her, the shadow of Coulter, plodding, deadly and waiting, in the background.

They were back at Corralitos, now, and the darkness was about them as they stood in the patio. Coolness and the smell of night came down upon them from the heights, and Carolina looked for a moment at his tall, lean form in the shadows and said, "I sent for you because I think that you should be riding north soon—after Kirby."

"I was going tonight."

"Why tonight?"

This night he was to meet McCanless in Broken Wheel. He said, "A man rides in the night, no one sees him on the trail."

A *mozo* came from the house, bringing a tray with coffee, and put it on the table. Landry wondered if she had planned it this way. Carolina said, "Have some coffee with me. You do not have to leave immediately."

"Any time before midnight." He sat down at the table and curled up a cigarette while she poured coffee.

There was in this moment here, while they were surrounded by the darkness, a kind of intimacy which stirred up in him warm, pleasant sensations. He knew, too, that she sensed it, for it was in the low pitch of her voice, as she said, "You have dark currents of thought, deep channels of feeling that most people would never dream were in you. What are they, Frank Landry? What do you think?"

"About what?"

She was still for a long while. Then she mused, "I have often wondered what you thought of—me. I wonder what your opinion is—that final judgment of a person which comes from one's heart."

"I didn't know you cared about anyone's opinion."

"Not just *anyone's,*" she said slowly.

Landry let himself be momentarily tempted by this new mood. He knew that he had piqued Carolina Steele's feminine curiosity, and that she was now giving that interest in him its play. Recalling her abrupt questioning of him about

Mary Wayne, he played into that line. "I'm not much of a hand at judging women," he said laconically.

"You're evading," she challenged him. "You did not fool me about that Wayne girl. There is something—*was*, at least—between you two. Don't deny it."

"Perhaps."

After a short silence, Carolina Steele said, "Answer my question: what do you think of me? Are people justified in hating me? Am I such a person as you have been told?"

Landry pushed back his chair and slowly rose. "Don't take advantage of me," he told her. "Remember, I'm just part of the help here."

He started away across the patio.

"Frank—wait." Her voice came after him. He turned, and in a moment she came and stood near him, looking up at him through the darkness.

All her life, Carolina Steele had been too busy with other considerations to fall deeply in love. In her climb to power she had found it expedient to use men, and she had never scrupled over employing her charms to bend them to her will. Men she had known, and none had she loved, for the opposite sex had been variously a barrier and a weapon to be forged to her needs in the only way possible for her. Landry's coming had subtly worked to change this attitude, for he was not of the stamp of those men whom she had known before. His indifference, his very arrogance, challenged all that was basically feminine in her. Even in Carolina Steele there was that atavistic germ of desire to be dragged away by her hair to a caveman's lair. Now, here with this man who both repelled and attracted, she spoke her woman's mind.

"You are not just another man to me," she said huskily. "Are you blind that you do not see that?"

The light from the window cut across her face, showing the liquid warmth of her gaze and the invitation which lay in her slightly rounded, full lips. His hunger for a woman, and for this one in particular, rose up in him, and then he put his hand on her hips and swayed her to him. Her eyes closed, and with a little sigh she put her arms over his shoulders and drew his lips down to hers.

Her mouth, warm and wet and full of surrender, met his, and then she pressed her body close to him, and he could feel the softness of her breasts and the rapid excitement of her breathing against him. For a long time he held her that way, and when he let her go and stepped back, she still clung to him. He could see the wild light of complete release in her eyes, and he thought of how much she had to give a man, and was tempted to take it.

"Tell me, Frank," she murmured. "Tell me—"

Almost, it came to his tongue, for her magic was strong. And then, fighting his way free of it slowly, he said, "There's a hell of a lot of woman in you, Carolina. And strangely enough, it's mostly lonely woman. A thing I never knew before."

He had hit at something deeper than want. Her face changed, and she said slowly, "The way I have come has been a lonely way. I suppose that by ordinary standards I am not a very good woman. But then, you know that."

For a moment he felt pity for her, and a leveling of all mortals to the common denominator of clay. He said, "I wouldn't give a damn for a woman who didn't have a wide streak of bitch in her."

She screwed up her face, and then she laughed. "That's not very gallant. I suppose you meant it as a compliment."

"Just as the truth. Why can't a woman have her hungers even as a man can?"

She stepped back, wondering at him. "Not many men think as you do," she said wryly.

"Perhaps it's just as well."

"Yes, perhaps it is." After a short silence, she said, "Would it be foolish to think that here at this place, sometime, when things are settled and peace has come to this country, I might ever get to know you, and you me, and that we could both find something a bit richer and fuller in life because of it? Or is it simply that this is the nighttime and we are ever so slightly mad at this moment?"

"I'll tell you about that," Landry replied slowly. "Moments like this come along, without regard for what has gone before or what will come after. They are just a little piece of time, and a man is a fool not to take them and use them for what they were meant to be. When you start asking questions about them and trying to place them in some kind of a plan, they blow up in your face, like a soap bubble when a breeze hits it. You're a strange woman, Carolina. It would take me years, perhaps the rest of my life, to get to understand you—"

She realized that again he had slipped away from her. Her voice was a little bitter as she said, "I'm not that deep."

"Yes, you are. You hire me, and then you put a spy on my trail. The next thing, you kiss me, and talk of a future that seems to do with us both. What goes on in that mind of yours?"

She watched him a long time. "So you found out about Coulter."

"He's not too clever," Landry explained. "But you ought to have known that if I were playing a double game, I'd watch for someone at my heels."

Surprisingly, she laughed. "Now that you know, what are you going to do?"

"I'll let it remind me that we may have our moments like this, but that you always keep the long and narrow view."

She had her moment of light regret, now. There was in this man a powerful attraction, yet her innate wariness told her that the unexplained things about him could be dangerous ones. Still, she said half-wistfully, " 'Just a little piece of time.' And now this moment has blown up in our faces, hasn't it, Frank?"

"We'll have to see about that," he said. And then he paused, listening. A moment later they both heard it, and they turned as the sound of a running horse came near and into the yard. Voices sounded quick and excited by the bunkhouse, and then someone came running over the yard.

"Something has happened," and Carolina Steele went

quickly toward the veranda. Landry followed. A man came running through the darkness, saw them and stopped.

"They hit the 'W' outfit," he said. "One of the boys picked up some lead, and the herds are scattered."

"Did you give them a fight?" she asked sharply.

"Couldn't. They stayed out in the pasture. Threw some lead into the shack as they left."

Carolina Steele ripped out a stiff, manly oath. "Do I pay you to run and hide under the covers when trouble comes?"

"Like I said," the rider began, "we—"

Landry took command. "How many men you got down there?"

"Four."

He turned to Carolina. "It looks like the beginning of your war. Your Pitchfork and 'W' spreads will be first."

This was not the woman who had melted in his arms only a moment ago. Now her voice was hard and shrill as she said, "Let them try it! They'll get their war!"

"With Kirby and part of the crew on the trail?"

She swung about, frowning. "That's right," she said reluctantly.

"What should we do?"

"Cover up until they get back from the north. Send Hagberg and part of the men over to the 'W', and as many more over to your Pitchfork place. When the others get back, you can bust Ardoin and his crowd wide open."

She turned to the rider. "You heard that. Go tell Hagberg those are the orders. Hurry!"

The man said, "That won't leave too many here—"

"Do as I say!" The man left, and in a moment they heard the commotion of preparation, the scuffling in the corral as the riders caught up their mounts.

The woman finally turned to Landry and stood looking at him soberly. He said, lightly ironic, "You see, all it takes to kill the magic is a little trouble with cows—"

"But good heavens," she exclaimed petulantly. "When you are being robbed, you cannot think of romance—"

"Of course not." He turned away.

"Where are you going?" she demanded.

He stopped, staring at her through the shadows. "I am going to kill your brother, as you asked me to."

He heard her gasp. Quickly she stepped toward him, and it was anger that twisted her face and ground down her voice. "You damned blackguard," she cried. "You—"

Landry laughed. "So you do have a conscience. I wondered about that." He paused. Then, "How will you feel when you're boss of the country? Will you sleep soundly at night?" Then he was gone.

Carolina Steele stood staring after him, fighting with a strange mixture of emotions. After a while she heard a lone rider head out of the yard, taking the road toward Broken Wheel and the north. It had grown cold, now, and suddenly she shivered and turned toward the house. As she came to the light, she became aware that tears were in her eyes, and she dabbed at them savagely, telling herself that his insolence would anger a saint.

Landry rode into Broken Wheel's dark stillness well on toward midnight, coming in in a roundabout way, and stopping frequently to listen down his back trail. He had had the sense of being followed, and once as he had halted in pines, with the wind sighing overhead and the sound of burbling water coming up from somewhere below, he thought he had heard the clatter of a horse's hoof striking stone on the trail behind him. For a long time he had waited but had heard nothing more.

Now he sat idly on the leather, noting that only an occasional light hit the street. Before the Longhorn two or three cow ponies were hitched, but across the way at the Casino, the rack was full. McCanless' crowd was in town.

Presently Landry pulled into an alley and waited. After a while he heard the slow, cautious approach of a horse at the walk, and then he saw movement against the blackness. A moment later, Coulter edged out of the darkness, his head bent forward, peering into the town's dark funnel, sifting the shadows and probing the street. The man passed Landry, the dim light from a nearby window showing the still, wild face of the gunman briefly before he rode into the shadows.

Coulter passed on down the street, and at the Longhorn he got down, tied, and spent some moments examining the horses at the rack. Then, one lone man in the deserted street, he stepped across the way and looked over the brands on the horses before the Casino. Afterward, he recrossed the street and entered the Longhorn. With that, Landry rode on, toward the alley at the end of the first block, coming thus to the Casino's rear. A few moments later he entered the saloon through the back door.

Jim McCanless sat at a table there, playing stud with three others. From the front came the sound of animated Spanish, and Landry knew that the *vaqueros* were awaiting the night's orders.

McCanless heard the door open, swung about. He recognized Landry, spoke to the others, and they went away toward the front of the saloon. As Landry sat down, McCanless said, unsmiling, "What in hell kept you?"

Landry said, "Shut up. I don't run errands for you." Then, as the big man's face hardened, he added, "There are a couple hundred Corralitos steers in the Lagos pasture. Just a walk for your boys."

McCanless' eyes gleamed. He leaned over, poured a drink, and said, "Pretty close to the main ranch. Remember, I've got to keep my job, too."

"There are only about six hands left at Corralitos. The others are at the 'W' and the Pitchfork."

"How come?"

"Ardoin's bunch raided. Now, want to do business?"

McCanless smiled a slow, white-toothed smile. "How do I know I can trust you, friend?"

Landry shrugged. "How?"

"It could be a trap," McCanless said thoughtfully. "I wouldn't trust my own mother, where money's concerned. Let alone you. Tell you what: you come with me until the boys try the thing out. Then, when they say the word, we'll do business. All right?"

"Where do I go with you?"

"There's an old line shack a few miles north, between Ardoin's place and Wayne's. We can go up there and have a couple of hands of poker until my *jefe* comes with word it's all right. If it isn't—well, it'll be a long time until they find you." He gave Landry a hard grin.

"That's all right," Landry agreed.

McCanless clapped his hands. "Luis." A dark man came running, and McCanless explained in rapid-fire Spanish. The dark man said, *"Si, como no?"* He looked at McCanless and at Landry, flashed a smile and left. A moment later they heard the saloon clearing, and afterward the bursting run of horses.

McCanless squared his big shoulders. "Well," he said. He poured whiskey into two glasses. "We'll have one to bind the bargain and then hit the trail."

They drank, and McCanless shoved back his chair. "Let's ride."

"You're impatient," Landry said softly. "Aren't you forgetting something?"

"What?"

"One dollar a head. Two hundred dollars. Payable now."

McCanless frowned. "Damn it," he complained. "I don't have that much with me. You know I'd be good for it. After all, you could tip my hole card if I didn't make it good."

"Cash in advance," said Landry.

McCanless looked at him with exasperation. He said impatiently, "I'll give you my IOU. How's that?"

"Better than nothing," Landry conceded grudgingly.

McCanless took a stubby pencil from his vest and fished until he found a scrap of paper. He scribbled, handed the paper to Landry. "That do?"

Landry read, " 'IOU two hundred dollars for two hundred head at $1.00. Jim McCanless.'

"I think that will do," he said slowly, rising. "I believe that will do the trick."

Chapter 14

THE TWO other men at the bar finished their drinks, laid money on the wood and nodded to Grady, then left the saloon. Grady ambled up the way, pocketed the silver, and put glasses and bottle under the bar. Then he went down and stopped in front of Harry Wayne.

"Finish up, Harry," he grumbled. "A man can't stay open all night."

Wayne raised a vague glance. "You've still got customers. What's the idea of running me out?"

"They just left. You're the last."

Wayne stared at him a moment, then he took the bottle in his hand, corked it, and fished in his pocket for money. He found none, and as his empty gaze came up to Grady, the latter said, "It's all right. Your credit's good. But I've got to get off my feet, sometime."

Harry Wayne turned away and Grady said, "Good night, Harry." Without replying, Wayne went unsteadily toward the door and came into the street. It was deserted now. The rowdy departure of McCanless' *vaqueros* almost an hour ago he had not noticed, nor had he seen Coulter when the gunman had come into the Longhorn, stayed his time, and left to scout the town further for Landry.

Along the street, now, the last lights were winking out. A blue-black blanket lay over the sleeping town, and the stars had begun to light the dust of the street, laying a lightly silver haze over the stark shapes of the buildings. Harry Wayne sat down on the edge of the plank walk and had a drink. A roaming hound trotted toward him, came up and sniffed curiously, then went on about its business. Wayne did not notice when the light from the Longhorn went out. But after a while he heard a step behind him, and Grady said, "Harry, you ought to be home in bed."

"Go away," Wayne said loosely. After a moment Grady turned inside and locked the door, afterward ambling flat-footedly up to his quarters over the saloon.

Wayne sat there, having the rest of the bottle and trying to find the answer to his conflicts in the liquor. It came over him that he would never again know the feeling of freedom that had been his before Carolina Steele had shown him the lush promise of her body. The days of free-ranging and careless living were gone from him, and they had taken with them his ability to look in his mirror when he shaved. He felt unclean, lost and defeated, and the feeling was inside of him and out, based upon the hard realization that even should he marry Carolina Steele, the justification for which he had been searching could never be found. Knowing that, he knew, too, that without it he was irrevocably lost.

Harry Wayne took the last pull at the bottle, threw it into the street, and sat for a long while with his head hanging between his knees. Finally he stirred and looked long and dully into the night, and then he got up and walked down toward the livery stable. He found his horse in the darkness and saddled, and after a brief confusion in the stable's darkness, he led it to the street and mounted, heading south toward Corralitos.

He arrived there toward two in the morning, sobered and soul-sick. He had expected a challenge, and was prepared in his ultimate desperation, to meet it. Not even a dog barked as he rode into the yard, passed the unlighted bunkhouses and came to the Casa Grande. A Mexican woman answered his knock, long after he had begun to pound. She brought a candle and a frightened face, and when she looked at Wayne by the candle's light, she would have closed the door. He thrust his foot inside and pushed his way in.

"Qué quiere usted, señor?" She was frightened.

"Call doña Carolina," Wayne said heavily, and when the woman started to protest, he snarled a curse that sent her scurrying to do his bidding.

He saw the light from the lamp she was carrying precede her into the room. She looked at him, tight-faced, and gave him no greeting as she placed the lamp on the table between them. "Why did you come here?"

At this moment she was beautiful to Harry Wayne, and in the sleep-misty eyes and the lovely dishevelment of her golden hair, he found once again the reason for living. She had drawn a silken gown tight about her, and he saw the full contours of her body with a choking rise in his throat.

The whiskey and his days of self-abasement gave him the answer. "I've come for a settlement, Carolina. I've waited as long as I can."

She studied him, outright dislike in her gaze. "You were a fool to come here," she said at last. "Don't you realize that this is dangerous?"

"Almost as dangerous as riding to cut a Corralitos herd," he said bitterly. "Almost as dangerous as owning land that Corralitos wants—like Steve Landry did. Isn't it, Carolina?"

Wrath whipped color into her cheeks as she flew around the table at him. "Keep your damned mouth shut! Now, what do you want? Tell me, and get out of here before some of the men find you."

Slowly he shook his head, his eyes burning upon her. "The same thing, Carolina. It never changes. Only, this time you can't stall me. When are we going to get married?"

Carolina Steele had tossed fitfully in the night after Landry had ridden away, full of strange hungers and ridden by thoughts that were new to her. Her pride had been hurt at the same time that her desires had been aroused; she was filled with doubts about him, and consumed by her desire to mold him to her preconceived pattern. He had awakened in her needs long unfilled, and brought to her by a phrase the enormity of her cruelty. The feeling of insecurity, the fear of unknown things, had dogged her to the brink of sleep and clutched at her as she rose from slumber when the maid called her. Now, nervous and irritable, she no longer desired to finesse this game. She drew a long breath, and her lips fell into a tight line. "All right, Harry, here is your answer: *never!* I would not marry you if you were the last man on earth."

The bluntness of it made him pale, then disbelief came over his face. "You don't mean that. You're just angry."

"I mean it."

Still he did not believe her. She was angry, nothing more. "All right," he said spitefully. "Have it your way. And I'll see to it that this whole damned country knows the kind of game you've played!"

"Just so," she shot back. "And I will see to it that your family and your friends know precisely the part you took in it!"

He sagged and the fight ran out of him. Seeing this, Carolina Steele loosed her contempt. "Yours is the rebellion of a sheep, Harry. Now, get out of here and never cross my path again. We are finished, do you understand? *I never want to see you again.*"

There was no doubt about it, this time. He read it in the contemptuous curl of her lips, the open disdain in her eyes. Something behind her gaze made him crawl inwardly, and he knew, suddenly, that it was her hate of the loathsome thing that she had made him become. He stared at her for a long while, and finally said in a pinched voice, "It was all a lie—"

"All of it. I used you. You helped me to get what I wanted."

Distantly, remotely, he muttered, "You told them to ambush us the day we cut."

"I did! Could you expect me to let them take my herd?"

Harry Wayne knew in this moment that she had ruined him. He thought, briefly, of killing her, and then it came to him that this would in no ways undo his own private ruin. One shot, one slap, even one savage curse, could have saved him from himself, for it would have been in days to come a remembrance that he had struck out at the agent of his abasement. Instead, he chose to tell himself that the greatest expiation is admission of a wrong willingly done, with the consequences fully in mind. Only for a second did he recall that he had never been quite sure of her honesty, and he pushed that thought aside, finding not even anger in it. As of that moment, Harry Wayne was a different and a wholly lost man.

He turned without looking at her, and walked out on the porch. For a moment he stood there, slack and empty, and then he got aboard and headed his horse down the trail toward Broken Wheel.

Almost as he left, Coulter stepped through the door. He had come stealthily into the yard on his way from town, and had stood in the shadows outside, overhearing most of this conversation.

Carolina snapped at him. "Do you always sneak around like that?"

He waved the remark aside. "I've got something to tell you about that fellow Landry. Figured it couldn't wait until tomorrow."

Remembering what Landry had said about Coulter's following him, she said, "Never mind that. Later. Right now, go after that man who left here."

"Young Wayne?"

"Follow him and do not come back until he is dead."

Coulter said, "Now listen. He's got friends here. Maybe—"

"I leave the details to you," she said coldly.

He waited a moment. "This calls for something special," he said pointedly.

Carolina Steele frowned, then after a moment she turned and left the room. Presently she returned, thrust a bill at him and said, "After this, special work goes in your monthly salary. Understand?"

Coulter nodded, glanced at the bill and at her for a fleeting second, then left. A moment later she heard his horse start up in the yard's gravel. She picked up the lamp and went back to her room.

Landry and McCanless reached the line shack in the foothills of the Buckhorns about two in the morning. Here above the desert the early morning air was chilly, and Landry built up a fire in the rusty stove, from wood which still filled the box at one side. After that they played stud warily for an hour, until the disinterest of a two-handed game overcame them.

McCanless stretched, yawned and said, "Enough for me. We could shove that same dollar back and forth all week." He went to the bunk, spread his coat on the dusty pad and lay down.

Landry sat smoking and riffling the cards unconcernedly. At last McCanless said, "Well, it's about time you told me."

"What?"

"Corralitos, friend. Remember? You work there. How do you like it?"

"Well, middling," Landry replied deliberately. "I'm just wondering how *you're* going to like it from now on."

McCanless' face slowly sobered. "Me? Why should I find it any different?"

"Well," Landry said slowly, "it's just that Kirby Steele's out of the picture."

McCanless rose, eased to the table and sat down. *"Dropped* out?"

"She sent him north with the herd. The plan is that he won't come back."

Landry knew that he was on dangerous ground, and he read the confirmation in McCanless' face as the other sat slowly back and weighed him, pondering Landry's words.

"It seems to me that you know too damn much," McCanless said softly. "How did you get hold of this?"

Landry waited a long time before he played his last card. "If you think I'm doing this for charity, think again. I know what your plans are about Carolina Steele. You want to marry her and get your hands on Corralitos—"

"Like I thought," McCanless growled as he pushed back his chair, "you're a spy! By God!"

"Now, just take it easy." Landry leaned across the table. "You can have her, and Corralitos, too, for all I care. But before you get 'em, friend, you're going to need my help!"

"What do you mean?" McCanless growled.

"Kirby will be taken care of, but that won't clear the track for you. The fellow who planned the job with her, and who shoots Kirby down, is the one who comes in for the payoff."

"That's a damn lie!" The scar along McCanless' jaw stood out against the crimson of his face. "What in hell are you trying to pull here?"

"She's always played you for a sucker," Landry said calmly. "Usin' your beef, and all the while playin' fast and loose with another man—"

McCanless let out a low rumble of anger and lunged, but Landry had anticipated it, and he swung his fist at the other's chin. It shook McCanless, and by the time he recovered, Landry's gun covered him.

"Now listen, damn you," Landry said tightly. "I'm in a position to help you. But if you want to act like a fool, I'm pullin' out." He backed toward the door.

McCanless glowered, rubbing his chin. "All right," he finally conceded. "Come and sit down." He came back to his chair and Landry, still holding his gun ready, dropped into a seat.

"You can put that thing away."

Landry holstered his gun. "She planned this thing with Harry Wayne," he said. He saw the angry surprise run into the big man's face. "Wayne will put Kirby in the shade, and then she and Wayne will be married. Corralitos and Running W together."

McCanless said, "That's a pile of stuff to swallow, from you."

"Don't believe it. Find out for yourself. She's been meeting Harry Wayne for months. He's been her front in half of these land grabs she's made. Go look at the Register of Deeds, and you'll see it. Wayne told her that his old man and Ardoin were going to cut that Corralitos herd, and Darby Wayne was killed because of it. Tomorrow, Harry Wayne will be on his way north to kill Kirby. Then they'll get married, and where'll *you* be? Now, does that sound like I'm lyin' to you?"

It was a shaking moment for McCanless. It uprooted all his brash confidence, and scattered the remnants of his egotism to the winds. He sat for a long time, looking at Landry, his dark eyes burning hot, and suddenly he shoved his chair and rose. "I'll kill her," he said hoarsely. "By God, she can't play fast and loose with me like that!" Abruptly, he turned toward the door.

"Where are you going?"

"To Corralitos. Either you're a goddamn liar, or she's a double-crossing slut. I'll find out."

"Now wait a minute," Landry said quietly, knowing that at this moment his whole strategy hung by a raveling thread. "You're forgetting something: what have I got to gain by telling you a lie?"

The logic of this worked into McCanless. "If you bust into this right now," Landry said, "you make her sore if I *am* lying. If I'm telling the truth, you'd kill her and you'd lose Corralitos. You'd better take it slow, friend."

Finally McCanless growled, "Suppose I do? Then what?"

Landry rose deliberately. "Let me handle the Corralitos end. You go back south, and I'll find out how things are when Wayne gets back. With what you and I together know about her, you can force her to do what you want. But you need *me*. Don't forget that."

"What's the deal?"

"I'll have her send for you to bring a herd along in a few days. She won't suspect anything. But when you come, bring all the *vaqueros* you've got. I'll ride out to meet you, and give you the latest word on the thing. Then, you can do with her as you please." He waited. "Five hundred dollars, after that, and I ride on. How do you like it?"

Before McCanless could speak his mind, they heard the sound of a horse coming up outside. A moment later Luis, the Mexican *jefe*, came in. *"Est á bien,"* he told McCanless. *"Ya estan los reses en camino al otro lado.* All is well."

McCanless turned slowly, facing Landry. "It's a deal," he said heavily. "And don't wait too long to send for me!"

Then he went quickly outside. A moment later Landry heard the horses start up. He stood looking at the door. "Don't worry," he murmured. He put out the light, went outside, and stepped aboard, heading the black higher into timber where he would make a solitary camp for a couple of days.

Behind him on the floor of the shack, lay one of his spurs, which had come loose in the moment when he leaped up and drew on McCanless. He did not notice its loss until he made camp early in the dawn of the day, high on the mountain's flank. Then he considered the loss trivial.

Harry Wayne rode as in a dream through the night, knowing that his world had come to an end, and that the day should not find him in this country. He thought, dully and momentarily, of killing himself, and then abandoned the idea by telling himself what he had heard others say: it was the recourse of cowards. He was aware sometime in the morning that his horse was passing through Broken Wheel, and it awakened him to the fact that the animal was heading homeward under the urging of instinct. With that, he pulled to the left outside town, and an hour later was climbing through the foothills of the Buckhorns, toward the abandoned line shack which once the Running W had shared with the Pitchfork.

Weariness sat through him like the hand of death, and when he off-saddled and went into the cabin, it was some moments before he noticed that the stove still had a fire in it. Mildly surprised, he assumed that Pitchfork riders, caught by the night, had stopped here and then gone on, early. It was toward morning.

It occurred to him that he might spend a day or two in this spot, while he made his plans and decided which way to ride. Return to the Running W he never could. Nothing in his whole frame of past reference could ever again come before his sight; it would be hard enough to live with such things in his mind. He made his half decision, threw more wood on the fire, turned the lamp low and stretched out on the bunk.

He must have dozed presently, for the sound of the door opening merely touched the edge of his consciousness. It was Coulter's flat voice which brought him awake.

"Sit up, Wayne."

He opened his eyes and stared uncomprehendingly at the man in the middle of the room holding a gun on him.

"I've got nothing against you, Wayne," the still-faced man said. "It's just a job has to be done."

It came to him then. "Coulter," he said quickly, "I don't know what this is about. But listen, don't shoot me. I'll pay you. I can get money—" Then his eyes sprung wide as he saw the look on the man's face.

"No good, Wayne," Coulter said slowly. "It's too late."

"Give me a chance! Don't shoot me like a dog, Coulter! Give me—"

The explosion rocked the room, and Harry Wayne shrugged sharply forward. In a moment he raised slow, sick eyes to the gunman and his mouth opened to speak, and again the gun roared. This time Harry Wayne fell back on the bunk, a dark round hole in his forehead beginning to send forth a trickle of blood down over his temple. His hand lay on his chest, and after a while it began to slip with the weight of his arm, and presently it fell dangling toward the floor. Then he lay still.

Coulter broke the gun, took the spent cases from the chambers and pocketed them, then replaced them with fresh cartridges from his belt. He slipped the gun back into the leather, walked over and looked down at the dead man for a moment, then he blew out the light and went outside. The chill breeze of morning came down out of the hills, and he turned up his coat collar as he mounted and headed back down the mountain.

Chapter 15

AN IDEA had grown in Kirby Steele's mind as he led the Corralitos herd north toward the railroad. He could not remember precisely how it had begun, nor the moment when it first took root. It was something which came from the long hours of riding with the bright sky above, the swish of grass at the side of the trail, the low, even beat of the marching cattle as a backdrop for his thoughts. There came to him at these times a flow of the essence of time itself, past and future, and it made him reexamine his place therein. Lying at night under stars that seemed to reach down to within an inch of a man's hand, and watching the blue-black, light-studded reaches of infinity, Kirby Steele had a sense of rediscovery of a thing that he had lost.

He lay now at the edge of pines, his head pillowed on his saddle, and found in the vastness overhead a humble solemnity that was new for him. Pine scent made the night sweet, and the freshness of the wind was the freshness of wide spaces and mountain heights, and he had a feeling of cleanness that was somehow a vaguely remembered thing. It had begun when he rode away from his sister and Corralitos; it had stayed with him and grown, and each mile was like a scouring away of things that he had hated and had been in spite of himself.

It was quiet here in the night. The herd lay bedded down a hundred yards away, and there was from them no noise save the occasional blowing of a horse as the guard circled the herd. A low sighing ran through the pines, and a few yards from him men slept the deep and dreamless sleep of exhaustion. He reached out with his mind for what had been the key to his destiny, and the effort left him dissatisfied and confused, for there was in this too much of a harsh remembering.

At some point in his life, all stabilities had ended. The sure and known things which had anchored him in both time and space had disappeared, and it was because something had gone out of him which held them. He could not place that point exactly. And because he could not, he let his thoughts feel back carefully into the past, trying to recapture something of the flavor of old times. His boyhood, the university, the war, in none of these things did he find the answer. And then, somehow, he remembered that night when he had fired the library of his home and driven away with Carolina. It came to him, then, that he could never go back. Beyond that point there was a gap, a chasm which the years had made it impossible to bridge, leaving him groping hopelessly in a void when he tried to narrow down the focus of his thoughts beyond it. It was a thing of which he could never again be quite free.

He pondered this problem at some length, not able even to define precisely what he meant by Kirby Steele's freedom. At last he concluded that the definition was bound up in the idea of complete liberation from Carolina. He had come back from the war hungering for war's antithesis; for the presence and the friendship of someone who stood at the opposite pole from greed and violence and the baseness of men. Had he found that, it might have saved him, but he had found in his sister one whom the war had hardened and warped in a way that it had not done to many men.

Kirby Steele thought of that for a moment, and the admission came through that Carolina had been more lost than himself. Neither had been able to find their way out of the forest of their personal tragedies, and each had blurred for the other whatever saving paths might have presented themselves. If she had failed him, he had not helped her in her lostness. There was no answer to it now, to that wholly mistaken and hateful association of theirs. But for Kirby Steele it had ended for all time.

It was not that he believed that he could return to yesterday. Today's skies are never quite the same as yesterday's, even though they, too, are blue. He knew, also, that a man may draw his face long for so many years that the facility for laughter, for the carefree song, the light touch, can be irrevocably lost. No, the hours piled up into days and they into years, and the changing of a man's bone, his flesh and his blood was merely the visible change: His spirit changed with it. And yet, the spirit had its remembered and nostalgic roots leading back into the past, threading a kind of unity through one's total chronology; and if a man might never quite turn back to the lost past, he could, at least, reach out after the memories of what he had lost along the way, and shape them into the semblance of mileposts for the future. Once he had taken the wrong way. Now, he might not find the other, but he had turned into his back trail, and somewhere he would find again the place where the forking of the trail pointed the other way.

Kirby Steele felt a great satisfaction as, at last, he was able to formulate that thought clearly. Then, just before he fell asleep, the strange and oddly unrelated thought passed over his mind that the only man whom he had been able to call friend in all these long years had been Swede Hagberg—a moronic killer.

Ardoin's crew hit the Corralitos herd shortly after midnight. The simultaneous burst up of firing and the mad run of the herd jerked Kirby Steele out of his sleep. In one brief, confused instant of roaring bedlam, he saw the herd sweeping past the wagon, twenty-five yards away, the flash of gunfire in the darkness, and then he was out of his blankets and strapping on his own gun.

Shouting rose above the noise of the herd's run, and he recognized Ed Ardoin's voice, thundering, "Get 'em all! None of 'em ride back!" And then lead began to whine toward him as he saw his men firing into the darkness a few feet away. A horse and rider plunged into the camp and the rider fired twice and then reeled out a string of curses as he was hit. The horse skittered on across camp, out of control, and two more riders came in, fast, as a sharp exchange of fire passed between them and his own men who had run for the cover of the wagon. The next moment the camp was overrun as he heard the cries of men and of horses taking lead, and it came over him that this was the end of the trail drive. Ardoin had come in force and had struck by surprise. Crouching low, Steele made a run for the pines.

As he reached their cover, he remembered that he would be afoot in enemy territory. Turning, he ran back toward the melee. Luck was with him. A horse and rider loomed twenty feet from him and he took careful aim and fired. Even before the man fell from the saddle, he grabbed the reins. The next moment he was aboard, and even as he headed the animal into timber, he heard a querulous shout, "Where in hell is Steele? Get Steele!"

Wind whipped into his face, and branches tore across it in his headlong flight. He felt the straining of the horse beneath him, the long, reaching strides, and knew that the animal was climbing, drawing a long, sweeping circle around the flank of the hills toward the summit. After a while, when the animal's blowing was heavy, he reined down and halted, listening carefully back through the night. Hearing no sounds of pursuit, he pushed on, the gait easier now.

That hard voice, singing out in the darkness amid avenging gunfire, told Kirby Steele that he was hunted and his life was at stake. Therefore, he did not delude himself into thinking that it ended with cattle, as far as Ardoin was concerned: too many fatal ingredients had gone into the making of this moment. He thought, ironically, that retribution had come quickly upon the heels of the forming of his hard decision, and then he had but one thought: he would not let it overtake him.

He reached a level stretch where the trees swept back.

Now stars gave light and his vision adjusted to the darkness, and he saw that he was upon a trail, almost a road, which cut across the top of the hills. He was high up and would go higher as he followed this way. The cold wind off the heights blew against him, and the stars were clear and close over his head. He set his horse into a steady canter and pushed on.

Kirby Steele was three hours from the scene of the raid when he felt the falling away of the trail beneath him. He slackened his pace, feeling caution rise, and as he rounded a bend where the trail dipped sharply, he saw ahead the shapes of a few houses, all dark save one from which one dull finger of light fell into the darkness.

Now he halted and considered this situation. He was without food for fast flight, and while he did not believe that Ardoin would pick up his trail for some time, he would need a horse with reserves of speed and endurance if they should. Realizing that this would be his chance, he lifted the reins and went cautiously forward.

The town was merely a half dozen shacks lining the trail which passed directly through. There was a hitch rack and the litter of rusted wagon tires and scrap iron before one building, which would be a smithy's shop. Another was a store, and the light came from a two-story building, which was a hotel, judging by the outside stairway leading to the second floor. No horses were in sight.

Reassured, he rode on and got down before the hotel, which he now saw was also a saloon. As he hitched, a faint lingering odor of dust in the air caused him to lift his head quickly, tensed and alert. For some seconds he waited, feeling a vague uneasiness, watching the shadows and slowly reassuring himself. Then he remembered that it was toward morning, Ardoin was far behind, and he himself had stirred up some dust. With that, he stepped inside the place.

A sleepy-looking saloonkeeper looked up from a greasy newspaper, weeks old, and regarded him steadily.

Steele came to the bar, laid a coin on the wood and said, "Give me the bottle."

The barkeeper, still silent, lifted bottle and glass and put them on the counter. Steele had his drink and another, then he saw that the man was watching him with a narrowed-down interest in his gaze.

"I want some grub and a horse," Steele said. "You got 'em?"

The barkeeper nodded. "Both." He looked at Steele craftily. "It's a good horse. Cost you something."

"They always to. Right now, get me something to eat, then throw some grub together. I'm in a hurry."

A knowing, snag-toothed grin touched the barkeep's lips. "Most of my customers are." Then he turned away toward the rear of the saloon.

"Where are you going?"

"To get your bait of vittles."

After a moment Steele said, "All right. But step right along, friend."

The man gave him a strange smile and went toward the back. Kirby Steele looked back at the bottle, poured another and sipped it slowly, his back to the door. There was in him a kind of uneasiness that was not wholly reasonable. He felt certain that he had gained hours on Ardoin, yet the smell of dust hanging in the air outside was the same smell that lingers minutes after a bunch of horsemen have passed, and that fact bothered him. Analyzing his preoccupation, he knew that reason was against his mild fear, and he decided that it was because escape, now, meant more than it would have meant before—

"Just stay right there, Kirby."

It was as abrupt as a door suddenly slamming shut. Yet Kirby Steele did not even start. It was Ed Ardoin's voice, and he knew that he had been trapped the moment that the first word hit his eardrums. And just as quickly, he made his fatalistic adjustment. Deliberately, he lifted his glass and drank his drink slowly, savoring it and knowing, beneath thought, that he might never again know the good taste of raw liquor. Then he put the glass carefully down and said, "Can I turn?"

"Want to go for your gun that way?"

"No," said Steele softly. "Not just yet."

"Turn. I've got you covered."

Keeping his hands bar-high, Steele slowly turned. Soberly, he looked at Ardoin a long while, and then his ever-present curiosity rose and he asked, "How did you know?"

"You shot Sam Bowman out of his saddle. He recognized you and saw the way you went. There's a short cut to this place and we took it." Then he let his guns slide back into the leather.

Steele saw that. "You going to take me in?"

"No," Ardoin shook his head. "You stay here, Steele."

Kirby Steele nodded. "I thought it would be like that," he murmured.

"Any time you're ready," said Ardoin. He was very still, waiting.

Steele said sardonically, "It won't take long, and I have no desire to drag it out. I'm not too good with guns, personally. I suppose your men are outside?"

"We beat you in by about fifteen minutes," Ardoin said. "We waited out back."

"The dust." Steele frowned. His mind went back to an earlier thought. He had hoped to find the forking of the trail which would take him back to a certain place in the past, but he had started too late. And now it seemed to him that all his trails had been clouded and obscured by dust, so that the sign which would have taken him on the right one had never appeared. He had read them all wrong. In this moment he knew with a great, blinding certainty that there is a distance down the wrong road which one may go safely, and beyond which there is no turning back, that once beyond that point, the forking of the right road down the back trail can never again be found. The irony of it hit him, and his saving philosophy rose up, bringing him his old cool, Olympian detachment.

"Ed"—he smiled his crooked, thin smile—"what would

you think if I were to tell you that this moment has nothing to do with cows or land or money? That it is merely a matter of two roads?"

"You can't talk yourself out of this," Ardoin said, low and thick. "It's too late."

"Precisely," said Kirby Steele. And then he went for his gun. It was a gesture and nothing more. Ardoin's slugs ripped into him before his own gun had cleared the leather. The shock of it arrested him and he lurched forward, staggered and waved drunkenly for a moment. Then, drawing upon his will, he raised his gun painfully, with both hands, toward Ardoin. Ardoin's gun crashed again and Kirby Steele shook. At the same moment, fire came through the front door, a hail of lead that lifted him from his feet and slammed him sideways to the floor, where he moved once and lay still. When Ardoin reached him, Kirby Steele had already set foot upon the longest road of all.

Men came in through the front door now and stood around Ardoin as he looked down at Steele. There was the stiff, wondering silence that all men find in the presence of sudden and violent death. A man murmured, "Funny. I always figured he was a coward."

Ardoin looked at him, troubled by something deeper than thought, and said nothing. The bartender now came forward from the back room. "You'll have to get him out of here," he grumbled. "I'll help you tie him on his horse."

"He stays here," Ardoin said. The others started to file out of the place, leaving wondering glances upon the dead man on the floor, who seemed small and of little consequence, now that arrogance and power had been stripped from him.

The barkeep said, "Not much, friend. Take care of your own dead."

"Damn you," Ardoin suddenly swung and struck the man in the face with the flat of his hand. "Do you want to go with him?"

Fright and surprise stabbed at the barkeep's face. "Now,

listen here," he whined. The look on Ardoin's face beat him down.

"The ten dollars I gave you includes the price of a funeral," Ardoin said. "And, by God, you'd better bury him deep—you damned Judas!"

With these strange words Ardoin went quickly out of the place, not looking at the man who lay sprawled on the floor.

Chapter 16

SWEDE HAGBERG rode into Corralitos shortly after noon, and Carolina Steele, having coffee in the shade of the veranda, watched him as he got down by the corrals and then came on to the house. He stopped on the steps, and eyed her with his flat, dead gaze.

"What is it, Swede?"

"There's somethin' fishy goin' on. It's been quiet as death over at the 'W' ever since we got there."

"What did you expect? Daily raids?"

Hagberg shook his heavy head. "I'm not much on the brains," he growled, "but it seems funny that you leave Corralitos without enough guns to protect it right when things are hottest."

It was a worry beneath greater preoccupations for the woman, too. Still, she said, "Is that your only reason for riding over here?"

"No. Is there any word from Kirby?"

"Should there be?"

"You shouldn't have let him go alone," Hagberg said. "I wanted—"

"Alone! You call nine men as a crew going alone?"

Hagberg said doggedly, "Kirby's used to depending on me, and you know it."

Even as she started to reply a hard-driven horse came into the yard below the bunkhouses, catching their attention and swinging it that way. The rider reined down and came on

jadedly, his mount blown and sweat-streaked, and in a moment Carolina recognized one of the hands who had gone
north with the trail herd. She sprang to her feet noticing that
the rider carried one arm in a bloodstained sling made from
his neckpiece.

"Hazen! What has happened?"

The rider got shakily out of the saddle, came to the steps
and shook his head. "Ardoin smashed us. Herd's gone. Crew
wiped out—Kirby, too."

Carolina Steele paled. "Ardoin," she whispered. "Ardoin
did this?"

"We didn't have a chance. He stampeded the herd and
shot down or run down every man of 'em—I was lucky to
get away." He sat down on the steps, just short of collapse.

It was a double blow to the woman. A wild, raging voice
of suspicion told her that Landry had failed her. *Where had
he been? What had he been doing while Ardoin stole her
herd?*

She was thinking in terms of dollars lost, and it was a
panicky feeling. She did not hear Swede Hagberg until he
said again, "You hear? I'd kill you if you weren't a woman.
You sent Kirby away and kept me here!"

Her attention swung back to the gunman, now, and she
saw him merely as an irritant in her broader preoccupations.
With thousands of dollars lost, with the enemy striking back
at her, with her whole plan set back, he talked of Kirby! Almost she screamed at him, "Shut your damned mouth and
get out of here! Do you have any idea what this loss means
to me? And you stand there muttering about Kirby!" Beyond
fear now, she rushed at him.

Hagberg felt one sharp sweep of her nails on his face, and
then a big hand shot out, pinioning her hands together. He
twisted, venting his cold grief in this form, and saw her face
go white. The anger left her eyes and fright grew up there.
"Let go!" she shrilled. "You're breaking my wrists."

The rider on the steps looked up. "Let her go."

"Shut up." Then, to the woman, "You never liked him.
You wanted him to be killed. It's your fault, as sure as—"

"Damn you," she moaned. "Let go of my hands."

"I'll let go. But remember this: I aim to get revenge for Kirby. I'll help Ardoin bust you! And then, I'll hunt you down, and so help me God, Carolina Steele, I'll kill you with these two hands!" Suddenly he threw her backward and turned. She spun away across the veranda and collided with the wall. Dazed for a moment, she was thinking, not of Hagberg, or of Kirby, but of her loss. "All these years," she told herself. "All this careful planning, and now this great blow!" Almost, she forgot that the cattle she lost had been mostly stolen cattle in the first place, and that the loss was not therefore a real loss. She saw only that the past of want and hunger and of never quite enough of anything could overtake her again if this kept up, and it was a frightening thought, if a warped one. After a long while, she saw that she was alone with Hazen, and she said, "Are you *sure* that they took the whole herd?"

"Yes."

"How do you know they killed Kirby?"

"I made a run through the hills after the raid, and about dawn I came to this little place where he'd been shot down. A fellow was makin' a hole for him."

She let that pass with mild satisfaction over the top of her thoughts. At last she squared her shoulders and said, "Go over to the Pitchfork and send the crew there home. Then you can rest up. Have one of them bring the others from the 'W.' "

The man looked at her narrowly. Then he got up stiffly, muttering something, and walked a bit shakily toward his horse.

It occurred to her that there was something else, perhaps. "By the way," she called after him, "thank you, Hazen." He looked at her coldly and reined away.

Through the afternoon, Carolina Steele was torn with doubts, suspicions and fears. She paced the veranda, and wandered about the yard, feeling herself alone in a hostile world in which every hand was turned against her, every plan drawn with the intent to ruin her, and it was a frightening sensation. Now, she remembered the stark fear of past poverty, and she alternately pitied herself for her loss and reassured herself that it was a financial blow which she could weather. It was only when she drew before her mind the fact that Kirby was dead that she began to overcome her fears and to take a sober inventory of the situation. After all, Corralitos was *all* hers, now. There was no longer fear of some future in which their animosities would burst into uncontrollable friction which might result in her loss of even a portion of it. And yet, in her consciousness, lodged the idea that something had gone wrong with her plans—a vague fear arising from the unexpected show of force by Ardoin. And when she thought of this, she fumed with impatience with Landry, with Coulter for not having reported in to her after following Harry Wayne, with the fact that she was here almost alone, with only a handful of men.

Such was her mood when Landry returned.

Even as he came up the steps through the deepening shadows, he sensed the hard and deep currents working through her, and was prepared for what they would bring.

She looked at him, unwelcoming, and said, "I am glad you are back, Frank. Did everything go as—we had planned?"

Landry knew that she had learned of her loss. It was in her face and her too-tight control of her voice. He rolled a cigarette, leaning against a pillar, and blew out smoke before he answered. "No," he said dryly, "it didn't."

"Why not?"

He felt the readiness to pounce, the tightly balanced control. "Ardoin followed that drive," he shrugged. "A thing we should have thought of." Then, eyeing her warily he made his guess. "But why tell you things you already know?"

"What do I know?" she demanded quietly, and Landry knew that his facts would have to check against those already in her possession. He spoke on the assumption that Ardoin had carried out their plans as they had been made.

"You probably know more than I do. You lost your herd, and Ardoin killed Kirby. Unless someone got back here with some news, it'll be awhile before we know the details."

"Why?"

"They hit 'em at night." She did not react, and he knew that he had passed this test. With that he let a slow displeasure show on his face before he said, "Why all these questions? You suspicious of me, Carolina?"

"You split up the crew and sent them away from here," she said with a hard dubiousness. "You talked me into sending Kirby north."

"That's what you wanted."

"I wanted *you* to see about him. In the name of God"— again the thought of her loss swept over her—"do you think I wanted Ardoin to wipe out my crew and steal my cattle?"

"You're acting like a damn fool," he said harshly. "We might have expected Ardoin to use some sense and hit that herd. Why get panicky just because your enemies use some intelligence?"

"Intelligence!" her voice rose angrily. "I should be philosophical about it when they ruin me financially, kill my brother—"

"You can stand several of those before you're down to your last dollar," Landry said dryly. "They took back cattle you stole from them. That going to break you up? As for Kirby—you wanted him killed."

"I was a fool! He at least had the interest of Corralitos at heart. Swede Hagberg, too, gone. The others who fought for this thing—dead." She got up and paced the length of the patio. Suddenly she stopped in front of him. "Who is there to fight this fight now? A foreman who stands by and watches my enemies ruin me, and then speaks of being philosophical!"

Landry let her finish, and stood watching her. He knew, now, that his own position had worsened, and that she had gone as far with her self-commiseration as he could let her.

He laughed ironically. "Good riddance, every one! You were sick of Kirby. He's gone. You never liked Swede. You say he's gone. You're tearing your hair because you lost a dollar or two in that herd. How much did you have invested in it? Besides, we'll get 'em all back. Your trouble is that you got panicky when the other side did what any damn fool would do anyhow. Not only that, but you put Coulter on my trail to watch me like you were afraid I was going to run off with the family silver—"

"What would you think if I told you he had something on you?" she demanded spitefully.

"Damned little. I'd never lead him into any funny business, knowing he was on my tail. Ever think of that?"

"He could fool you—"

"Shut up and listen to me." He knew that his best chance lay in overriding this mood of hers with a harder one of his own. "If you're so sure that someone is crossing you, look closer to home. The man you've got to be afraid of is your little friend, Jim McCanless."

She hesitated a moment, her face sobering. "I don't believe that!"

"Proabably not. But he's stealing you blind. Furthermore, I know that he helped Ardoin plan this thing."

"That's a lie!"

A great unconcern came into Landry's eyes. Then with a shrug, he turned away. She rushed after him, caught his arm and flung him about. "Don't you dare turn your back on me! Who do you think you are—?"

Landry grasped her by the shoulders and shook her. She tried to claw his hands off, but he pushed her backward toward a chair and set her down with a force that jolted the wind out of her. Beyond speech, she glared at him.

"This is your last chance to listen," he said firmly. "And so you'd better come to your senses. The night I left here, I saw McCanless and Ardoin talking together in Broken Wheel. I thought that was funny. I followed Ardoin, and he met McCanless in back of the livery stable. McCanless told Ardoin that this herd would be on the trail, and that Kirby would be with it. Now, don't ask me how he knew. If he's like you said, maybe he's got his spies here, too. McCanless offered to cut back for Ardoin to Pitchfork range as many as he could of the cows you've taken in the drifts. Two dollars a head. Ardoin was to gun down Kirby and leave McCanless a freehand here at Corralitos."

As Landry spoke, she began to listen with interest, her anger giving way to a cold, contained absorption. Now she said, "Either you are the world's worst liar, or this is the most damnable thing I've ever heard of."

"You'll have to decide that."

"Why didn't you tell me this sooner instead of reciting that beautiful story about Ardoin using intelligence?"

"I said your *enemies* were using their heads. This is not all that McCanless has done. He's been rustling your home range, here at Corralitos."

"What?"

He had that feeling that comes at showdown, just before the last card is flipped over. He drew a slow breath and said, "After Ardoin had gone, I talked to McCanless alone. I decided to test him. I offered to go into business with him, rustling off you. He took the deal, and ran off two hundred head from the Lagos Pasture."

There was a piling up of shock and surprise in Carolina Steele, and she waited a long while before she said, without conviction, "You expect me to believe that?"

Landry fished in his pocket, took out the IOU which McCanless had given him. He handed it to her, saying, "You know his handwriting?"

She looked for a long time at the paper which confirmed McCanless' duplicity. On every side of her, she now felt, was treachery, thievery and scheming. For just a moment it was almost too much for her. Had she been another woman, she would have wept. As it was, she was a long time in finding the words to say, "Everyone? Is everyone against me?"

Landry resisted the temptation to remind her that she had accused McCanless of just this thing when she asked Landry to become her foreman. "Not quite. I'm going to win this thing for you, yet."

She lifted a slow, tired gaze and stared at him. "What have you in mind?"

"When I saw how far he'd gone against you, I told him to get a drive together, so that he could make a sale and at the same time run off some more beef that I would set up again in the Lagos Pasture. He fell for it. You're to send for him in a few days."

"And then?"

"Why," Landry said, "he stays. Six feet under."

It had grown dark now, and he could not read her face. But as the silence wore on, he sensed that his plan found favor with her. Presently she said, "I have sent for the crew to come back—"

"Good. They can oil up their guns for our sweep at Ardoin."

"At Ardoin?"

"I told you," Landry said firmly, "we're going to get that beef back."

After a long moment she rose from her chair and came toward him. In a low, altered voice, "I did you an injustice. Can you forgive me?"

Landry chose to ignore the peace offering. "It's all right," he said. "You've had enough to upset you, losing your herd and—your only brother." Then he turned away.

"Where are you going?" The irony passed over her.

"To scout up that herd. It oughtn't to be hard to find."

"Do so," said the woman, with decision coming back into her voice. "And I shall send a rider tonight to McCanless, telling him to bring that herd up. He will be here night after tomorrow." With that she turned toward the house.

Landry went on toward the corrals, mounted and took the trail toward Broken Wheel, on his way to Pitchfork to notify Ed Ardoin that the time had come for the final blow at Carolina Steele.

*   *   *

At about the time Swede Hagberg rode into Corralitos
to ask about Kirby Steele, Ed Ardoin and Drav McLain
were dropping down from the heights of the Buckhorns,
cutting across the east-west traverse near the abandoned
line shack which had once served both the Running W and
the Pitchfork. They had left the others of the raiding crew
to split up the recaptured herd, and to hide it in the hills for
a few days until they could test Corralitos' reaction to this
blow.

They rode tired and lax in the saddle, Ardoin not without
a weariness of spirit that was hard to define. It was an
emptiness, the feeling of something that had gone from him
with the killing of Kirby Steele, and from it sprang a kind
of unease that was new to him. He had had his hatred of
Steele, and had suffered under his arrogance. Yet, now that
Steele was dead, he knew that it was an empty triumph, for
as they rode with the fear of Carolina's reprisals sitting in
the saddle with them, he recognized that he had shot down
in Kirby Steele only a shadow, a symbol. Corralitos would
go on as long as Carolina's evil genius rode free and un-
contested. He remembered, wonderingly, Steele's last words
about a "matter of two roads." There had been something in
the man's last moments, a cold, resigned courage that Ardoin now admired, and there had been for him, too, that moment of feeling that he had made a mistake, just as now
there was a light sense of regret.

The trail had now dipped through the foothills, and occasionally it showed them the broad sweep of desert beyond.
Even as it came over him that this was familiar country,
Drav McLain pulled up and muttered, "Funny. I wonder
what that smoke means."

Ardoin reined in. "What smoke?"

McLain pointed to a clump of trees ahead and below
them. A chimney reared its stone head over the tops of the
pines, and from it came a thin, blue wisp of smoke.

"That's the old line shack," McLain said. "We haven't
used it for God knows how long."

"I was thinkin' that. We haven't either—"

They sat for some moments watching the chimney. Ardoin finally said, "We'll go up and have a look." They reined on down the trail.

When they were within fifty yards a horse whinnied. Ardoin shot a look at McLain, who said nothing but loosened his gun in the scabbard. A moment later they turned up the trail to the cabin. A horse was tied outside, minus gear, and slobbering and showing its hollows with thirst.

"Running W," Ardoin read the brand. "Well, by God—"

"Harry's horse," McLain said in a strange voice. "And it ain't had a drink in a hell of a long time."

Wordlessly, they got down and stood facing the shack. At last Ardoin said, "Well—" and together they went up the path to the porch and opened the door.

What they saw stopped them dead in their tracks. Ardoin muttered a low curse and turned a sick face to McLain. Then he went slowly toward the bunk where Harry Wayne lay, and stood looking down at him.

In his mind at this moment was Ardoin's feeling for Mary Wayne, together with a compassion that went beyond pity. And, suddenly, out of the dark recesses of his deeper feelings, flashed the thought: *Why had Landry insisted that Harry Wayne not go on this raid?* Jealously eager to believe the worst, his old suspicions roused within him, and he told himself that there had been some dark and mysterious reason for that insistence. Too much of this whole thing had been taken on blind faith from Landry, who had, from the start, wanted it that way. He heard Drav McLain say, "This will go hard with Mary—" Then a cold, self-contained rage swirled up in him.

"Let's get him on his horse," he said tightly. "I'll help you take him home." And they began the unpleasant task of readying Harry Wayne for his last ride.

Ardoin had mounted and taken the lead rope of Wayne's horse, when Drav McLain turned back to the cabin. "Maybe we left something," he explained, as he went inside. A few moments later he came out, grim-faced. In his hand as he came up to Ardoin's stirrup he held a spur—a deep-rowled silver spur with a distinctive handworked design on the leather arch-strap. "Ever see that before?" he growled.

"By God, yes! Landry wears spurs like that. Noticed 'em first off."

McLain put the spur in his pocket and mounted. As they pulled away he said, "It was layin' on the floor—almost under the table."

They rode in silence to the Running W, each busy with his own thoughts, and Ardoin's running into the deeper, darker channels. It was toward evening when they came into the yard. Their approach had been noticed, and as they halted it was a tight-faced group of men who eased Harry Wayne's body out of the saddle and placed it on blankets on the ground. Then Ardoin saw Mary Wayne come out on the porch, and in her face he read that she knew. He went slowly toward her.

"Mary," he began, but she brushed past him, white-faced, and he went up on the veranda, knowing not how to comfort her.

The men opened a way for her. Drav McLain spoke the necessary words of explanation while she stood there, pale and self-controlled, and when he had finished she said in a small voice, "Bring him into the house. Some of you boys get his place ready—beside his father." Then she turned away.

Slowly she came back to the veranda. Without really seeing him, she looked at Ed Ardoin and then, as the men came past bearing their burden into the house, she looked away into the distance, dry-eyed and tight-lipped.

As always, there was in his mind the fact of her aloneness, and always, too, his undying hope. He said at last, "Mary, I—there's no way to tell you—"

"You needn't, Ed. I understand how you feel. Thank you."

"You'll need someone now," he said, gently insistent. "I just want you to know—"

"I know," she said. And it was as though a door had closed with finality.

The men came out of the house, Drav McLain with them, and went on to the bunkhouse while he stayed with the girl and Ardoin. It was then that she faced them.

"The whole country rode against Corralitos," she said, "and I did not even know that it was to happen. Apparently Harry did not, either. What is it that has pushed the Waynes aside from their neighbors and the interests of all the people here?"

There was no reply. Still dry-eyed the girl said, "Don't tell me. My feeling is that you cannot. But answer me this: is it true that Frank Landry's spur was found in the shack where Harry was killed?"

"The gospel truth, Mary," said Drav McLain.

She turned her gaze upon the distance, and finally she drew a long breath. "I believe it now," she said to no one in particular. "I did not want to, but now I must. It was Landry who betrayed my father. He is at the bottom of most of the troubles which have come to this place with him. He tried to shoot you, Ed, that day before the Court-house, and now—Harry." She waited a long time. Then, in a low voice, "He will murder no more of our people in the name of Carolina Steele!" Suddenly she whirled and ran into the house.

Drav McLain looked at Ardoin. "You'd better go home," he said. "Come back for the buryin' in the mornin'." Ardoin started to protest, but McLain said sharply, "Use your head. You're no use to us here now."

As Ardoin rode out of the yard toward Pitchfork, he was nursing a small feeling of triumph, together with the bitter knowledge that Mary Wayne would never be for him. It was a source of satisfaction to him that she had now iden- tified Frank Landry with all the piled-up disaster of recent days. There was, of course, the unanswered question in his own mind: *Had Landry, in fact, killed Harry Wayne?* If he had, why was he helping to break up the Corralitos herds and ruin Carolina Steele's range empire? Beside these queries, Ardoin placed his feelings for the girl, and knew that for him it mattered only that she hated Landry. He felt

no sense of guilt for withholding facts that might have
cleared him, only relief that his personal role imposed silence upon him. He would have wished a greater opportunity to harm Landry, had it been possible. So thinking,
cherishing his dark dislike, he rode homeward, and arrived
there as dusk was falling, to find Swede Hagberg waiting
for him.

Chapter 17

ARDOIN got down, off-saddled and watered his horse, and all the while Swede Hagberg watched him from the porch. Ardoin knew that now Swede would have heard about Kirby Steele, and he had no illusions about how far his friendship with Swede would protect him if Hagberg knew that he had killed Steele. The gunman's silence and his patient waiting had an ominous smell about them, and Ardoin considered these things fully before he turned his horse into the corral and headed for the house.

Hagberg's first words dispelled his immediate fears. "I came to join up, Ed," the Swede said. "I've left Corralitos."

It was a bit too sudden. Ardoin said, "Well." He fumbled for his makings, curled up a smoke, and all the while he was feeling about for the key to the situation. Finally he asked dryly, "What happened to you and Corralitos?"

"The woman," Hagberg said. "She sent Kirby north, where your bunch killed him."

Ardoin watched narrowly. "Had it comin'. Somebody killed Darby Wayne, too. They'd kill me the same. Once these things start, you kill or be killed."

The Swede waved a big paw. "I ain't sayin' no. But I wanted to go north with Kirby and she stopped that. She knew that something would happen to him and she wanted to make sure he wouldn't come back. She killed him."

Ardoin could see no point in indicating the flaws in this logic. He merely said, "So you want to join us. Why?"

"To help you bust Carolina."

It would be only a matter of time until Hagberg knew of the fight in the saloon high up in the Buckhorns. There was also concerned here the matter of his personal pride. He had fought his fight with Kirby Steele honorably and according to his lights, and he would stand by the results before any man. He said softly, after a moment, "You ought to get this straight, Swede. I met Kirby in a saloon in the hills. I gave him a chance for a fair draw. He was a little slow." Then he waited.

The answer came after a long time. "I figured that," the Swede said. "It's hard to say this. Let's say I had two friends, but they was enemies. They fought fair and one of 'em was killed. It might have been the other, and I wouldn't have liked it better either way. But this other person, the woman, is really at the bottom of it, because if it hadn't been for her, they wouldn't have had to meet, maybe ever. She made it so they had to shoot it out. She's the one I'm after."

While he spoke, Ardoin wrestled with devils. It was clear to him that Hagberg was willing in this matter to take his final judgment back to fundamental movers. If he believed that Carolina Steele had planned this thing, and would hunt her down for it, why should he not know the truth? It did not occur to Ardoin that he had shared in the planning of Steele's end. He saw it as the work of Carolina and Landry, and himself merely an incidental agent. Nor did it come to him with any force that he was betraying Landry. There was that whole hazy and bitterly clouded area of his emotions centering around Mary Wayne and his feeling that she was in love with Landry. Furthermore, he told himself that with Harry Wayne's death, there was justification for his breaking, now, the confidence which he had given and taken with Landry. He listened only momentarily to the clamoring of contrary evidence, then said, "Carolina Steele wasn't the cause of Kirby's death."

"How's that?"

"Listen. Landry hired out to Corralitos to help me bust it up from inside. He figured out that deal of sending you boys over to the fake brands, the night we hit 'em. He had Carolina send Kirby north with the understanding that he would kill him himself. But instead, he planned with me to do the job, and to take her herds into the bargain. Swede," he paused, "Landry's the man you're after."

There was a moment's long silence. Hagberg said heavily, "I ought to have gunned him down when I had the chance."

"Never too late," Ardoin said softly.

"No. Never too late." The Swede waited, adjusting his pattern of thought to these new developments. "I'll get him for that, now. I'll—"

"What are you waitin' for?"

"Well," mumbled the Swede, "there's Carolina."

"One thing at a time. We'll take care of her. When you've done your job, you ride with us. There's a bunk and a plate for you with the rest of the boys."

The strange and obscure forces which moved under Hagberg's skull did so slowly, but relentlessly. Kirby was dead, and he had loved him. He had thought that Carolina was primarily responsible, but now it appeared that Landry was the author of Kirby's end. It was merely a matter of minutes to relate Landry to the central idea, which was revenge, revenge of the kind which finds an outpouring of dumb grief in striking down the agent which caused it. When he had made this decision, he started abruptly off the porch.

Ardoin said with surprise, "You goin' right now?"

"I'll be back. But I've waited long enough to settle up with that fellow." Then he left, and in a moment he was taking the trail southward toward Broken Wheel and Corralitos.

Ardoin listened to his departure, looking into the night and wondering that his only feeling was one of relief. Now he alone would carry the secret of Frank Landry's collaboration against Corralitos. Time was long, and it worked many changes. With time, Mary Wayne would forget Landry, and with her forgetting would grow her need for a man and the necessity of a strong hand at the Running W. For just an instant it came to Ed Ardoin that he harbored a perversity beyond all understanding, and then he pushed that

damaging admission aside and went into the house to his
supper.

Landry did not reach Broken Wheel until well toward ten
o'clock at night. He had ridden slowly, thinking his
thoughts, and finding no urgency at his back. He realized
that his game was about played out. Such poisons of dissen-
sion and corrosion had been loosed that he himself could be
destroyed with those against whom they were directed. His
salvation lay in precise timing, and in unswervingly right
judgment, if he were to come through unscathed. He considered these facts and made them a part of him, and then he
turned his mind fatalistically to other things.

Landry had no way of knowing that Mary Wayne now
blamed him for her brother's death, nor yet that Ed Ardoin
had betrayed him to Swede Hagberg. The only certainty in
this whole game for him was the grim satisfaction that every
moment now was drawing him nearer to a settlement with
Steve's killer, and the hard corollary knowledge that the
deeper he went into this game the greater grew Mary
Wayne's hatred of everything that he stood for. He did not
like to think of Mary Wayne, now. With the days and his
deeper involvement in this morass of treachery, the very
thought of her had begun to leave him with an obscure kind
of pain and an unsatisfied hunger which he did not want to
analyze. Before him lay still the final blow at Corralitos, the
wrecking of Carolina Steele's empire of hate, and beyond
that point lay a hazy and unsatisfying future whose texture
he cared not now to test.

He rode into Broken Wheel at a walk, finding the town
almost deserted, with spare and dim lights coming from the
hotel and from the two saloons. Seeing ponies racked before
the Longhorn and the Casino, it crossed his mind that he
might find Ardoin here, and he reined in at the Longhorn
and sat for a moment in the saddle, looking over the animals
racked there. In the darkness he could recognize no brands,
and presently he got down, tied, and afterward walked
among the horses, examining their brands. He found no

Pitchfork markings and with that he started across the street
toward the tie rail before the Casino.

Halfway across, he heard a horse coming on at a canter,
and he stopped and swung about in the dust, and saw Swede
Hagberg bearing down upon him. Recognition hit Hagberg
at the same moment, and he pulled up sharply, fifty feet
away, all his cold and dogged attention centered upon
Landry. Neither spoke here in the silence of this dead and
dusty street, and Landry knew that this was a moment which
held the culmination of Hagberg's long and stubborn animosities. Knowing that, Landry waited, making himself
ready.

"I was lookin' for you," the Swede said heavily at last.

Landry said, "Now you've found me. If you want to play,
get off that horse."

Hagberg waited a long time. It seemed for a moment that
he would speak, and then he edged the horse easily forward,
saying nothing, until they were ten paces apart. Then, watching Landry, he swung the animal crossways of the street, stepping slowly from the saddle with the horse between him and
Landry. In the dust, he flicked the animal on the rump and it
trotted over to stand with the others at the tie-up. Hagberg
spread his feet, planting himself solidly in the street's middle,
and now he said softly, "It's been a long time in coming."

Landry studied him with a narrowed-down care. He
knew that Hagberg drew crosshand, a flashy, two-gun draw
that annihilated with a hail of lead. But unless the first shot
was good, a slower draw, followed by a well-placed shot,
could stop the big man cold. Such was Landry's summation
of his chances before he said, "I don't want to kill you, Hagberg. For some reason, I can't hate you."

"Try," said the other in a flat voice. "I find it easy where
you're concerned."

"Why?" asked Landry curiously.

Hagberg waited a little while before he said, "You're a
double-crosser. In a way, I'm sorry that I can't wait to let
Carolina handle you. You and Ed Ardoin have framed her.
You framed Kirby—my friend. *The last man you'll ever*

frame—" The sound of the words on his tongue and the thought behind them whipped sudden fury into him and he bent suddenly forward in a crouch, his hands streaking for his guns. They came up out of the leather ridden by wrath and urgency, and for the first time in his life, Swede Hagberg shot blindly and too fast, with just a little of heart-break behind his wild anger.

Landry drew as Hagberg moved. As his gun came up he cocked it, and he pivoted to one side as the first tearing salvo shrieked past him. He lined the sights on Hagberg's right arm just above the elbow and pulled the trigger, and he saw Hagberg's body jar sideways as the slug shattered through muscle and bone, sending the gun in that hand into the dust. In the split second of failing fire he heard the Swede's grunt of pain, and even as he drove another deliberate shot into the gunman's left arm, fire exploded from Hagberg's other gun and a searing pain and a rocketing blackness filled with shooting fire thudded into his brain, driving him to his knees, stunned and then into the dust. He heard dimly and from afar Hagberg's moaning as, his arms dangling limply, the shattered bones' grating friction brought the sweat of agony to the big gunman. A whirling, windy world of confusion swam through Landry's head, and he held on to consciousness with all his determination, painfully identifying each sound that reached him and clinging to each as he fought off the thing that would sweep him under: Hagberg's curses, strained, helpless, wild, were an anchor, and so, too, was the sound of men running through the doorways of the saloons and into the street, even though their comment was confused and senseless to him. He hung there, struggling, for a long while, and heard someone way, "Well, the Swede got him. Deader'n a poled beef." Then a voice said, "Stand back. He's creased. Be all right in a minute." And afterward he felt a man's hands, rough and hard, under his shoulder, and then he was sitting up, leaning against the man's knee. With that, he knew that he would not die, and he had the strange thought that he was glad because now he could see this thing through for Mary Wayne's sake.

He opened his eyes, and light from a saloon stabbed at his aching brain. He shook his head, and put his hand to it, and his fingers came away bloody.

"He damn near got you," said the man holding him, and he looked up into Lon Wilson's thin, morose face.

Landry took several long, deep gulps of breath, and the world came back to focus, leaving only the agony of his splitting head. He got up, then, with Wilson's help, and he took his neckpiece and held it to the wound on his temple. Now, sickness of another kind came over him as he thought of what Ardoin had done to him. It came to him that he had entirely misjudged the man's capacity to hate, and yet it puzzled him that Ardoin should have done this thing at the very moment when their game was ready to pay off.

Shakily, he came back to his surroundings now, and found that he was trembling. An eighth of an inch would have made the difference—would have split his skull and sent Hagberg's slug bursting through his brain. He pushed that thought aside. A man came running down the street with a leather bag, and knowing that this would be the doctor, he stepped forward.

Men opened a way for him, and he said to Hagberg, "As soon as you can, ride. The next time I meet you in this country, I'll kill you."

The doctor turned to him, frowning. "You'd have done better to kill him anyhow. He'll be lucky to keep these arms at all."

"So much the better," Landry said dryly, turning away. "He was too fond of guns." He went to the boardwalk and sat down in its edge, full of weakness, his head aching powerfully and the wound burning now. For a moment he thought he would be sick. Then, after a while, he raised his head and saw that the street had cleared of men, and that Lon Wilson stood before him in the dust, holding Hagberg's guns and watching him narrowly through the darkness.

"You want these?" Wilson asked. "He'll never use 'em again."

Landry looked at the sheriff quizzically. "No arrests, Sheriff?"

After a long while the other said in a dry tone, "Self-defense. I saw the whole thing. I even heard it all—every word the Swede told you before he cut loose."

"So," Landry said softly, "you know what I'm doing at Corralitos."

"I knew all along," Wilson said softly. "I found a letter on Steve Landry, when I went over there to *investigate*"—his voice slurred the word bitterly—"and it was from his brother—Frank Landry. I knew the minute you hit town who you were."

Again Landry knew the feeling of precariousness that had become almost a part of him. After a while he said, "Funny—maybe Carolina Steele ought to see it."

He heard the sheriff's long, soft sigh in the darkness. Then the man said, "No. I'm glad you came. Maybe you don't know the feeling of needing an answer, like I do. I've got it now." He turned and threw Hagberg's guns into the dust of the street where they had first fallen. After a moment he unpinned the star from his vest and tossed it after them. Then he turned slowly toward Landry. "I'm a trail boss," he said, and there was a change in his voice. "I know cattle. And I know when a string is played out. So long." He turned down the street, a new purpose in his stride, his back straight.

"Good luck," Landry said. "You can tear up that letter."

Wilson looked back for just a moment. "I already did—when I found it." Then the night swallowed him up, a man who had had his fill of meaningless servitude.

Landry sat there many minutes in the night, getting back his strength, and holding the neckpiece to the wound on his head. After a long time, it had ceased to bleed, and he sauntered up the way to the livery stable, wet his neckpiece and washed the blood from his face and hands. After that, he rolled a cigarette, his hands still a bit shaky, and took the goodness from the tangy smoke, feeling strengthened by it.

There was in him now a small conflict, for he knew not quite how he should face the immediate future. The fight with

Hagberg had shaken him, physically and psychologically.
And there was still the question in his mind what Hagberg
would do with his knowledge of Landry's role at Corralitos.

The street was deserted now, as he made his way back to
the hitch rack, where his mount was tied. He stood for a long
while with his hand on the horn, looking down into the
blackness of the dust, seeing nothing. For a brief moment he
thought of Lon Wilson, throwing his star into the dust and
riding out into the night, away from this maelstrom of hate
and clashing motives, and he was tempted fleetingly to do
likewise. He did not notice the stealthy form of Coulter
watching him from the shadows, from where he had seen this
whole thing in the street. Nor did he see Coulter slip on down
the street in the darkness, after a moment, and station himself
in an alleyway on the dark north end of town, waiting.

Finally, Landry made his decision. There could be no
turning back now. Ardoin had betrayed him, but Ardoin was
necessary to the final play of this game. Therefore, he must
ride to the Pitchfork. Knowing that, he swung aboard and
pointed his horse north, riding at an easy walk past the lights
of the town and so out toward the road leading to the Buckhorns.

As he went past the alleyway where Coulter was con-
cealed, the gunman ghosted easily from his hiding place into
the middle of the street. He drew his gun and took dead aim
at the black bulk of Landry, less than forty feet away. His
arm stiffened, and his finger began to squeeze the trigger.
Then, imperceptibly, the pressure eased, and as Landry's
outline was swallowed up in the darkness, Coulter lowered
his gun and slipped it back into the holster. He stood looking thoughtfully into the darkness for some moments, then
he headed back down the street.

A first-quarter moon left a slight tinge of silver on the
night as Landry rode into Ardoin's yard. He passed the corrals and came to the water trough, noting as the black dipped
its muzzle that the lights in the bunkhouse were out. A gleam
of light came faintly from the house, and Landry got down,

tied his horse to a pole of the corral, and went across the yard.

The light came from a back room. Cautiously Landry circled the house and came at last to the back where light shone full into the night from a kitchen window. Ed Ardoin sat at the table, brooding over a cup of coffee. He was alone. Landry eased onward, and stepped across a small back porch to the door. Even as he reached it he heard the quick movement inside, and as he came in Ed Ardoin, half out of his chair, faced him with drawn gun.

As the surprise went out of Ardoin's face, Landry said, "You're jumpy, and by God, you ought to be."

Distrust stood out on Ardoin's face. "What do you want here?"

"Put your gun away, Ardoin."

Ardoin wavered. Then, as Landry took out his makings and curled up a cigarette, Ardoin eased his gun into the holster on the chair back and shifted around the table, pulling the chair with him and sitting down opposite Landry. Landry blew out smoke. "Your little game didn't work," he said cooly. "I met Hagberg in Broken Wheel."

Ardoin paled slightly. Now his hate for this man had doubled, for Landry knew that he was without honor. "I'm sorry," he said in a dry, hating voice. "I'm damned sorry that it didn't."

Landry lounged to the table and sat down. "I could rough you up," he said calmly, "or I could shoot you. I thought of doing both, on the way over here. If it would serve any purpose, it would be a pleasure."

"I'd like for you to try," Ardoin said softly.

"I'm curious about you. One of my failings. I guess that's why I didn't kill Hagberg."

Ardoin said nothing. He had his pride, and it was rooted in unbending belligerence.

"What have you got against me, Ardoin?" Landry asked musingly.

It was the way he asked it. It put in one small lump all the hidden animosities running between these two men, and it

spread miles wide the differences which made each what he
was and said that nothing would ever bring them together to
let them see eye to eye. It brought the hate unbidden into Ardoin's glance as he watched Landry.

"You came into this place walking with your head high
and a chip on your shoulder," he said. "You're too proud for
ordinary men, and you've got a way of looking down that
damned long nose of yours at others as though they were
dust. We've all got our faults, but you see 'em and make a
man conscious of them. You're too damn sure of yourself to
get along with men who are troubled and having their wor-
ries. I could forgive you that"—he waited a moment, and the
wash of emotions made his eyes bright and caused his
hands, on the table before him, to tremble a little—"but you
walked into the life of Mary Wayne in some way that I don't
understand, and when you did that, I was pushed out. If that
sounds small to you, all right. She was the biggest thing in
my life. That's why I told Swede Hagberg that you helped
frame Kirby Steele. I'm not one damned bit particular who
kills you, Landry. Just so it's done."

Now, when he had finished, Landry remembered many
things out of their association which added up to this moment. In a way he felt sorry for this big man, for he had his
own understanding of how deeply a man could feel about
Darby Wayne's daughter. Still, he knew that there was more.

"Let's have the rest of it," he said evenly.

"Harry Wayne," said Ardoin with hard implacability.
"You told me to leave him behind so that you could butcher
him in that shack over in the Buckhorns."

Landry waited while the shock of it came and went. "And
why did I do that?" he asked.

It was a weak spot in Ardoin's hypothesis. After a while
he said, "I'd like to know that. I'd also like to know what
your spur was doing there, where we found Harry."

Now Landry remembered the loss of that spur. He was
thinking, too, that he knew the reason for Wayne's death,
and he wondered in this moment if he had protected the secret long enough. He said, "I met McCanless that night in

the shack to frame up a deal to smash Corralitos. To do it, I
had to get McCanless mad. We had a tussle. When I rode
into the hills later, I saw I'd lost that spur. That's the God's
truth. If Harry Wayne was killed there, he came after we left.
I had nothing against him, and you know that."

"Why did you insist that he be left behind?" Ardoin asked
quickly.

It came to Landry now that he could go only so far alone.
Harry Wayne was dead. Protecting the boy had all along
been merely for the purpose of protecting Mary Wayne from
shame. But this man, who misunderstood, loved Mary
Wayne—loved her with an insane kind of jealousy which
might guarantee his keeping the secret, too. To this consideration in Landry's mind was added the fact that matters
were reaching the bursting point in the battle against Corralitos, and he needed understanding cooperation from Ardoin, if not the kind of collaboration that grows from
friendship. He made his decision.

"Harry Wayne was in love with Carolina Steele," he said.
"I saw with my own eyes the two of them meet in her room,
and that was the night before his father was killed. I saw the
records at the Courthouse which prove that he bought
Steve's ranch after it was called derelict. He was the only
one who could have told her about your plans to cut that
herd. But how could I have let that be known? You know
what it would have done to his sister—what it would still do
if she knew."

Ardoin had studied him as he talked. At last he said
softly, "Is this the truth?"

"You can find part of it on the record. And you know that
I didn't inform about that cutting party. You know what my
plans have been from the start."

After a long while Ardoin nodded. "All right. Now, what
about this plan to smash Corralitos?"

"McCanless is bringing a herd north tomorrow night. He
thinks Carolina has crossed him, and she thinks the same about
McCanless. They'll be at each other's throats. He's bringing a

crew, and the Corralitos crowd will all be back home. It's the chance we've been waiting for. It's the payoff, Ardoin."

"What's the plan?"

"You ride in late. Come like the devil and all his angels. Every man and boy who can sit a horse. I'll see to it that the Corralitos crowd is afoot and that they stay that way."

After a long time, Ardoin nodded, his face long and sober. "The end of Corralitos," he murmured. "It'll be good to breathe free air again—"

Landry rose. He stood looking down at Ardoin for a moment, then said, "It's hard to tell what will happen tomorrow night to you and me. Just in case I don't see you again, I want you to know that, as men go, you're at the bottom of the heap."

Ardoin colored. Forgotten now, by both of them, was the necessity for working together, as their basic dislikes rose once more between them. Ardoin said meagerly, "I never liked you. I guess I'll always hate your guts."

"You could have made this thing easier," Landry went on implacably. "You've kept me in the grease with everybody, just because you had to keep your mouth shut to make our game work out. But when this thing is over tomorrow night, mister, we'll have our reckoning. I'm not going to be the goat forever."

"Yes, you are," Ardoin said softly. His eyes had grown hot and mean. "Nothing will change for you tomorrow night. I know what you have in mind—squaring yourself with Mary Wayne. But you've misjudged me, Landry. You think that I wouldn't tell her about Harry, that I'd keep it a secret, to save her from hurt. You have the idea that now I might shift from you the blame for Darby's death and Harry's. You'd like for me to be grateful and do the right thing by telling everybody that *you* were the one to plan the end of Corralitos and break its stinking control of this country. But you're wrong, friend. Before I'd give up Mary Wayne and let you have her, I'd see her in hell!"

Landry took a step toward him. Ardoin threw up a hand. "Wait! Don't get fancy with me. You need me now, because you've played this game as far as you can go under your power alone. You're up to your neck with Carolina. If I don't bring my bunch tomorrow, you've got to ride out and leave the jackpot behind. You've held the whip hand up to now, but it'll be different from here on. Landry"—his voice rose and he leaned across the table—"as far as I'm concerned, no one will ever know the truth about what you've done to help. All the rest of my life I'll drive it home to Mary Wayne that you killed her brother. I'll hold that spur before her eyes and lie until she believes it. And as for what Harry Wayne did—betrayed and killed his father, sold out his sister and his friends—I'll keep that from her just so long as you stay away from her!"

Landry said softly, "You'd do that? You'd add that blow to what she's already suffered?"

"Yes. I'd do anything before I'd give her up to you. And don't get the idea that you could tell her. She wouldn't believe you. And if she did, she'd hate you!"

They looked at one another for a long while, and it came to Landry that Ardoin was slightly mad, that there was on this subject a blind spot in his moral fiber and in his mind.

"The bottom of the heap," he said softly, and then he turned away. He went into the darkness and around the house to his horse. With a numb feeling inside, he rode back toward Corralitos, asking himself how the victory would taste if it were compounded of defeat.

Carolina Steele had had time to take stock of the situation after Landry had ridden away to scout the stolen herd. The passage of time calmed her and brought her a more detached view of events. She saw now that her fears had been exaggerated, and that the loss had appeared great chiefly because she was used to winning. She knew herself well enough to know that any change in that pattern temporarily disoriented her and loosened a fury of exasperation out of proportion to the changes themselves.

Sober reflection told her that she had been foolish to mistrust Landry. His proof of McCanless' duplicity was, to her

mind, the best evidence that he was working for her interests. Even, she admitted, his manner of getting such proof
had its cleverness, for McCanless was nobody's fool. She
found, too, added comfort in the fact that Kirby was out of
the way, and there was no regret to cloud that comfort. She
could see ahead only minor obstacles now, and it came to
her that the future could be very good, indeed, since this
great issue was irrevocably decided. And as she thought of
the future, she remembered the night when Landry had
taken her in his arms and shown her his hunger, and had
aroused an answering hunger within her. Yes, she told herself, the future could be good—and it was not beyond the
realms of possibility that such a man as Landry might share
it with her.

Such was her mood when she heard a horse come into the
yard and stop by the corrals. She got to her feet and went
that way.

Landry heard her step and turned. "You rode late," the
woman said.

"I located most of the herd. The bulk of them are on Ardoin's place, in a high pasture about three miles from the
ranch house."

"Good." She suddenly felt at peace, for this was a falling
away of her greatest worry. For a moment it crossed her
mind how foolish she had been to react as she had to this
man when he came back from the north.

Landry pushed the black into the corral. "It's late," he
said. "You sit up worrying all the time?"

"I'm not worried. I've been thinking of you. I'm going to
say a thing that is new for me, because it is not my custom
to make apologies. I'm sorry I acted the way I did."

Landry kept thinking of Harry Wayne. This woman's
claws were sheathed in velvet. Did she once think with regret of Kirby Steele? "There's nothing, really, for you to
worry about," he said. "After tomorrow night, you'll be sitting on the top of the world. You know that, don't you?"

"Yes," she said after a moment, "I think I will."

There was a little silence, now, and Landry said, "I passed

through Broken Wheel. There's a story in the bars that Harry Wayne was found shot to death in the Buckhorns."

He heard her sharp intake of breath. She said calmly after a moment, "I suppose it's too bad. But after all, he was on the other side. Those things happen."

Landry let go a hard, short laugh. "It's about time you played straight with me," he said. "After all, you need me. Don't try to hold out. I know that Harry Wayne was spying for you."

"How do you know that?" her voice was sharp.

"I saw him go to your room. I know that he told you about his father's plans to cut your herd."

"You know too many things," and suspicion had come back into her voice.

"I don't know nearly enough. And don't start freezing up on me now, changing that mood of yours again, just because I'm wise to you. I'm getting tired of your keeping me in the dark, and still expecting me to fight this fight for you. I've a mind to tell you to go to hell and ride out."

A note in his voice impressed her. "Let's not be at loggerheads," she said more reasonably. "There is too much ahead for us here after tomorrow. As for Harry Wayne, he became a real trouble to me, and had to be gotten rid of. Why should I bother you with *that?*"

Her cold-blooded detachment again amazed him. Somewhere in some twisting and warping experience in her life, Carolina Steele's conscience had died utterly, and she had not noticed its loss. "Yes," he said dryly, "I have enough to do, planning to get rid of Kirby and McCanless for you."

"Don't be cruel," she reprimanded him.

There was really nothing he could say to that. Presently he said casually, "This is off the subject, but there is something I want to know and you can tell me. I think I know the answer, but I've got to make sue. Who killed my cousin— Steve Landry?"

"Why should *I* know?"

"Because," he lied, "McCanless told me the night I met him that you would know the answer to that."

Through her mind flashed in an instant the danger which this man could represent to her should he find out the truth about the ranch she had gotten from Steve Landry. She had the knowledge, too, that she had only him, now, near her to fight on her side: Kirby, Swede Hagberg gone, McCanless turned against her, Coulter undependable and ready for blackmail—she must hold to this man's loyalty and allegiance at all costs. And because her plans for him went beyond this, she must make him believe that he had her confidence; must quiet his suspicions and center them on her enemies.

She laughed a dry, unamused laugh. "How clever of him! It was he and Kirby who engineered the whole thing. They wanted his land. They killed him and forced Harry Wayne to purchase it and assign it to Corralitos, to—to me, Frank!" She paused and took a step nearer him. "That was only one of the many reasons I feared them both, believe me. And then Harry Wayne came threatening to tell you about that purchase if I did not give him money. Rather than face blackmail the rest of my life, I—" Then she paused, her voice frightened and confused.

Landry thought, *She lies as though she believes it.* He played his part, however, saying, "I think I understand, Carolina."

She turned back to him. "Frank, you will never know what it means to me to have you here, to see this awful thing straightening out under your guidance, and to know that in the future we—we might have a decent life—" Her voice broke ever so little. Then, when he said nothing, she continued. "You do believe me, Frank? I can prove this. I can show you the records in the Courthouse to prove it!"

"You didn't answer my question," Landry said. "Who killed Steve Landry?"

She waited a long moment. Then she spat out, "Who else but the man who sold me out to Ed Ardoin? Who else but *Jim McCanless?*"

Chapter 18

MARY WAYNE watched Drav McLain and the Running W crew ride away into the gathering dusk on their way to the rendezvous at the Pitchfork with Ardoin. She had taken this news of the final blow at Corralitos almost with unconcern, a thing which worried Drav. He had wanted a pair of riders to stay behind with her, for something in Mary's manner had aroused a prying apprehension in him.

"No," she had said firmly. "Take every man with you. I wish it that way, and my father would have wanted it so." And McLain had been convinced by her reference to Darby Wayne.

There is a point beyond which repeated shock stimuli fail to bring a response; Mary Wayne had reached that point. The loss of father and brother would have been enough, but there was the additional hard conviction, sitting like a leaden weight upon her consciousness, that Frank Landry had been responsible for their deaths. There was in this girl a depth of emotion which she herself had never suspected, and Landry, the tall, hard stranger to this country, had awakened all the strong currents of those depths. Somehow, in a way that she could not have explained, he had made her come alive, and for a little while she had entertained such dreams as may come only once in a lifetime. The dashing of these fantasies, and the sudden realization that they had been built about one whom she should hate, left her feeling warped and ill. And with Harry Wayne's death, she knew that she must strike

back, could now do so for another reason than wounded
pride and disillusionment.

As Drav and his riders grew small in the distance, she
went to her room, changed to her riding clothes and then
went to the corral and caught up her favorite saddler. Just
before mounting she went to her room and took from a bu-
reau drawer a small revolver. This she slipped into a pocket
of her divided skirt, and then she went from the room. Passing through the living room, she caught sight of her father's
picture, and she put down a twinge of pain and went quickly
out, her lips drawn tight. In a moment she was in the saddle,
riding southward toward Corralitos.

Coulter had drunk up all the profits of Harry Wayne's
death. Since the night at the cabin in the Buckhorns, he had
hung over first one and then the other bar in Broken Wheel,
enjoying a sense of leisure and of time on his hands and
money in his pockets. He was back on the payroll, there was
a fight in the country, and his measure of contentment
swelled high.

The night meeting of Hagberg and Landry had sobered
him sufficiently to realize that there was still a job to do. In
his whiskey-hazy way he had almost followed the impulse
to shoot down the man he hated, as Landry rode out of town
after the fight. And then it had come to him that he still had
Carolina Steele's bidding to do, and he had turned his back
on sure vengeance, knowing that Landry could wait. He had
been impressed, too, by the fact that the matter might not be
as simple as he had thought. Landry's maiming fire upon
Swede Hagberg had sobered Coulter considerably.

Now it was a day later, and he had emptied his pockets
and partially cleansed his brain of the alcoholic backwash
that had hung there for days. Money had again become a
problem, and he knew that now was the time to report to
Carolina Steele, make big his lie about Landry, and then finish him off as conveniently as possible with the approbation
of the mistress of Corralitos.

Thus, full of his slow and abiding hate for the man who

had humbled him, he had a last sundown drink at the bar of the Casino and went outside to the rack, where he climbed aboard and rode out of Broken Wheel into the south.

The day had somehow been good for Carolina Steele, filled with a sense of some unfolding destiny. She had had time alone to think of recent events, to evaluate them, and to place herself in the forward flow of others which would come from them. The results had been to her liking. First of all was a deep and secure satisfaction in the belief that she had won Landry definitely and convincingly to her side by her feigned frankness in discussing Harry Wayne's part in her past, by her placing of the blame for Steve Landry's death upon McCanless and Kirby. In her talk with him last night, she had felt that Landry accepted her explanations as truth.

In a way, she was glad that after today there would be no need for more lies, no necessity for intrigue to gain her ends. She would have gained them. Ardoin would still be there to be reckoned with, but that reckoning would come swiftly and he would no longer stand in her way. This was the opening of the final act.

She had her moments of remembering, too, much of the harshness of the more remote past: the days when she and Kirby had first come to Texas, and even beyond that, to the war and to the privation, the suffering, yes, the hunger and grinding want that she had suffered in those days. Thinking of these things, she remembered them with a rising tightness within her, and knew that it was the remnant of her old fears: the fear of want and the dread of poverty which then had stood constantly at her shoulder. Because she was neither introspective nor objective, she knew only pride and relief in the road down which she had come since then. Her sense of accomplishment was dulled not in the least by the fact that she had ridden over men's souls and their bodies in her flight from the fears she now remembered. Rather, she remembered them gladly and a bit arrogantly from the perspective of her wealth and her power, knowing that they could never again be anything but memories for her. Perhaps, one day, when she had grown old and most of the necessity for her having been ruthless had slipped into the past, she could afford the luxury of being thoroughly moral, of scrupling with regard to her relationship with those who stood, even shakily, in her way. But that would come later.

Now it was growing late, and she knew that Landry would be waiting at the Lagos pasture for McCanless to come. She had asked him to do this, for she wanted to talk with McCanless, to throw his duplicity into his teeth, to enjoy the sight of him squirming, denying his guilt, even while Landry waited in the darkness outside to dispose of him.

An association of ideas crossed her mind, and as she remembered that McCanless had always hungered mightily after her beauty, she recalled the night when Landry had held her, close and hungrily. She thought of him now, warmly, and with a small, rising want of her own, and presently, with a half-smile, she rose and went to her room and after searching through her closets, she took down her most beautiful gown. It was of glistening gold silk, with a bodice of sea green, and she admired it for a while before undressing and slipping into it. Afterward, she looked at herself in the glass, sensually pleased with the manner in which it sheathed the fullness of her hips and displayed the soft mounds of her breasts. She had a moment of idle amusement as she thought of dallying lightly with McCanless before she flung her accusations at him. And then she thought again of Landry, and a more secret idea caught musingly at her lips and caused her to assess herself more closely in the mirror.

What she saw pleased her, and with another idea partially formed for her future, she turned away from the glass just as a heavy step sounded from the front of the house. She stopped, listening. Now she heard the clattering arrival of many horses and the rapid-fire ripple of Spanish, and knew that the *vaqueros* had ridden into the bunkhouse, and that it would be Jim McCanless in the front room. In that moment she heard his voice, strangely hard and arrogant, speaking to a servant: *"Que venga la señora.* I want to talk to her!"

Landry saw the *vaqueros* ride off toward Corralitos, leaving behind only a small guard with the rustled Mexican cattle. He saw Jim McCanless speak a last word to his foreman, and then ride toward where he waited. It was almost dark here in the Lagos pasture, but Landry could see the stiffness in the big man's face as he came close and leaned on the horn, watching Landry through the heavy dusk.

"All right," McCanless said, "we're here. What next?"

Landry was thinking, *He killed Steve.* And as he remembered, he fought with the urge to draw his gun and make an end of it here and now. Still, he said, "Up to you, McCanless. Your job."

"I know that," the other growled. "But what have you found out about Carolina and Wayne?"

Landry was thinking that this had been a losing game for him, too. He would face this man before many hours, and one of them would die. But in bringing matters to this point, he had so involved himself, had played so fast and loose with human hates and lusts, that he had defeated his own purpose by leaving himself merely the emptiness of revenge. He looked closely at McCanless and asked himself if just knowing that this man was eaten of worms would be enough. And with the answer came the unsatisfactory knowledge that the future lay behind him and he had merely brushed it in passing. Knowing, too, that the next time he walked into Corralitos, he must do so with drawn gun, he said, "He was to come over tonight. You ought to just about catch 'em by the time you get there."

McCanless let go a rippling of profanity. "Kirby?"

"Wayne killed him. Now he's coming to collect."

"Like hell he is!" And McCanless swung his horse about.

"Wait a minute."

McCanless halted. "Well, what is it?"

"I don't have to tell you that she'll try to lie out of it."

McCanless muttered something and put spurs to his

horse. The rapid beat of the hoofs died away, and Landry sat there, hugging the darkness, waiting for them to get a start on him, and feeling a strange, empty sense of relief that it was almost over. There had been so much of lies, of the poison of the human spirit, that he felt himself unclean and ill. He thought, now, of Mary Wayne, and told himself that after all she was merely an attractive girl whom he had met a few times and kissed once, and this explanation did not satisfy him. The feeling was there of how much this whole affair had brought down upon her, and he wished mightily that she might know the truth someday. The association of ideas brought Ardoin to mind, and then he knew that it was time to ride into Corralitos and spring the last trap which would clean this country of the thing that had ridden it.

It was an hour later when he arrived at the ranch. He had ridden slowly, and now, as he got down beyond the barns, a shadow against the shadows, he was thankful that the new moon would be up late, and that it was now dark. Even as he watched, the last light in the *vaqueros'* bunkhouse winked out. The other, too, was dark. There were lights in the Casa Grande, and he thought wryly that McCanless and Carolina Steele would be in there now, facing each other with their hates, their passions and their mistrusts. He pondered that briefly, feeling very old and very wise in a way that left him with an obscure kind of sadness. Then he stepped softly around the barn through the dust and came to the corral.

It was filled with the Mexican and Corralitos horses. He set up a low whistling as they saw him and started, then waited. After a moment, working slowly so as not to frighten them, he hoisted the poles from one section of the corral, one at a time. Then, with the opening made, he stepped inside and with slow care hazed the animals singly and in pairs through the gap. Without commotion they scattered into the night. Corralitos' defenders were afoot.

*   *   *

Coulter was high in the hills toward Corralitos when he heard behind him the commotion of a bunch of riders, pushing their horses hard. He halted for a moment; then as the drumming roar swept on, he decided against running ahead of them. Pulling his horse off the tail into pines, he waited. As they rolled down on him they broke the pace and slowed to a trot. There were many of them, and he heard their talk as they went past and knew that it was Ed Ardoin and Drav McLain with their riders and neighbors. He heard a man say, "By God, it'll be good to smash Corralitos for a change." And after that a man replied, "Change, hell! This is the final one."

The tail of the cavalcade was nearing. Coulter thought quickly. This changed his plans. Perhaps, after all, he no longer worked for Carolina Steele. Not after this bunch got there. Still, there was Landry. Let them have Corralitos. He would have his inning with the man whom he hated. As the last riders came by, Coulter pulled noiselessly out of the pines and eased into their wake. It was too dark to distinguish one from another, and he felt safe. He rode along for several yards behind them, and finally a rider turned in his saddle, watched him a while, and called out, "You, back there! Close up!"

"I'm comin'," Coulter grumbled in an altered voice. "Horse is a little lame."

And then Ardoin's voice came from up ahead, "Let's ride. Go in burnin' powder, and burn it until the last bullet's gone!" The next moment they were sweeping forward at a run, the cool breeze off the Santisimas beating against them and whipping the smell of dust into the night's breath.

At sight of Carolina Steele, Jim McCanless caught a swift breath. For an instant her beauty was a warm, remembered thing, and then he knew that another man had claimed her, that she had taken it from him, and a blind wrath rose up in him, making him hate her.

He said, "Dressed for him, I suppose! Well, he'll play hell havin' you, Carolina."

She was taken aback by this approach. Frowning, she said sharply, "What are you talking about?"

"You know, damn you. You and Harry Wayne."

"Are you crazy?"

"Sure," said McCanless with slow, heavy rage. He took a step toward her, feeding his jealousy on her beauty and finding it a lash to the boiling violence within him. "Sure I'm crazy. Crazy to ever have believed you, you lying slut!"

She paled, her face pinched with anger. Then color rushed into her face. She stood by the table, and on it was a heavy glass-ball paperweight. Suddenly she swung this into her hand and threw it at him, all her strength and her outrage behind it. He ducked, but it caught him on the shoulder, jarring him. "Name me that, will you?" she screamed. "You who spoke so mealymouthed of protecting me! And all the while robbing me—"

McCanless had gone backward a couple of paces. Now he was unsure, disoriented. "Robbing you?" he growled, watching her. "You've got a nerve—"

"Stealing my cattle and plotting with Ed Ardoin to run off my herds. Two dollars a head. Two dollars a head and a little love speech with every one, damn you, McCanless." Fury had gripped her now, and the big man stood rubbing his shoulder and glaring at her in perplexity. This thing was not going as he had planned. The initiative was slipping from him; she was putting him on the defensive.

"You can't talk yourself out of this," he said harshly, rallying. "I don't know what lies Harry Wayne filled you with, but this I'll say: he'll never have you, Carolina. So you need *me*, do you? Yes, to do your dirty work, while you play around with him. Using him as a spy. Plotting with him against Kirby. And I, like a damn fool, telling you that *I* would protect you from Kirby. How you must have laughed, Carolina, while I was telling you that, and all the while you had Wayne primed to follow Kirby north and kill him, so you and he could be married and build your great empire of cattle. Corralitos and Running W. A great plan, Carolina.

But it won't work out. You've pulled your last double cross—"

"Who told you these things?" her voice rose shrill and brassy, and her eyes, on his face, were round-sprung and staring.

Something in her voice and on her face shocked McCanless into soberness. He stopped, looked at her narrowly. Then, as she stepped toward him, he said, "None of your damned business. You can't explain Harry Wayne—"

"Harry Wayne is dead!" she shouted. "Do you understand? Dead! Killed by Coulter in the Buckhorns. Would I have a man killed whom I was going to marry? Now—what is this damned nonsense that you've been talking?"

It was a slap in McCanless' face. He stood looking at her, slack-jawed and confused, trying to adjust himself to his beliefs and his desire to believe. "Dead?" he muttered. "Wayne dead? You—you *didn't* plan on marrying him?"

The woman said bitingly, "I might ask *you* what you were doing, bargaining away my cattle at so much a head to Ardoin."

"You're crazy. I haven't seen Ardoin since the meeting in the hotel."

"And you're a liar. You met him at night in Broken Wheel, less than a week ago."

"Where in hell do you get these fairy tales? I did no such thing—" Then he stopped. He watched the woman closely, and slowly, a light began to break over his face. "Carolina," he said, grimly querulous, "who has been . . . ?"

But she was ahead of him. Slowly, thin-lipped, she nodded her head. "Jim," she said carefully, and her voice was flat and dead, "tell me exactly why you came here tonight. What you have been told and who told you."

"I was told that you have been playin' a double game with me. That you and Harry Wayne were planning to kill Kirby up north, then get married. I was told that he had done the job and would be here tonight. And, Carolina"—he waited a moment, and his heavy face grew dark and tight with threat—"the fellow who told me that was the same one who told you that I was stealing from you, and workin' with Ardoin. *That man was Frank Landry!*"

Realization had come to her slowly, but the blow was hard as she watched another of her quickly formed and temporary worlds topple before her eyes. For just a moment she would have wept, and then that passed, and she felt the cold emptiness of an utter defeat come through her. Now, in this moment, her mind raced over the events which had transpired since Landry's coming: Kirby's trip to the north and his death; the loss of her herd; the splitting of the crews between her Pitchfork and Running W spreads; this, and—yes, even the play before the Courthouse and the manner in which he had come to join Corralitos. She knew with a panicky feeling that her talk with him last night had, also, been to an end, and now, too, she knew that he was no cousin of Steve Landry.

In this blinding moment of realization, Carolina Steele knew that the end was very near. She knew, too, that she stood here vulnerable and alone, and she had a small flash of panic as it came over her how nearly she had thrown over the one man over whom she still had control. The fact of Landry's Judas kiss passed like a cold hand over her heart, once, wrenching deep and powerfully inside her, and then she pushed aside such sentiments and her powerful instinct for self-preservation asserted itself. She let her gaze on McCanless' face grow softer, with the mood she needed, and said, "Jim, for once in my life, I have been a great fool. I was ready tonight to turn you away. For that, perhaps, I deserve to be left alone. But you and I started out together. If everything else falls, we fall with it, together. I must tell you that I believe we are in more than ordinary danger from—Landry. I say that because he has been cleverer than I, and to do that, he must have a powerful reason to hate both of us. He has destroyed people who helped me. Tonight he meant to have us destroy one another. Do you see that?"

He studied her, knowing that she was as false as himself, and yet, finding a reckless, daring kind of satisfaction in the fact. After a moment, his dark face eased, and the brash white smile, characteristic of him, showed fleetingly. "You know something, Carolina?" he said with a kind of amused irony. "From the day I first saw you in Rockport, longer ago than I care to remember, I have known that you and I would probably end with our backs to a wall. We're not good for one another. You have no more damned heart or principle than I have, and God knows that I wouldn't trust a man like myself. But there's a funny thing about that—I'd rather end that way, with you, than be in any other place with someone else."

She showed him now a kind of tenderness that might have been real. "Jim," she murmured, coming toward him, "we'll never be such fools again. We—"

He laughed ironically. "You don't have to act for me. If we get out of this thing, you'll try to sell me out again. I know that. But I won't let you. The thing now is to get the boys up and on their feet—"

"Why?"

"We're going to have company tonight, Carolina. I can see his game. Ardoin and his bunch will hit tonight. This was to be the payoff. He damned near got us. But it didn't work. Now, *where would he be?*"

"He went to meet you, didn't he?"

"Yes," McCanless said. "That means he'll be comin' back. All right. When he does, I'll be waitin' for him."

Landry's voice cut between the man and the woman: "Wait right here, McCanless. I'm back."

The surprise of it spun them with the force of a whiplash. McCanless made a swift movement toward his hip, saw the gun in Landry's hand and froze.

"Raise 'em," Landry said, "real high." Slowly, hate darkening his face, McCanless raised his hands. The woman stood looking at Landry, a hard kind of scorn on her countenance, and behind the angry brightness of her eyes an obscure thing that might have been admiration.

"You have done well," she said coldly. "But if you think—"

"You, too," Landry said dryly. "Way over your head."

"I will not. If you think that I had a gun and wouldn't use it on you, think again."

"Get 'em up," Landry snapped. "You're at the end of your tether. Or did you think that I'd let you off just because you told me that McCanless killed Steve Landry?"

McCanless whirled. He looked at the woman, then at Landry. "She told you that?"

"She sold you out. I was to cut you down tonight so you'd be off her neck, like Kirby."

A string of oaths tumbled from McCanless' thin lips. The woman's eyes, on Landry's, had gone hard and dry. She shot a look at McCanless. "It's a lie, Jim. Can't you see that he's still trying to split us up? Don't let him. He hasn't won this thing yet."

Landry said, "She decided to kill you when I showed her that IOU you gave me."

McCanless looked from one to the other, and finally he let out a great sigh, and decision had come into him. He said without rancor, "You're Steve Landry's brother, aren't you?"

"That's right. I came a long ways to find you."

McCanless shrugged. "She's the one you want." He nodded toward Carolina Steele. "She's no damn good."

"I will kill you for this, McCanless," the woman breathed.

"She planned the whole thing," McCanless went on. "She's planned everything bad that ever happened in this place."

Carolina Steele swung around facing him. For a moment she glared, then turned back to Landry. "Now listen to me," she said in a low, tight voice. "I have fought with men because I had to, and I have fought their way because it was my only way of winning. In this country men take the lives of those who are against them, or who are not strong enough to hold some thing another wants. Does it make me less good to do that because I am a woman? Darby Wayne and Ed Ardoin and any other man could do the same thing, and in them, because they are men, there would be a virile kind of virtue to such acts. But because I am a woman who dared to fight as ruthlessly as men do, I am condemned by men themselves. I hate you. I hate you all because you are such preposterous damned hypocrites. You raise women to a pedestal and insist that they stay there, and then when you find out that an occasional female is better than any dozen of you put together, you pull your long faces and act as confused as a small boy who has been brutally told that there is no Santa Claus. Now, Mr. Landry, I did not kill your brother. The one truth at least that I told you was that McCanless stabbed him to death. But I'm not afraid of you. Give me something to fight with, and we will see who wins the last battle of this war!"

He had watched her, not without a reluctant kind of admiration, as she talked. He did not notice the stealthy lowering of Jim McCanless' upraised hands to a level with his shoulders, nor the taut, watchful gaze the big man kept on him during Carolina Steele's speech. Nor did he hear the first swift step on the porch. Mary Wayne's voice cut through the thread of this moment like a knife as she stepped inside, her gun aimed at the room, and said behind Landry's back, "Carolina and McCanless, keep your hands up. And you, Landry, drop that gun and raise yours."

It happened in the next, outrunning second. Landry started to turn, then caught himself. And out of the corner of his eye he also saw the sudden, climactic movement of a hand and saw the swift glint of the blade that leaped to McCanless' hand from the sheath behind his neck.

In the same instant a shot burst up outside and a man's shrill cry, long and high, split the night. The drumming rush of oncoming horses rose up boiling through the night, and the light at the side of the room went out in a shattering crash of glass. Landry's gun swung around and he drove two shots at the place where Jim McCanless had stood, and the thunder in the room was rolled under by the roll of heavy firing which spread over the yard, toward the corrals, to the back of the house and centered quickly in the direction of the bunkhouses.

In that split second, too, Landry heard a cry, sharp and anguished, then the sound of a body falling and afterward a low moan. There was commotion toward an inner door and at that swift sound of movement he let go another burst. The shrill whistle of a hurled object sung past his ear and he heard the thud and the quick, humming vibration of a steel blade as a knife stuck in the wall at his back. Then he raced across the room after McCanless.

Chapter 19

LANDRY heard McCanless stumble over furniture and utter a wild curse; then he lost the sound of flight for a moment in the thundering racket outside. He came to a door leading out upon a corridor, and at its far end he caught the sound of swift retreating footsteps, and sent a shot echoing that way. Then he ran down this hallway and in a moment came out on a back porch. Sound throbbed angrily in the air about him. Ahead in the darkness, down the house's side, he saw a figure round the end of the patio and raced after it, coming thus to the front of the house.

Lance points of fire flicked through the darkness, and the roll of gunfire was a steady, hammering thing in the night. Before him horses scuffled and circled wildly in the gravel of the yard, and he went out into the boiling melee, sky-lighting a number of riders wheeling their excited mounts to the shelter of the buildings across the way.

A man ran through the shadows before him, stopped, fired three shots at the bunkhouse, and dashed on into the gloom. In a small break in the shooting Ed Ardoin's voice rose high above the commotion, "Pour it in! Pour it in! Don't let 'em make a break for it."

He wondered where McCanless would have gotten to, and knew that he had been cut off from his men. He went on across the yard, coming into a crazy, wild maelstrom of plunging horses, of darting riders, hazy in the night, and of guns bellowing vengeance at the two bunkhouses from which a deadly round of fire now came in a steady stream. A careening horse hit him and threw him against a pole fence, shied away again. The rider above him was cursing, pulling at the reins and firing methodically at the bunkhouses.

"Get down from there, or you'll get hit," Landry shouted. The rider hesitated and swung about in his saddle. Then Landry saw him lurch. He gave a cough, swayed in the leather and his body bent toward the ground as Landry caught him and pulled him free of the saddle and laid him on the ground close up to the fence. The man tried to say something, but Landry heard only a bubbling breath. The man's legs flexed and he lay still.

Landry rose, his mind racing. He heard someone yell, "Not me, you sonofabitch! I'm on your side!" Above the drumming gunfire came the crash of broken glass and a man shouted, "Give it to 'em! Don't let 'em make a run for it." The firing rose higher, like the roll of approaching thunder. From the second bunkhouse came a high, derisive yell and a taunting Spanish voice which broke suddenly in the middle on a choking note. From near by in the darkness a man growled, "Damned *Mexicanos*. Maybe they'll stay where they belong now."

Ardoin's men had cleared their milling animals out of the fight now. It had turned into a siege. Landry walked away, circling the corrals. He bumped into a man in the darkness and this one said, "Watch your step."

"Ardoin," Landry said. "It's comin' your way."

"Yes," Ardoin said shortly and passed on.

A small bunch of men passed Landry, running. "They'll come out with their hands up," one was saying, "or they'll come out feet first." Their boots clattered off through the gravel toward the heaviest sound of firing.

He kept on his way until he could see the looming shape of the big barn before him in the night. Now he made his step stealthy, stopping frequently to probe the darkness and to listen. He reached the door and eased inside, and the odor of hay, mingled with the pungent, nitrogenous smell of manure, rose to his nostrils. Underfoot was soft earth and rotted straw, damp and loamlike. He went forward into the gloom, cat-soft, every sense awake and feeling through the darkness about him.

A sound brought him to a halt. It was a quick, heavy sound, not usual in a place like this. A board had been stepped on, and it had struck another piece of timber. He waited, holding his breath, then drifted forward again. Now he was toward the rear of the barn, facing the corner where baled hay and straw were stored. He waited. Time dragged on. There was no sound. After a while he caught a stealthy rustle in that corner.

"McCanless," he said, "come out of there."

There was no reply. Presently, "No hurry. I'll stay here until I kill you."

Again silence. A thing began to nag at his mind, and he said, "If you lost your gun, say so and I'll fight you bare. That's your choice."

For a long time, now, there was no sound. Landry began to think that he had been mistaken. Then, from a far corner, McCanless' voice sneered at him out of the darkness, "How do I know that?"

"I'm not here to argue," Landry said softly. "I know where you are, and I'm comin' after you."

"Wait." A curiously temporizing note was in McCanless' voice. "Let's talk this over, Landry. You got things all wrong."

"No. I've got them straightened out, now." Again he went forward.

"Listen—" McCanless' voice had moved. It came to Landry's mind that he was standing between that voice and the dim light from the barn's front doorway, that McCanless had maneuvered it that way.

"Listen, Landry. What makes you think that I—" For just an instant there was a hesitation in the sound of the voice, and in that fractional moment Landry threw himself low. The hurled knife split the air where his body had been. He felt the wind from it on his face. On one knee, he aimed at a

darker blot against the darkness before him and fired. He
heard the bullet slam home and McCanless' groan. Then a
pain-logged voice cried, "Christ Jesus! Give me a chance to
defend myself—"

"You didn't give Steve a chance," Landry's cold voice
went out through the darkness. "You didn't give Carolina a
chance back there in the house. It's not your way to kill. You
didn't take the chance I gave you. You tried to cross me. Remember those things when you're roastin' in hell, McCanless."

There was a long silence. Landry began to think it was
over. Then he heard a breath, ragged and gasping, and afterward there was a slow, painful movement in the darkness.

"A poor . . . way to die." Horror clung to the strained
words. Again silence. "I'm gettin' up. I'm comin' . . . after
you—" There was a sudden, desperate movement ahead of
Landry, and he saw the great bulk of the man rise up in the
shadows, heard the harsh, ragged breathing. He cocked
the gun and pulled the trigger and heard the shot ring
through the old barn and die away in little concentric circles
of sound which left the eardrums lingeringly. The shape of
McCanless blurred against the lighter darkness and slowly
collapsed with a muted thud on the ground. He heard a bubbling word: "Butcher—like butcherin' a steer—"

There was sickness in Landry along with a mad kind of
anger now, as he said tightly, "Eye for an eye. Better than a
knife in the back, McCanless." And for the first time he realized the extent of the wild thing that had driven him all the
way from Montana to this moment in the night of the Santisimas, a thousand miles away.

The past came down over him now, and he stood sus-
pended in space, in time, with his whole existence revolving
about the heavy, dying breath of the man before him. After
a long while there was movement in the straw ahead of him,
and he thought wildly, "Goddamn him. Why doesn't he
die?"

McCanless' whisper, strained and fading, came to him,
"Man—never knows—about a—woman." The breathing

rose quick, rasping, harsh. Landry took a step forward, slipped his gun into the holster. Then he stopped as a whisper came out of the shadows and died away on departing breath, "A beautiful—devil—"

For a long while Landry stood there, numb and suddenly empty, washed clean of feeling and having the impression that more than McCanless' life had ended. After a long while he brought the identification of this thing down to himself, and he knew then that it was because there was nothing, really, ahead of him now. With a sick and hollow feeling, he turned and went out through the darkness toward the dim shape of the barn's doorway, suddenly conscious that the racketing sound of firing outside had become sporadic and uneven.

As she had stepped into the room, Mary Wayne had known only a deep, cold satisfaction that Landry was here with her other enemies; the fact that he held a gun on them had been only a momentary surprise. Then, the swift burst up of action had left her no time to analyze the situation or to search for motives or explanations. When the lights had crashed out and the battle had rolled down upon Corralitos, with Landry firing in pursuit of McCanless, she had stood for a moment confused and uncertain, and then she had heard the moaning of Carolina Steele in the darkness on the floor in front of her.

She went quickly to the table, found matches in a drawer, and struck one. Then she bent over Carolina. Instantly she saw the red stain in the woman's side, and noted the paleness of her face, her lips. Carolina opened her eyes to the light, and her gaze was distant, bright with pain.

"Help me to my room," she said in a strained voice. "Light the light there." Then her eyes closed again.

Mary Wayne went down the corridor, found Carolina's room, and lighted the lamp. She came back, knelt and helped the woman to her feet, heard Carolina's low, anguished moan as she rose. By the time she helped her down upon the bed, she knew that Carolina Steele had played her game to its end. She stood looking down at the woman, and found herself trying hard to hate her and only half succeeding. After a long moment, Carolina's eyes flickered open and she looked at Mary for a long, solemn moment. At last her lips moved, and she said, "What was there between you and Landry, Mary Wayne?"

She felt the color rise into her cheeks. "Nothing. I came here to kill him."

The woman studied her with her wise woman's eyes. Then, slowly, she shook her head. "You are lying. Sit down here beside me a moment." Mary sat down slowly, Carolina's eyes on her face, filled with pain and yet with another thing. Presently the mistress of Corralitos said, "I have done you a great deal of harm. I am not sorry. But now, I am going to do a thing that may have good in it. Listen to me, Mary Wayne—"

From his place by the corrals, Ed Ardoin watched the diminishing fire from the bunkhouses thin out and grow fitful. He turned to Drav McLain, who was crouched a few feet from him, slamming shot after shot into the riddled building. "'Bout over," he said.

"There's the *Mexicanos*, yet." Drav waved his gun barrel toward the spare bunkhouse where the *vaqueros* kept up a token resistance.

"They'll give up when the others do. Got no damn interest in the thing, anyhow."

At that moment a loud, exasperated voice shouted from the besieged building, "Ardoin!"

"Say your say." Ardoin saw now that the firing from this bunkhouse had ceased.

"You take the pot, Ardoin," the heavy voice replied. "How do you want it?"

"Come out with your hands up. Take it or leave it."

There was a short silence. Then, "We're comin' out. Hold your fire."

Ardoin shouted an order and then turned to McLain. "How's it feel? Boy, how's it feel?"

Drav let go a pleased chuckle. "We did it. By grab, we did it."

"You go take over those men. Take very gun and start 'em out of this country right now. If they're still here when the sun comes up, they'll be dead when it goes down. I'm goin' to the house to see what Carolina says about it."

He turned away through the darkness. It was all over now. Corralitos was broken. The evil and arrogant thing which had ridden these ranges was no more. From today, a man could breathe freely, could grow up as the country grew. Soon, there would be just law for all; the railroads would come, and Broken Wheel and the surrounding ranges would grow away from the past and face into a better and a brighter future.

As he came to the veranda, he saw a light coming from the deep interior of the house. Stepping into the room he halted, catching sight of the broken lamp and the overturned furniture. Then, suddenly, he saw the dark red blot on the floor. He knelt to touch it and his fingers came away sticky. Frowning, he drew his gun and stepped down the corridor toward the light.

Mary Wayne now stood beside the bed, and she wheeled to face Ardoin as he came in. He growled, "Mary, what are you doing here?" When she looked at him coldly and said nothing, his glance turned to the bed where Carolina Steele lay, lovely in her gold-and-green gown, her face pale and drawn, her eyes closed and her hand held tight over a darkening stain on her side.

He stared at the woman, then stepped to the bedside. Senselessly he said, "You're hurt, Carolina."

She opened her eyes and looked at him. After a while she said in a faraway voice, "It will be an empty victory for you." And then she closed her eyes again.

Ardoin looked at Mary Wayne, but she had a blank gaze for him. "I could get a doctor," he said uneasily. Somehow, it was not a part of his plan that this woman should die here, unattended, surrounded by enemies.

Carolina heard this and opened her eyes. "Ed," she said softly, "you are a fool."

Mary Wayne went to a stand, poured a glass of water and brought it to the bedside.

"Drink, Carolina."

Carolina Steele turned her face toward the girl. She looked at her a long time. At last she said, "I remember something now that seemed foolish when I heard it. Kirby once told me that I would make a great mistake, and that I would pay for it alone, and that there would then be no one but enemies around me. I suppose that this is the moment, but—"

"I do not hate you, Carolina," Mary Wayne said. "Not now—"

It was then that Landry came into the room, his face sober and thoughtful. He met Ardoin's stiff, hostile glance, and looked fleetingly at Mary Wayne, then came to stand by Carolina Steele's bedside.

She looked up at him, and for a moment a strange and renewed light came into her eyes. Seeing her, Landry thought of her words in defense of herself, just before McCanless' knife struck. He thought, swiftly, too, of the men who had fallen to her relentless drive: Darby Wayne, his son, Kirby, Steve, even McCanless and the scores of obscure and little men who had sold their valor to her at a stated price per month—all these she had used up, had thrown between herself and the obstacles to her forward sweep, and now they were gone, and she had lost her wild and daring gamble with fate. She must have read something of his thoughts in his gaze. She started to say something, and shut her lips. For a moment she turned her head away, and a spasm of pain racked her. Then, slowly, she turned her face toward him and in a moment she said, "I've waited for you to come. I want you to know that—that you have broken only Corralitos!" She shut her eyes tight against the pain, and after a moment she opened them again, and now, as she looked at him, Landry had the feeling that she did not see him. Her voice was very far away as she whispered, "It could have been—

different. I am sorry only that you won. Will you do something for me?"

"Yes," he said.

She looked at him, or toward him, he knew not which. "You were my kind of man," she said with the last of her remaining pride and arrogance. "Give me your hand."

Landry bent and took her hand in his. She closed her eyes, then, and was still. For a long time Landry stood like this, not noticing that Mary Wayne had turned quickly away from the bedside and now stood looking at nothing, toward the wall. He expected Carolina Steele to make some gesture, say some last word; and then, as the moments passed, he knew that she had taken the only way she knew of showing him that she, Carolina Steele, had not been beaten, and that she had forgiveness within her and asked, unbowing for whatever measure of the same he might accord her.

He stood there, knowing that in this moment it would be very easy to feel sorry for her, but finding that impossible. He really did not know how he felt about her, now that she was dead, except that she was very beautiful, lying there, and that there were formless thoughts centering about her which told him that there had been in her great potentialities for good, as well as for evil. Almost, for a little while, he grasped the fullest meaning of what she had once told him: "The way I have come has been a lonely one—" Then it eluded him, and he bent over and placed her hand on her bosom and turned away from the bedside.

Without looking at either Ardoin or Mary Wayne, he went quickly out of the room heading toward the front porch. It was all over, now, and he was weary and sick of death and of violence, and not wholly proud of the part he had played in the game.

He stopped on the veranda, thankful for the cool wind beating against him, and feeling its fresh goodness slowly clearing out his brain and washing over his spirit. In a few hours, another day would dawn, and it would find him out of this country, free—almost free—of the turbulent and wrenching memories of what had passed. He fished in his vest for the makings, curled up a smoke and drew the tangy fumes down inside him, taking some of the harsh bitterness of it for his very spirit, and then he stepped down the yard toward the barn where he had left the black tied in the darkness, hours before. He saw now that the new moon had ridden free of the peaks, and he was glad that there would be a few hours of partial light for the trail he would make this night.

He stood for a moment, his hand on the horn, and then he crushed out his cigarette under his boot and tested the cinch. Then, ready to swing aboard, he was halted in the act by a voice behind him.

"This is it, Landry," Coulter's flat voice said. "Right through the back. Got anything to say?"

He waited a moment, and his only feeling was one of a strange kind of unconcern. The thought occurred to him: *It goes on, even after she's dead. It will never end, for once started, these things consume everyone who touches them, and everyone has been touched by this.*

"Nothing to say." He was surprised by the sound of his voice and by his own indifference.

"You made a mistake by beatin' me up," the gunman said. "You made another by chasin' me off the place. No man would take that. No man would ever let you walk the earth after you'd done that to him. If you hadn't been so damned high and mighty, I'd have given you an even break. But you don't deserve it, damn you, and—"

The crashing bellow of a gun rocked out on the night, and Landry heard a grunt behind him. Surprised that he was alive, he turned. Coulter stood swaying in the pale moonlight, his face twisted, his eyes burning at Landry. For a moment he tried to raise his gun, mumbling and mewling in a tone that was almost a sob of frustration. "Luck," he gurgled, "always—luck—" Then, suddenly, the strained life thread snapped and he pitched forward, dead before he hit the ground.

Drav McLain stepped out from the side of the barn and

said, "Put your hands up. You'll get a fair trial. You saved my life, and I owe you that."

It was overmuch of arrogance, of conflict and hate for Landry. He had had enough. "Take you gun off me, Drav," he said. "I'm riding out."

"You fork that horse, you're a dead man."

Landry saw Mary Wayne come around the barn's end, and the sight of her stopped his hard reply. She came straight to Drav McLain and pushed the gun aside. "Go away, Drav," she said, looking at Landry. "I want to talk to him alone." And a note in her voice caught hard at Landry.

"No," Drav said stubbornly. "He killed Harry, and he'll have to prove to a court that he wasn't responsible for Darby's death."

There was a short silence. Then the girl said in a small voice, "He didn't kill Harry, Drav. I know who did—and why." And with that Landry knew that Carolina Steele had paid off the debt to him in the only coin she had to give.

Drav mumbled something and turned away. He stopped, looked back at them, and then went away toward the bunkhouse where the Corralitos riders and the *vaqueros* were catching up their horses, under the guns of Ardoin's men, and riding away into whatever trails they chose leading out of this country.

They stood looking at one another for a long time, and then the girl came toward him, slowly and wordlessly. Near him she stopped, and now he could see that there was a mistiness in her eyes as she turned her face up to him.

After a long while she said, "Carolina told me—everything. Oh Frank!" Then she was in his arms, sobbing softly into his bosom.

He let her weep for a while, and then he raised her face, cupping her chin in his hands. "I'll be everything to you that a man can be to a woman," he said earnestly. "I'll try to make up to you what you've lost."

Now she smiled, and blinking back the tears she shook her head. "It will have to be the other way, Frank. I will never doubt you again. Never as long as we live."

It was then that Ed Ardoin, stiff, hard and unrelenting, rode around the barn, headed outward toward the north. He saw them and stopped, sat looking at them, baffled, beaten and soul-weary.

After a long while he said, "Good-bye, Mary. I just want you to know that I wouldn't really have used that about Harry to hurt you, this fellow from beating me out."

Landry saw the girl stiffen, and she said, "All right, Ed. I can accept the apology. I am not sure that I believe you. But I shall try to remember that you did this because you thought you loved me."

"More than anything," he mumbled. "And—well, I guess I hope that *you'll* be happy." With that, he reined away.

Something of the somberness and hurt in that stiff figure touched Landry. He said, "Ardoin, no hard feelings. Maybe I'll get used to you."

Ardoin pulled up and turned in the saddle. His voice was hard, dry and hating as he said, "You won't have the chance. I'm riding on. From the time you came to this country, I lost interest in it. Now, I'd rather live in hell. If it's any satisfaction to you, you can be sure that I'll always hate you." And he went on down the trail, a hard, unbending man who knew how to hate, but who had never found the meaning of love.

With his hard words hanging between them, they turned away toward the house, sober and silent. As they passed Coulter's body, huddled in the dust, Landry stopped and looked down at the gunman. It came to him with a confused lost feeling that here, in the space of a minute, they had seen the essence of life in this country: undying hate and wild, fatal violence. He said, "Maybe Ed's right—this country is not much good. There's a curse on it, Mary. And I wonder—"

"No," the girl said softly. "It's like all other places. It is corruptible by corrupt people, and it can be as good as others may make it. Don't forget that, Frank. We can make it good, and we can forget the evil and the violence that were necessary to save it. Someday—"

He looked up at her, and the wind was blowing down off the Santisimas, fresh and clean in her face, coming off the timber with pine scent and the pureness of mountain waters behind it, and catching at the coppery wisps of her hair in a dancing, moon-polished way that moved him. It came over him that she was right, that the next day that dawned would find Frank Landry on no drifter's trail, but rooted to this hand and anchored with responsibilities reaching as far as he could see into its future.

Suddenly he smiled. "I see now. I know what you mean. In a small way, another world has been born here."

They looked at one another for a moment and then she laughed, a light, happy laugh. "More than that," she said, taking his hand in hers. "It's a new *life*—"

Her happiness caught at him. "Mary," he said, "it comes to my mind that I've never told you—"

She smiled and led him away toward the lighted bunkhouses, where Drav McLain was issuing the orders for the restoration of peace. "There's plenty of time," she said complacently. "All the rest of our lives. All the rest of our days—together."

SIGNET BOOKS

JUDSON GRAY

Introducing a post-Civil War Western saga from
the author of the Hunter Trilogy...

DOWN TO MARROWBONE

Jim McCutcheon had squandered his Southern family's fortune
and had to find a way to rebuild it among the boomtowns.
Jake Penn had escaped the bonds of slavery and had to find
his long-lost sister...
Together, they're an unlikely team—but with danger down
every trail, nothing's worth more than a friend you can count
on...

❑ 0-451-20158-2/$5.99